ROBERT STEAD was born in Middleville, Ontario, in 1880. Two years later, his family moved to a homestead near Cartwright, Manitoba. At the age of fourteen Stead left school, his only other formal education consisting of a few courses he took in 1887 at the Winnipeg Business School.

In 1898 Stead founded a newspaper called, variously, *The Rock Lake Review*, *The Rock Lake Review* and *Cartwright Enterprise*, and, finally, *The Southern Manitoba Review*. He moved to Alberta in 1910, and within two years settled in Calgary, where he joined the editorial staff of the *Calgary Herald*; he later directed publicity for the colonization department of the Canadian Pacific Railroad. He moved to Ottawa in 1919 to become publicity director for the Department of Immigration and Colonization. From 1936 until his retirement in 1946 he was publicity director for the parks and services aspects of the Department of Mines and Resources.

Although Stead published five volumes of light patriotic verse, which had extensive sales, his major literary achievement rested in fiction. Apart from the thriller *The Copper Disc* (1931), all his novels have western settings on the prairies or in the foothills. His early fiction shows his indebtedness to the popular genre of romance, yet his development as a novelist parallels his increasing concern with realism and his artistic dedication to the authentic fictional depiction of prairie life.

Recognizing that true genius was rare, Stead set himself the modest ideal of being an honest worker with words: he always aspired to "take words – the tools of thought – and use them with the care that good tools deserve."

Robert Stead died in Ottawa, Ontario, in 1959.

GRAIN

ROBERT STEAD

AFTERWORD BY
LAURIE RICOU

Copyright © 1993 by McClelland & Stewart Inc.
Afterword copyright © 1993 by Laurie Ricou

First published in 1926 by McClelland & Stewart
Reprinted 1993.

This New Canadian Library edition 2010.

Library and Archives Canada Cataloguing in Publication

Stead, Robert J. C., 1880-1959
        Grain / Robert Stead ; afterword by Laurie Ricou.

(New Canadian library)
Includes bibliographical references.
ISBN 978-0-7710-9430-9

        I. Title. II. Series: New Canadian library

PS8537.T42G73 2010   C813'.52   C2009-904844-2

We acknowledge the financial support of the Government of Canada through the Book Publishing Industry Development Program and that of the Government of Ontario through the Ontario Media Development Corporation's Ontario Book Initiative. We further acknowledge the support of the Canada Council for the Arts and the Ontario Arts Council for our publishing program.

Typeset in Garamond by M&S, Toronto

McClelland & Stewart Ltd.
75 Sherbourne Street
Toronto, Ontario
M5A 2P9
www.mcclelland.com/NCL

1 2 3 4 5   14 13 12 11 10

GRAIN

ONE

The eleventh of April, 1896, is not generally known to be a date of special significance, yet it was on that day, or, to be more exact, that night, that the hero of this narrative made his entry into a not over-hospitable world. Perhaps the term hero, with its suggestion of high enterprise, sits inappropriately upon the chief character of a somewhat commonplace tale; there was in Gander Stake little of that quality which is associated with the clash of righteous steel or the impact of noble purposes. Yet that he was without heroic fibre I will not admit, and you who bear with me through these pages shall judge whether or not the word is wholly unwarranted.

His advent in the Stake family and in the little farm settlement of which it was a unit, was not, of course, quite unexpected. Perhaps his eight-year-old brother, Jackson junior, a thin, dark-eyed, silent boy, who found himself suddenly the recipient of a night's entertainment at the neighboring farmhouse of Fraser Fyfe, was the only one in the immediate circle to be taken entirely by surprise. But, even with the added interest of the unforeseen, Jackie refused to be deeply stirred by

I

the latest family acquisition. He regarded the little, puckered, wrinkled morsel shyly and without comment, but with an inward sense of depression which sent him presently to the fields in search of venturesome spring gophers.

To Mrs. Stake and her husband the impending event had been an occasion for serious consideration and concern. It was eight years since Jackie's arrival, but time had not entirely dulled the memory of that experience.

"You'll have a good doctor this time," Jackson had comforted his wife and himself together. "Doctor Freeman is well spoken of in the neighborhood."

Susie Stake clenched her fingers under the blankets in foreboding. "Good enough, I guess – if he gets here in time. So was Doctor Blain a good doctor, but he didn't get here. . . . Mrs. Martin —"

Jackson's great, hard hand found hers and pressed it in a passion of inarticulate sympathy. Mrs. Martin, at the age of twenty-four, had been rewarded for her contribution to the State – the third in as many years – with a bed under six feet of frozen clay. The incident was too recent to be disregarded. Susie Stake herself had stood in the snow by that open grave, and wondered.

"It'll be spring," Jackson had argued, "an' the roads'll be open. Jackie was in January, an' a howlin' blizzard."

Gander's arrival had been under more happy circumstances. The snows of winter were gone, or nearly so, on the eleventh of April, and although the streams were full of ice-cold water, and a bridge on the most impassable of them had gone down with the current, trifles like these were no deterrent to Dr. Freeman. He came on horseback, swimming the streams that could not be waded, and drenched to the skin. For all his haste Gander preceded him by twenty minutes, and, before the doctor's arrival, had already sent his first lusty announcement into the world.

Dr. Freeman pronounced all well, and shared with Jackson Stake a pot of strong tea and thick slabs of bread and butter. He loitered for an hour, probably to justify the ten dollar fee which he would collect from Jackson in the fall – if the crops were good. Then he straddled his horse for home, and nature once more was left to take her course.

There is no means of knowing at exactly what date young Gander began making appraisals of his new environment. His immediate interests were few and he concentrated upon them with imperious determination. His disappointments he expressed in wails of incredible volume, and his approvals he gurgled with equal if less lusty enthusiasm. He had not asked for admission into the world; he had not at all been consulted about a matter in which he, plainly, was most concerned; but, now that he was in the world, he proposed that it should serve him.

Gander was utterly selfish. If he thought of his older brother at all it probably was with contempt and hostility, feelings which were reciprocated by young Jackson. If he thought of his father at all he no doubt regarded him as an enormous, shaggy, but not dangerous animal, given at times to grotesque antics apparently intended to be humorous, and an unseemly curiosity concerning his – Gander's – toes, hair, and absence of teeth. The suspension bridge of scalp across a chasm in his little skull was a matter of concern to this great animal, who had once or twice stroked his rough fingers gingerly across the gap, as though they might fall in. His mother he took for granted. She supplied him with all the needs of his little life – food, warmth, and attention, and upon occasion he would reward her with an amiable gurgle, quite without value on any market in the world, and yet unpurchasable by anything those markets have to offer.

If he took note of his surroundings beyond the wooden cradle in which he lay, the arms in which he was lifted, the rounded founts from which he drew his nutriment, he must have marvelled at the habitation which Fate had selected for his home. To him at first it would seem very big, although his mother found it inconveniently small, and filled with equipment of amazing variety and interest.

A huge bed occupied one corner of the room, and, next to his cradle, was the most important article of furniture. Here his father and mother slept. The bed could be screened off by means of a curtain, with gaudy figures on it, which could be stretched along a wire. This Gander held to be a wholly esthetic device for the display of the gaudy figures already mentioned, which at a later age he took to represent angels, and, still later, goblins. There was a stove, where a fire crackled cheerfully, and a kettle sang most amiably, puffing a vigorous white cloud out from its headless neck. When he was old enough to reach it he attempted to stem that cloud with his little hand – an experiment he was in no hurry to repeat. His mother rubbed baking soda upon the burn and encouraged him to play drummer-boy with his uninjured member by means of an iron ladle and a sonorous tin wash-pan.

The roof overhead was of boards – elm boards, as Gander learned when he was older – supported on rafters of peeled poplar poles. Over these was a layer of tarpaper, and, over that, poplar shingles nailed to the elm boards. Long before Gander's time the shingles had cupped with the weather, curling up at their discolored edges, and releasing small round knots which left small round holes in the space they once had occupied. When one of these holes coincided with a similar hole in the elm board below, or straddled the gaunt cracks which now gaped between the strips of lumber shrinking with the kitchen's heat, the fragile tarpaper soon gave way. Through the apertures thus provided Gander observed many a starry heaven, winter and summer, although his mother had a thrifty habit of stuffing the major openings with old rags upon the approach of frosty weather.

Frosty weather! Then, too, was something to observe. With an unreasoning disregard for the fitness of things, the early settlers always made use of shingle nails half an inch too long for the boards into which they were driven. It was the only shingle nail they knew, and that every nail should pro-trude through the board, splintering off a fragment at its end, they accepted as inevitable, very much as they accepted early sunrise in summer, and late sunrise in winter. In frosty weather each of these nail-ends became a condensing point for the household vapors, and a thousand little globules of ice formed in rows between the poplar rafters, dripping a little when the heat from the stove overpowered the cold at the other end of the nail, and recovering their losses through the long, crack-ling night.

"Have to strip those rafters an' cover 'em with buildin' paper, sometime," Jackson Stake remarked to his wife every winter.

"Yes," Susie Stake agreed. "Sometime."

The walls were of logs – round, poplar logs, the spaces between them chinked and plastered. The logs, like the boards of the roof, had undergone a drying and shrinking process which left the chinks and plaster hanging loosely between, like idle brake-shoes on a wheel. A well-directed poke with any rough instrument would sometimes dislodge a chink altogether, and afford a loop-hole through which young adventurers might watch for Indians. But this was a dangerous pastime, as Gander discovered when he had been caught at it and rewarded with one of his father's infrequent thrashings.

The floor, too, was of poplar boards, with the inevitable cracks between them. The Stake family residence, it seemed, consisted largely of cracks. Jackson himself had hauled the logs in the winter of '85, the first winter after he had filed on the homestead. Jackson's quarter was in brush country, not far from a lake, and although his own land provided no timber worth while, there were poplar and elm, and some oak, on the rougher Government lands that abruptly broke into deep ravines plunging down into the valley. Some of these logs he hauled to the portable mill at the head of the lake and had them sawn into boards and shingles.

Had Jackson Stake homesteaded on the open prairie further south his first house would, no doubt, have been of sods, with a sod roof covered with yellow clay that baked itself impervious under the hot sun; not so esthetic a building material as logs and plaster, but less subject to cracks. But the young settler carried from the wooded East in which he had been born a sort of superstitious fear of the prairie.

"That open country looks sleek enough, but so does a bald head," he remarked to his neighbor, Fraser Fyfe. "I like to see a few bristles stickin' through, if only to encourage cultivation."

Jackson's own sandy hair stood in thick curls about his big head, and he scuffled it with his fingers as he talked. There was a cheerful virility about him, and when he had promised Susan Harden a frame house with lathed and plastered walls and an upstairs she had said yes, not for the house, but for himself. But that was before he left the East, when he and his hopes were young. Gander was driving a four-horse team before the ribs of his father's frame house at last rose stark against the prairie sky. •

The boards of the floor had knots, like the shingles of the roof, but not so many of them fell out. Susie Stake's regular scrubbings kept the floor from drying up, and the knots held their ground. Indeed, as the wear of the softer lumber went on about them, they more than held their ground; they rose in little hummocks and elevations over the surrounding plain. When the table was set for company, as happened once in a blue moon, care had to be taken to set all the legs on the hill-tops, or all in the valleys beneath. "A teetering table," said Jackson Stake, "is mighty hard on manners, an' ours can't stand no unnecessary provocation."

As soon as he could walk Gander was allowed to visit the wide, wide world on his own account. He had already explored most of the farmyard by a process of propulsions which was neither creeping nor crawling, but a combination of both. Anchoring himself on his hands he would draw his right knee up to his wrists, then heave forward, dragging the left leg inert. From the standpoint of gracefulness it left something to be desired, but as a means of locomotion it was simple and effective. It enabled him to explore the stables, and, upon a certain great occasion, to make the acquaintance of the family pig. Young Jackson, who retrieved him, told at school that he didn't know which was which, but that was an exaggeration.

In course of time Gander made the discovery that both legs might be used in travel, and from then on he assumed an upright position, with intermittent relapses to the horizontal. As his effective range increased he roved further and further afield, pursuing gophers and butterflies, and proving all things by the child's simple test of thrusting them into his mouth. He

7

was fond of food in all its forms, but he disliked water, unless mixed with earth to the consistency of mud, when he found it very agreeable. He protested regularly against being put to sleep in the little box-bed which succeeded his cradle, but he loved to lie in the grass under the afternoon sun, and he gave his father and mother more than one uneasy hour by his protracted naps in distant corners of the farm.

He was fond of horses. He wandered among their feet at the peril of his life, but without mishap from that source. He was the foster-child of the family collie, Queenie, in whom he confided all his troubles, and who was usually the first to locate him when he wandered too far from home. He hated geese, having had a disastrous encounter with that masculine bully of the farmyard from whom he was afterwards to derive his appellation; but he admired the turkey-gobbler, who strutted around with his great tail spread until it scraped along the earth and his bulging blood-red neck threatening instant apoplexy. He had discovered that when this gentleman's vanity was at its height sticks might be thrown at him, from a distance, with reasonable impunity. Ducks he loved. He would sit by the duck pond for hours watching them turn tail-up as they grubbed among the grassy roots, or filtering juicy morsels out of the water through their broad, chattery bills. With hens he had little concern. He regarded them somewhat as a small boy regards girls, as objects of slight interest and no possible importance. He liked his mother, tolerated his father, and hated his brother Jackson. But he loved Queenie.

It was when he was three years old that an incident occurred which annoyed him somewhat, and which needs to be told. A man with a black coat and a funny collar buttoned behind arrived that day at the Stake homestead, in time for dinner. That the event was of unusual importance Gander knew by the production of his mother's only white tablecloth, by the killing of one of the hens which thronged the kitchen door, and, in particular, by the wholly unwarranted scrubbing to which he himself had been subjected. He afterwards recalled that the hen had been killed before the arrival of the stranger, which suggested collusion on the part of his mother, but that point had escaped him at the moment.

The stranger spoke to him pleasantly, but Gander maintained a haughty aloofness. He had suspicions. He observed that the visitor's vest went right up to his collar, and he surmised that he was without a shirt, but he kept this deduction quite to himself. Had he known to what indignities he was to be subjected it might have been a different story, but for the moment the discomfort of a clean wash and clean clothes was balanced by the prospect of hen with dumplings, and one must take the bitter with the sweet in life, mustn't he? Through some error his mother referred to the savory stew before her as chicken. Gander was about to mouth a prompt correction when he was brought up short by one of those telepathic despatches which mothers were able to broadcast long before the discovery of radio. He lapsed into a bewildered silence. Obviously strange doings were afoot.

It was Jackson Stake's practice to ask a blessing before meals – a commendable hang-over from his Puritan ancestry. The exact purport of this ceremony Gander had never been able to learn, as his father always confided in his plate, rattling the words off in a great hurry, as though in fear of being caught at it. It was Gander's belief that the purpose of the blessing was to give everyone an equal start – a purpose which he thwarted as often as possible by surreptitious plunderings in his potatoes and gravy. To-day the stranger was asked to say the blessing, which he did in a quite audible voice. Gander caught enough of his words to gather that they involved, in some way, the Stake family; they were not mentioned by name, but by suggestion or allusion so obvious that even Gander could not be misled. He watched his father closely and was somewhat disappointed to find when the long blessing was finished that relationships remained quite cordial.

The meal was a trying one for Gander. He had coveted intensely one of the "chicken's" drum-sticks, but the first went to the stranger, and the second, in defiance of all precedent, to his father! Gander expostulated against this outrage, and although his mother sought to convince him that the neck was a particularly choice morsel, he gulped his dinner through a mist of indignant tears.

Matters improved when the meal was finished. The visitor read from a book, and even sang, an exercise in which the boy joined lustily. Suddenly he found himself quite the centre of interest. His father and mother were standing, with Gander between them, and the stranger in front. They were answering a number of questions, somewhat hesitatingly, Gander thought, and in a low voice, as though in fear of being overheard. Then, quite without warning, the stranger splashed a few drops of water on his head.

Gander's first impulse was belligerent, but the stranger spoke to him so pleasantly that it was impossible to impute hostile intent, so he let the incident pass with a dignified rebuke.

"I ain't dirty," he said. "I got washed before dinner, dang it all!"

The "dang it all" was his own mature and triumphant climax, borrowed from his father's vocabulary, and absolutely unused until that very moment. Gander prided himself upon having carried it off rather well. In the hubbub which followed his remark he failed to catch the fact that he had been christened William Harden.

And not one of them knew that his name was to be Gander!

TWO

By all the rules upon which insurance companies base what they call the expectation of life Gander should have been dead long before he reached his tenth anniversary. In that brief decade he had piloted his little ship, quite without medical interference, through the seas of those infantile diseases, measles, whooping cough, and scarlet fever. Gander regarded these as mere incidents, annoying for the few days during which they enforced his confinement in the house, but otherwise without significance. His attack by a malady known locally as the prairie itch was a more serious matter; it flourished in winter, when he wore his heavy woolens, and subjected him to genuine discomfort when he sat by the kitchen stove after being out in the cold. There he would scratch and squirm until it was time to go to bed. His mother gave him sulphur and molasses, and, when one of his numerous colds threatened to rasp the tonsils out of his throat, fed him on a concoction of onions boiled in vinegar.

Gander had not at that time read Genesis, nor, for that matter, has he yet, so far as I am aware, but he believed with our first parents that all the fruits of the field were given to man for his subsistence, and he conducted himself accordingly. Strawberries, raspberries, saskatoons, currants, chokeberries, rose-haws, "buffalo beans" – not commonly regarded as edible – found their way into his capacious little maw with no more serious results than may be set right by timely administrations of that well-known lubricant which every adult considers indispensable to the health of children, but which no one takes on his own account after he has reached the age of self-determination. He ate the leaves of every flower of the prairie, but was particularly partial to rose leaves and the purple blooms of the so-called prairie crocus. He gnawed the bark from the toothsome red willow, and he dug up "snake" root and ate it moist and earthy as it came from its natural element. He chewed the rank weeds and cattails that grew in the marsh at the head of the lake, and, under cover of the deepest secrecy, he smoked sections of porous cane which he cut from the shanks of discarded buggy whips.

His adventures with disease and foodstuffs by no means covered the range of Gander's hazards. Before he was ten he twice had fallen into the lake; once in summer, from a log upon which he had improvised a raft, and once in winter, when he skated into a fishing hole. In each case he managed to get out again, and, in the former instance, did not bother to go home to report the occurrence.

His winter plunge was more serious. By much coaxing Gander had persuaded his father to exchange the price of four bushels of wheat for a pair of skates. In those days the luxury of special skating boots, with the blades securely screwed to the soles, was unknown, at least in Gander's circles, or perhaps this adventure would not have taken place. Ten bushels of wheat for boots and skates would have seemed prohibitive to even so indulgent a father as Jackson Stake. The skates of that day could be attached to any stout farm boot, provided the heel or sole were not too badly worn away. Adjustments were made by means of a key, in the genial neighborhood of the kitchen stove; then one walked to the ice with his skates flung over his shoulder, and snapped them to place as he sat on a stone or a stump by the edge of the lake. Gander had done all this, and was swinging up and down the lake in great exhilaration of spirit, the ice ringing under his steel blades, when pop! into the hole he went. Some one had made the hole the previous day for spearing fish, and the tissue of ice which had formed during the night was not strong enough to bear the child's weight. He splashed over his head, but bobbed up again in an instant; flung out his arms, and managed to find handhold on some of the rough chopped ice about the hole.

"O-o-h!" said Gander, "it's cold!" his teeth already chattering. His first impulse was to shout for help, but it was a mile and a half to his father's house, and there was not a chance in a thousand of any one being within reach of his voice. No one – but Queenie! The dog had come down to the lake with him, and was off in the bush, hunting rabbits.

"Oh, Queenie, Queenie!" he called, and then, because he was essentially religious, he began to pray. "Oh, God, make Queenie hear me," he cried, "and I won't —" But before he had made any indiscreet commitments the dog appeared, racing toward him.

"All right, God," he said, his assurance returning. "I guess Queenie an' me can make it."

The dog came close to the black hole in the ice, now slopping water over its edge, and Gander, after one or two unsuccessful attempts, during which he was almost at the point of praying again, managed to slip one hand through her leather collar. "Now, Queenie, pull!" he threatened. "You pull me out or I'll pull you in."

The dog pulled, and Gander had enough presence of mind not to expect to be pulled out perpendicularly. He threw his body into a horizontal position, as in swimming. This brought one of his feet into contact with the solid ice at the opposite side of the hole. A thrust, a lurch, a scramble, and he was up in safety again. He whipped his skates from his boots and started on a run for home.

"Well, for the soul or sake o' me!" his mother exclaimed as Gander plunged through the door, panting to exhaustion, with Queenie at his heels. "What you been up to? . . . My land, did you fall in the lake?" She was on her knees beside him then, her heart suddenly choked with concern. Gander's outer clothes were a thick icy film, but his run had kept his body warm. The buttons were frozen fast in their buttonholes, so his mother ripped the trousers down the outside of the leg until they could be drawn off him. In a few minutes she had him in bed with a hot stove-lid at his feet and a glass of hot chokeberry wine in his stomach. Gander experienced a sense of delicious comfort, and presently fell asleep. When he awoke it was morning, and he was as fit as ever.

By the time Gander was eight he was shooting gophers with a muzzle-loading shotgun that had been in the family for at least a generation. He carried his powder and shot in old-fashioned horns made for the purpose, and re-loaded the gun himself, out alone on the prairies. First he would pour a charge of powder into the barrel – a barrel so long (and the boy so short) that he had to stand it at a slope in order to reach its muzzle – then force it down with a crumpled lump of paper in front of his ramrod. The powder must be well pounded down, after which the charge of shot is poured in, and held to place by another wad of paper, which need not be pounded down quite so hard as the first. Then you turn the gun end for end, raise the hammer, and examine the nipple cautiously, to make sure that the powder has come down all the way. If not, you will do well to drop a few grains of powder from your horn straight into the nipple; it may save you a mis-fire, and the annoyance of having to do it afterward. Having made sure that the powder has come down all right you take the box of percussion caps out of your pants pocket – the little box with the lid which never comes off easily and never goes on straight – and you press a cap home on the nipple. Then you let the hammer carefully down to place, and you are ready for the next gopher.

"A dangerous business!" you say. "Incredibly dangerous for a boy of eight!" Not so dangerous as dodging street cars and automobiles, which, we may remember, were not among the menaces threatening young Gander's life.

As a matter of fact, Gander met with only one mishap in all his shooting experiences. That was the summer he was ten. He had been hunting plover, and was walking homeward with his empty gun swung across his shoulder, when, cresting a ridge that commanded a small pond, he was astonished to see a dozen or more grey geese resting at the water's edge. It is an unusual thing for the wild goose to rest without sentries on guard, but fancied security may be the undoing of even a goose. The boy sank as silently as an Indian into the grass; then drew himself gently back over the ridge and out of sight. There he quickly reloaded his gun, pouring in twice the charges he would have used for plover, and then, his heart thumping like a drum, he wormed his way like a snake back up to the crest of the ridge.

Gander never had shot a goose; this was his chance of sudden glory. Steady, Gander, steady! What will they say at home when you carry in a great grey goose – maybe two of them? What will they say at school? What will that detested brother Jackie say, who is forever belittling your marksmanship? Gander raised his gun slowly. The blood was swirling in his head, but his hand was steady. There were two geese sitting right in a row; a long shot but a good target. Gander lined them with his sight, being careful to keep his eye close down to the breech. There they are, covered by it! Gander hugged the stock to his shoulder and fired the left barrel – he had grown into the habit of always firing the left barrel first, because that was the rear trigger, and his little arm was too short to reach the other trigger with comfort.

What happened next Gander never knew. When he awoke the sun was just setting – and it was mid-afternoon when he fired! He arose on his left arm, but a stab of pain flattened him again on the grass. His right arm seemed paralyzed. There was something clammy and sticky about his face. He rubbed his cheek and found a cut now choked with a plaster of dried blood. The discovery sent a strange creepy feeling up his spine. Had he shot himself? Was he dying? The tears came into his eyes – he was only ten – and the thought of dying alone on the prairie came as near to terrifying him as anything ever had done. He wished Queenie were there, but he had forbidden her to come on this trip, because, with all her amiable qualities, she had an annoying habit of racing in among the plover at inopportune moments. She was a collie, not a bird dog. Once again his religious subconsciousness asserted itself, and he began to pray. Then his eye fell on his gun, lying some paces away, and the sight stirred him to action.

He arose slowly. He got up on his knees, he stood on his legs. To his surprise and joy they did not collapse under him. Then he experimented with his right arm. It was stiff and sore, but he could hold it out. He even could swing it a little.

"I guess it ain't broke, or I couldn't do that," he consoled himself. And suddenly his heart was very light as he realized that he was not about to die, after all.

He picked up his gun and examined it. It appeared to be none the worse; it was docile in his hands. He stroked the long, lean barrel; it gave no hint of its recent treachery.

"Just a kick," he soliloquized, a little sheepish now over his scare. "But gee – didn't it spill me! Wonder what made it kick like that? I held it good an' tight." Then, his mind suddenly connecting up with recent events – "Wonder if I got a goose!"

He raced down to the water's edge, all his injuries forgotten. There were the tracks, right there in the mud. He hunted around. Just as he was about convinced that he had missed his mark he almost fell over a stout body in a clump of grass. He seized it. A grey goose – a great big grey goose! When he lifted it by the head it seemed almost as long as himself. With a whoop he gathered up his gun and started on a run for home.

"Pretty late out shootin', ain't yuh?" his father challenged, as he stood in the door. "Got your mother scared half – jumpin' jack rabbits, what's that? A goose!" His father was beside him with a great stride. "A dandy, ain't he? Good boy, Bill! But you're all over blood – should be more careful carryin' it. Good boy!"

It was the proudest moment in Gander's life. What were a cut face and a bruised arm to glory like this?

"Gun kicked a bit," he explained. "Nothin' much. Cut my face a bit."

"You might ha' been killed," his mother commented. "I'm scared to death some day you'll come home dead. Well, there's another goose to pluck an' clean an' stuff an' cook —"

"Gee, we ain't had a goose for a dog's age," Gander protested. He resented his mother's lack of enthusiasm. Hadn't he shot a goose, and he was only ten? He was beginning to feel that mothers didn't understand. His father did.

"What did you do – fire both barrels at once?" his father asked him. He had the gun in his hands, examining it.

"No – just the left. Look out for it – the right's loaded."

His father was dropping the ramrod down the barrels. "'Tain't!" he said at length. "No charge in this gun!"

The two men looked at each other for a full minute.

"Sure you loaded both barrels?"

"Sure. I came up on the geese sudden, with the gun emp'y. Then I dodged back behind the ridge an' loaded 'er – double charge in both barrels. But I only fired one – I'm sure o' that."

His father hung the gun on its two nails over the door before he spoke. "Guess you rammed both charges into one barrel, Bill," he said, solemnly. "It's a God's mercy you ain't killed."

Two days later Jackson Stake brought a new breechloading shotgun home from Plainville. "Take that, Bill," he said, "an' throw that ol' gopher-duster in the bone-yard."

Gander's eyes jumped, and he committed one of those rare indiscretions in the Stake household – he gave evidence of affection. He actually put his arms around his father. And Jackson Stake absent-mindedly rested his hand in the boy's tousled hair for a fraction of a moment.

"Well of all things!" said Susie Stake. "I bet that weepon cost the price of a load o' wheat."

"May be cheaper 'n a funeral at that," was her husband's dry rejoinder.

THREE

Gander had started to school the April he was five years old. Jackie was then thirteen, and too big to be spared from the work of the farm, but he walked the mile and a half with Gander to the prairie schoolhouse and presented him to the teacher, Miss Evelyn Fry.

"This is my brother Bill," he said. "Mother sent 'im to school."

Miss Fry regarded the little chap in the new cottonade pants with the pockets with some misgivings.

"Looks small," she said. "How old is he?"

"Five."

"Sure he's five, Jackson?"

"Well, he'll be five this week, if that'll do you," said Jackie, belligerently.

Miss Fry's second appraisal of Gander seemed more favorable. She had to be on guard against parents sending their children under school age as the easiest means of disposing of them. She meant that her school should not be exactly a nursery.

"All right, William," she said. "Are you going to be a good pupil?"

William was non-committal.

"I'm sure you are," she pressed, reaching down and taking up one of his lean hands in hers. An hour ago Susie Stake had scrubbed it clean as one scouring could make it, but the business of pelting clods of wet earth at venturesome spring gophers along the trail had left its marks of toil. Miss Fry was accustomed to soiled hands, with deep lines of mourning under the finger nails.

"I'm sure you're going to be a good pupil," she repeated, "and learn to read, and spell, and count numbers?"

Gander was in a difficulty, and he studied the dusty floor, as though in it he might find some solution of his problem. The fact is he had no idea what Miss Fry meant by pupil. But he was favorably impressed by this young person, so fresh and dainty in comparison with his over-worked mother, who was almost the only other woman he knew.

"Guess so," he compromised, twining his thin legs around each other as an outlet for his embarrassment.

"You will sit with Tommy Burge," Miss Fry told him. "Tommy, this is William Stake. Show him your desk and help him to feel at home."

The Burges lived south of the school, on the road to Plainville, and three miles from the Stake homestead. Gander had seen Tommy once or twice, and knew him by sight, but no acquaintance had been developed. He was as slim as Gander, with long legs and a fair face peppered with freckles in large flakes like oatmeal, a circumstance which had gained for him the cognomen of Porridge.

Jackie had left for home without further formality. He was a man now, helping his father to clean wheat, and he had been a little humiliated by having to go to the school at all, even to accompany his brother. Of course, Jackie attended school during the winter months along with the other big boys of the neighborhood, but that was different.

Tommy Burge took Gander in charge. "This is our seat," he explained. "If you got any books you can stick 'em in there," indicating a shelf under the desk.

"Ain't got any," said Gander. Thereupon the two boys for an instant looked into each other's eyes, blushed under the searching gaze of childhood, giggled, and Gander knew they would be friends.

Miss Fry rang a bell, and the children who had been playing outside while Gander was being introduced to his new surroundings came storming in. Storming is the word – there is no other for it. They jammed in the doorway, the bigger boys pushing or tripping the smaller ones and pulling the hair of the little girls, who squealed, and would have been offended had they been denied this playful gallantry. A stern word from Miss Fry checked the stampede, and the mass disentangled. As each child entered the room he or she developed an overpowering thirst, which deflected the procession toward the water pail sitting on a bench in a corner. There was but one drinking cup, and the water had been in the room since the previous Friday – this was Monday – but neither of these facts checked the thirst or, so far as ever could be learned, affected the health of the children. They drank in turns, and as each finished he threw what remained in the cup ostensibly on the floor, but actually on the legs of his companions. There was then a mild fight to be next in turn, in which the last user generally contrived to thrust the cup into a certain selected pair of hands – a mark of favoritism which never passed unnoticed or without comment.

Miss Fry regarded this behavior with disapproval. Before she had begun her career as teacher of Willow Green School she had entertained visions of well-trained and orderly children marching in double file to the "Left – right" which she would beat out with the precision of a drill sergeant. Her first day's teaching had been one of disillusionment. With a good deal of trouble she had lined the children up at the door, but just as her ruler began to beat time two of the bigger boys linked hands and rushed the whole group pell-mell into the school, almost trampling the teacher as they came.

"That's the way they load steers at the stockyards at Plainville," they explained to her proudly.

She had plans to stop all this – when she could. But she was only eighteen years old; she was a hundred miles from home, and a little terrified by this chaos of youthful energy. She noted the farm-bred muscles of her older boys and remembered that her parents had prophesied disaster. These boys were not accustomed to taking orders; if they obeyed it was because it pleased them to do so, or because they liked her – not because they were afraid of her. She took these things into consideration, and, being wise for her years, held her throne by judicious concessions.

When the children finally were herded into their seats they proved to be much less numerous than the rabble about the door and the water pail would have suggested. To be exact, there were just fourteen of them. Willow Green School District had twenty-seven pupils of school age on its register, but the attendance fell off sharply with the commencement of farm operations in the spring, when all the older boys, and most of the girls over twelve, were kept at home to help in the fields or about the house. True, there were always two or three new pupils – such as Gander – to take up the vacant spaces. So the dove-tailing of the generations goes on.

If Gander had been closely observant of his environment – he was not, as his entire attention was occupied with an

approving and sometimes suggestive criticism of a drawing
which Tommy Burge was perfecting under cover of his First
Reader, and which was confidentially understood to portray
Miss Fry, or an idealization of Miss Fry, as conceived by Master
Tommy; a sort of Futurist art, of bold strokes and conspicuous
angles, with height and breadth but without perspective – had
Gander been observant of his environment he would have seen
a room of four walls and a ceiling, with a door in the east,
windows in the north, and blackboards above the wainscoting
on the west and south. The walls were in need of whitewash,
and the woodwork, of paint – a detail which Gander would not
have noticed, had he been never so observant. Two rows of
desks made of soft pine lumber, which lent itself admirably to
the engraving of initials and other adornments, faced the
teacher's table placed at the west end of the room on a platform
raised a few inches above the floor. In the southwest corner
was a dilapidated organ, bought by the Ladies' Aid of Willow
Green School District with the proceeds of two box socials, as
an incentive to singing at the church services held in the school
on Sundays. On the south wall, over the blackboard, hung a
map of Canada and a map of Manitoba, both of which were
kept rolled up except during the period of geography lessons;
and on the west wall, over the teacher's head, was a lithograph
of Sir John Macdonald, for many years Prime Minister of
Canada, but now sufficiently dead to have his portrait dis-
played in a schoolroom without suggestion of partizan designs
upon the young minds exposed to its contagion. Even yet there
were rumblings in the school board and at the annual meetings
over the propriety of bringing the children under such sinister
influences, and a movement to hang the portrait of Sir Wilfred
Laurier beside that of Sir John had collapsed only when it was
discovered that to have it framed would cost two dollars.

One object did, indeed, catch Gander's attention, and he consulted his friend and mentor, Tommy Burge, thereon. It was a black daub on the plaster ceiling above the huge box stove which occupied the centre of the room, between the two rows of seats, and served the purpose, in cold weather, of rendering the remote corners somewhat less Arctic and the seats immediately alongside insufferably torrid.

"What's that?" he whispered to Tommy, indicating the daub with an up-pointed finger safe behind his desk from the teacher's view.

"Ink," said Thomas. "Bottle blew up."

This was interesting. This was something worth while.

"How?" Gander demanded.

"Ink was froze, an' Dick Claus put it on the stove to thaw, an' forgot about it, an' it blew up, an —"

"Thomas, I'm afraid you're talking more than is necessary. William, this is your first day in school, but you must learn not to talk during the periods of study."

Gander had no idea what was meant by periods of study, but he understood that he had incurred the teacher's displeasure. He squirmed in his seat and felt uncomfortable, until Tommy, with a couple of deft touches, revised his portrait of Miss Fry in keeping with the mood of the moment, and restored Gander's good humor. Gander giggled.

"William, what are you laughing at?"

No answer, but a terrific heart-fluttering under Gander's blouse.

"William, you must tell me what you were laughing at."

Gander tried to speak, but the roof of his mouth had gone suddenly dry, and he made only an incoherent gasp. And Miss Fry was actually coming down the aisle!

Meanwhile the ill-fated work of art lay under Tommy's reader. With conspicuous presence of mind Tommy added another stroke or two while Miss Fry approached.

The teacher looked at the drawing for a moment as it lay on the desk, then lifted it in her hand. "Who is this supposed to represent, Tommy?" she demanded.

"John A." was Tommy's prompt rejoinder. The politics of Tommy's father, Martin Burge, were well known to be the antithesis of that espoused by the distinguished statesman whose portrait hung above the teacher's desk. Indeed, it had been Mrs. Burge who had offered to supply, for the more appropriate adornment of the room, the picture of Sir Wilfred which she had obtained as a premium with a year's subscription to the Winnipeg *Tribune*.

Miss Fry crumpled the paper in her hand, lifted the lid of the box stove, and with great deliberation dropped the scrap of Liberal propaganda inside. "You ought to set your new seat-mate a better example, Tommy," she said. "No more of this nonsense, or you will stay in at recess."

Tommy and Gander were sobered by this episode, but not for long. Percy Marsh, who occupied the seat immediately behind, came to the relief of their drooping spirits. He contrived to drop another scrap of paper between Tommy and Gander. This, when surreptitiously smoothed out, revealed a poem by Master Marsh:

"Miss Fry
Couldn't hurt a fly."

Tommy spelled this out laboriously, grasped its meaning, and managed to convey it to Gander while the subject of the poem was working out a problem in division on the blackboard for the Second Class. Gander felt reassured, not so much by this information as by the temerity which dared to express it almost under the teacher's eye. The poem was given a timely touch by Tommy's capture of a fly, almost at that moment, from which he proceeded to extract the legs and wings for his own and Gander's amusement.

At first recess Gander was initiated into a game known as Pom, Pom, Pull-away. His instincts ran more to baseball, but a considerable pond in the centre of the school-yard made that game impracticable; besides, no one had a ball. Pom, Pom, Pull-away could be played on the relatively dry area beside the school. It consisted of choosing sides and placing two bases, on each of which a "prisoner" was located. To rescue the prisoner one had to run across the enemy's flank, and, if captured by them, became an additional prisoner on the base. The game was conducted to the accompaniment of a chant:

"Pom, Pom, Pull-away,
If you don't come I'll pull you away!"

For some time Gander remained in the safety of his home camp, as was becoming in a raw recruit, but as the game proceeded his courage rose. He saw other boys distinguishing themselves and the call to glory fell not unheeded on his ears. A little girl about his own age – Josephine Burge, sister of his seat-mate Tommy – in a pink calico dress which Gander thought very beautiful, was languishing in jail. Percy Marsh had rushed to her rescue, and, being one of the bigger boys, had drawn all the enemy's fire. They were pursuing him over the school-yard, and, in the midst of this deployment, Gander went "over the top." Silently and unnoticed he dashed to the aid of the prisoner, whose hand was outstretched toward him as far as her lithe little body would reach, because it was a rule of the game that the moment she was touched by one of her side she was free. Their hands met, clasped, and home they ran in triumph together.

"Hurrah for Billie Stake! Good boy, young Stake!" cried his comrades. Glory was his, and a new joy of life was upon him.

That was the first time he ever held Jo Burge's hand. . . .

At noon the boys ate their lunches squatted against the sunny side of the school building; the girls, always more fastidious, ate theirs from their desks inside. Miss Fry walked the half mile to her boarding-house on the Gordon farm, returning within the hour to resume her classes at one o'clock. Gander had brought his lunch in a school-bag which his mother had made from the better sections of a discarded grain sack, and he now produced it with some hesitation, being a shy boy, and struggling with an intense desire to go off somewhere and eat it by himself. But Tommy Burge had taken him under his wing, and before he knew it he had his bread-and-butter sandwiches spread out on his knees before him, and was attacking them with a will. There were two thick sandwiches, two cookies, and a hard-boiled egg. Gander noted that his luncheon – he called it his dinner – did not suffer by comparison with those about him, some of which consisted of bread and butter only; coarse, heavy bread such as Susie Stake would never have drawn from her oven, or, if she had, would have promptly thrown to her pigs or chickens.

They gulped their meal quickly, but interlarded it with conversation.

"You near caught it th' smornin', Porridge," Dick Claus – he of the ink-bottle episode – remarked to Tommy Burge. "Ol' Fry's on your trail, all right."

"Huh," said Tommy. "She ain't, neither."

"What you mean sayin' that was John A.?" Pete Loudy wanted to know. "Eh? I've a mind to bloody yer nose for it." Pete was Nine, and had the confidence of his years, especially when addressing Six.

"Don't take that, Porridge," one or two of the older boys, always eager for a fight which involved no risk to themselves, counselled. "Don' be scared of him because he's big. You can lick 'im, easy."

But Tommy had a well-developed sense of proportion. He knew – probably by experience – the difference between Six and Nine, so he smiled amiably upon Pete's truculent gestures, as though he were quite in sympathy with the champion of John A.'s memory.

Gander was less fortunate. His attention had been drawn to a portion of Peter's unfinished lunch; dark, soggy bread, incredibly uninviting. Gander was by no means fastidious but he always had been accustomed to wholesome food. This dark mass fascinated him and seemed to set some mechanism in his stomach in reverse gear. His intent observation did not escape Peter's notice.

"Well, what's a-matter with it?" Pete demanded.

"It's rotten," Gander observed, with great frankness.

This, of course, was too much. Pete bounced upon the little boy, punching at his head and face.

It was Gander's first engagement of any consequence and his tactics were simple and spontaneous. He wrapped his arms about his face and shrieked at the top of his voice. The other boys looked on, a little startled, but unwilling to interfere, partly from a wholesome respect for Pete's prowess, and partly from their natural human enjoyment of a fight. Only Tommy Burge, who felt a moral responsibility for his seat-mate, tugged half-heartedly at a broken end of Pete's suspenders.

Gander's screams brought the girls running out of the school. They formed a segment of a circle a little way from the centre of hostilities, horrified at the brutality of the master sex and eager to miss none of its manifestations. Suddenly from among them dashed a little figure in pink calico, and with cheeks blazing with indignation redder than her dress.

"Itth th' little Thtake boy!" she cried, and buried her fingers in Pete Loudy's hair. Her hands were small but her grip was astonishingly strong, and she had no squeamishness about her method of attack. Pete's shriek rose higher than the best of Gander's. He turned on his new assailant, but Tommy Burge, encouraged, or ashamed, as the case may be, by his sister's onset, seized him by the waist and down they went together. By the time Pete had wriggled loose his better judgment had cooled his fighting ardor. To hit a girl was considered bad form even in a school-yard where the boys fought with each other as their parents had fought with the wilderness – with the single idea of victory, and few compunctions about the method of attaining it. Besides, girls were notoriously tattle-tales. If he hit Jo Burge it surely would be reported to Miss Fry, and Pete had no great reserve of good conduct to his credit.

"Pete, Pete, tenderfeet!" the other boys ridiculed him, finding safety in his discomfiture. "Fightin' with the girls!"

"Didn't, neither," Pete defended himself, shame-facedly. "Whole fam'ly piled on me —"

Meanwhile Gander had disentangled himself, and, somewhat to his surprise, had found no serious injuries. A little miss, of whose acquaintance at that time he had not the honor, stuck a taunting finger in his face. "I know who your girl is," she said. "It's Jo Burge!"

Gander had no very clear idea what it meant to have a girl, but supposed it was quite reprehensible. Still, there had been something in that little tormentor's manner that suggested she would have been not unwilling to change places with Josephine Burge.

The incident excited within Gander an interest in Tommy's sister. During the afternoon he once or twice ventured to glance in Jo's direction, and, curiously enough, found that at the same moment she was glancing in his. A strange color flowed through Gander's dark skin as a result of these coincidences, and he found his attention distracted from a narrative concerning a cat, a hat, and a rat, in which Miss Fry had sought to interest him.

At afternoon recess the sport took another form. This was known as "Drownin' Out Gophers." The school water pail, a broken baseball bat, and such sticks or clubs as could be found, were the necessary equipment. On a dry knoll near the school several gophers were rejoicing in the sun of early spring after their long winter indoors and, sitting up staunchly upon their tails, were sending their challenging whistle forth to the world.

The game consisted in chasing a gopher into a hole and pouring water, carried from a nearby pond, down after him. When the hole was full of water the gopher, willy-nilly, must come out. The bedraggled, shivering little creature stirred no sympathy in the circle of children around the hole, each eager to prove his prowess by being the first to "lam" the victim. Half dazed with water and fright he would nevertheless put up a remarkable dash for liberty, twisting and doubling about among his pursuers' feet, and sometimes actually reaching another hole unharmed, but even in such case he only had postponed, he had not escaped, the inevitable end of the sport. More water would be carried, and again he would be forced into the open, more terrified and exhausted than before, until a merciful blow ended his suffering. Gander joined in the chase with shrieks of delight, and found running beside him, more than once, that little form in the pink calico. How she could run! Gander had counted himself speedy for his age, but this little girl was almost, if not quite, a match for him. As she ran her flimsy dress would billow high above her knees, but Gander and most of his companions were yet in the age of innocence. When, years later, he herded cows with Jo Burge, he used to think of those races.

At four o'clock Gander started for home, swinging his empty school-bag about his head and talking to himself after the manner of children who spend much of their time alone. As it happened no other pupils lived in Gander's direction, so he walked the mile and a half with no companionship except his own imaginings. These were busy with the events of the day, or, rather, with anticipated developments built on the day's events. The anticipations included a tremendous thrashing adminis-tered to Pete Loudy in the admiring presence of Josephine Burge; the persuasion of his mother to include another hard-boiled egg in his luncheon which he could share with Tommy Burge; and a little, elusive, shy half-resolution to gather a handful of crocuses for presentation to the most beautiful of all women, Miss Evelyn Fry.

Susie Stake watched from the south window for the coming of her boy from school. The promise (or threat?) of Genesis 3:16, postponed in the case of Susie Stake, was now being fulfilled. Minnie, two and a half years old, hung about her knees, and Hamilton, a babe of three months, occupied the cradle that once had been Gander's. These, with the growing herd of cows to be milked night and morning, the growing flocks of hens, geese, ducks, and turkeys to be fed and cared for, the growing area of garden to be planted and hoed and weeded for the growing appetites about her growing table, left the busy mother little time for sentiment. She had sat up the night before, making for Gander a pair of trousers from a new piece of cottonade bought in Sempter's store – the first occasion upon which Gander's trousers had not been salvaged from a worn-out pair of his father's – and a school-bag from remnants of a discarded grain sack, while the rest of her family slept the sleep of the unconcerned.

In the morning, above Gander's unavailing wails, his mother had scoured his hands and face and neck into some measure of cleanliness, made up his lunch, put in an extra cookie, told him to be careful of his new pants, and to be sure and do as Miss Fry bid him, kissed him, and sent him off to school. She followed his little figure down the path through the willows with something as like moisture in her eye as Susie Stake ever had time to entertain. More than once during the day, in the midst of her work, she had thought of him; when she saw his place vacant at the noon table it took her with a goneness under the waist which she would have been ashamed to confess, and by four o'clock she was beginning to send her glances down the road to the school. It was Gander's first little step into life.

It was after five o'clock when Gander came loitering along. Whatever sentiment or concern his mother had felt for him during his absence she now suppressed; it was a way with the Stakes to show no weaknesses toward each other.

"Well for the soul or sake o' me, I thought you was goin' to stay all night! Get off them good pants and go hunt the eggs."

FOUR

G ander attended school with more or less regularity
until he was ten years old. The qualification is ren-
dered necessary by those frequent interruptions
caused by rain storms, blizzards, illness and accidents – always
regarded as godsends by young Gander – temporary embarrass-
ments in the matter of wardrobe, and, it must be confessed, a
few occasions when he had deliberately gone gopher-snaring at
the cost of higher education.

Gander was dull; learning came to him with difficulty;
books were bothersome, and he was not disposed to be
bothered. After his first shyness had broken down he enjoyed
mingling with the other boys; he gloried in the games at recess
and during the noon hour; he never wholly disliked any
teacher, but he hated study. For Gander was a farmer born and
bred; he had an eye for horses and a knack with machinery; the
mysteries of the self-binder he had solved before he was nine,
but the mysteries of cube root he had not solved when he left
school – nor since. He knew more than any of his teachers
about the profession by which he was to make his livelihood,
and he regarded their book-learning as nonessential and

irrelevant – neither of which words would he have understood. He made chums of Tommy Burge, Dick Claus, and Freddie Gordon (of the school teacher's boarding-house), but particularly of Tommy Burge. And he developed a strange kindliness of regard toward Josephine Burge; a regard which, for all his blundering shyness, he in some way managed to disclose to the one individual who had most right to know.

The summer he was ten years old Gander began to take a man's place on the farm. Jackson Stake had added to the original homestead until he now had four hundred and eighty acres of land; rich, mellow, fertile prairie and scrub sod, with over two hundred acres under cultivation. His cattle and horse stables, his granaries and sheds, sprawled aimlessly about the log hut which was still his home, its numerous lean-tos marking, with some degree of precision, the periodical increases in his family; the new frame house, with lath-and-plaster finish, of which Susie Stake had dreamed for a decade and a half had not yet come into being, although every spring her husband had prophesied that if the crop "came off" the new house would surely be built the following season.

"What do you think about buildin' our new house this year?" she would say each May, when the prairie was a garden of flowers and a man's heart might be expected lightly to turn to rash commitments.

"Not this year, I am afraid, Susie; got to buy a new binder. Maybe next year, if the crop comes off."

Mrs. Stake was a bad but effective loser. "I'll believe it when I see it," she would close the discussion.

Meanwhile Jackson enlarged his stables and barns; abandoned the twenty-acre field idea which he had transplanted from his early Eastern environment to the broad measures of the West, and now farmed his land by quarter sections; abandoned the two-horse team for teams of four and six; abandoned the fourteen-inch single-furrow walking plough for two- and three-furrow sulky gangs; abandoned the broadcast seeder for the disc drill, and the six-foot binder for the eight; abandoned the grain sack for the bulk system of handling wheat; abandoned the old horse-power threshers whose metallic crescendo sang through the frosty autumn mornings of the 1880's for the steam and gasoline of the twentieth century.

Jackson Stake was but one unit in a hundred thousand who were making possible the great trek from the country to the city, a trek which never could have taken place but for the application of machinery to land, so that now one farmer may raise enough wheat to feed many hundreds of city dwellers. But if in this he was adding his weight to a gathering social and economic crisis he was quite oblivious to the fact; he saw no further than the need of bringing more land under cultivation, to grow more wheat; and even while he pursued this policy he would have told you that he lost money on every bushel of wheat he grew, and that it was the cows, the hogs, and the hens that held the farm together. And Mrs. Stake, had she been standing by, would have reminded him who it was that milked the cows, and fed the hens, and mothered the young chickens, and, perhaps, threw the chopped barley to the hogs. Mrs. Stake had a gift of mentioning such matters.

The summer Gander was ten he drove a two-horse team on the mower, and, later, a four-horse team on the binder. He was now a tall, thin boy, hump-shouldered from sitting huddled on his machines, grimy with oil and bleareyed with dust; knowing nothing about cube root but able to harness and handle four horses abreast, and filled with the joy of a man's accomplishment. He was still too small to be of much service stooking sheaves or forking hay, and his natural aptitude for horses and machinery led to his being made teamster of the binder and mower. His brother Jackie, now eighteen, and his father, followed him in the fields, working the long harvest days until after sunset to save the thirty dollars a month which a hired man would have cost. But for Gander's services the hired man would have been inevitable; the statement that he was filled with the joy of a man's accomplishment is, therefore, no figure of speech. True, Gander did not get the thirty dollars a month – nor did he expect it. He was working for his father and with his father, and that was enough. Gander was still in the tribal stage of development; his individualism was swallowed up in the family group.

Not so Jackie. Jackie discussed it with his father.

"Dad, I'm doing a man's work and I think I ought to get a man's pay," he said one day in harvest, as they sat in the shade of a stook for a few minutes after eating the four o'clock lunch which Minnie brought from the house. "I ain't a kicker, but I could get thirty dollars workin' on any other farm 'round here, and not work any harder, either."

His father chewed meditatively on a straw. There had been something in Jackie's mood in recent times which rather had prepared him for this conversation.

"An' how much would you get in winter?" he asked.

"Perhaps somethin', perhaps nothin'," Jackie returned, doggedly. "Or I could go into Winnipeg and hit somethin' for the winter."

"Hit a soup kitchen, mos' likely. I guess there ain't no jobs chasin' young fellows like you up and down the streets o' Winnipeg in January. Some fellows don' know a good home when they got it."

"I suppose you're alludin' to that log shack we eat and sleep in," Jackie retorted. "Yes, it's a pretty classy residence. You've been goin' to build a frame house as long's I can remember, with lath and plaster inside —"

Jackson senior paused in the mastication of his straw. His big red face hardened. When he spoke it was with the finality of an ultimatum.

"Lath an' plaster don' make a home, an' sometimes poplar logs do. I built that place with my own saw an' axe, an' you didn' help me, nothin' partic'lar. It was good enough for me then, an' it's good enough for me yet, an' any day it ain't good enough for you perhaps you'd better buzz round a bit an' find somethin' more to your likin'."

There was a silence in which both men gazed blankly at the shimmering heat away through the avenues of stooks.

"I don' mean that remark to be took too literal," the older man conceded at length. "You've been a good help on the farm – I'll say that for you – an' I'm not handin' you any grand bounce. What I can't understand is why you wan' to leave it."

"I ain't sayin' I want to leave, but I think I'm worth as much as other men that's gettin' paid."

"Well, we're not quarrelin' on that, either, but, there's more ways of payin' than writin' a check. You get everythin' you need. You charge it up at Sempter's store, an' I settle for it. Besides, I been payin' instalments on you ever since you was born, Jackie, an' before. Seems like the new generation nowadays don' take that into consideration. They think the old man should be like a stove-pipe – everythin' goin' out an' nothin' comin' in. I figger on bein' fair, Jackie, but it don' seem to be as you have any kick comin'."

"I know all that, Dad, but every time I want a dollar I got to go bowin' an' scrapin' to you, just like Mother does.

When I go into Plainville I see other fellows there with money to rattle in their jeans – workin' on the section, dollar and a quarter a day, and quit at six o'clock, and pay sure every month. They don't work as hard as I do, and if they want to treat some o' their friends to ice cream or – or – anythin' else, it's nobody's business."

Jackie was reaching the gravamen of his indictment. He paused, gulped, and plunged on:

"One day this summer you gave me fifty cents to go to a show – after I'd asked you for it – and I went and – took a girl along, and the tickets were thirty-five cents, and there was I standin' at the door tryin' to squeeze four bits till it looked like seventy cents, and the door-keeper – it was a travelin' show, and he didn't know me from a load o' hay – he says, 'Well, well, young man, what's the delay?' lookin' at me like I was a lump o' cheese. I'd a mind to soak him one for luck right there, but when you got a girl with you you got to be a gentleman, and just then Jim French came along – he's workin' on the section now – and says, 'What's a-matter, Jackie, old boy?' and I says 'Guess I must 'a' lost my money, Jim; had it down town a few minutes ago,' – lyin' a bit to cover my family pride, you understand – and Jim sticks a dollar bill in my hand and says 'Pay me any time you like,' and in he goes. Well, it made me so mad I felt like jumpin' the whole thing right there. I'm just a clod-hopper, a farmer's lout, but I got some feelin'." Jackie's emotions were not far from tears. He came to silence, swallowing hard.

His father took his time in answering. Then:

"Ever pay Jim back his dollar?"

"Well I guess I did. Very next time I was in town."

"Where'd you get it?" his father sprung on him. Jackie had walked into his trap.

"From you. Had to ask you for it, though."

"Yes – from me. An' you could 'a' got it before the show, just as well as after, if you'd said so, an' saved your wounded feelin's. An' it's my notion that a boy that gets money for the askin' ain't so darn' bad off as he might be. I don' get mine that way – an' never did."

Jackson glanced at the shadow of the stook, creeping around to the eastward. His legs were stiff with toil and he rose with a groan, but once upon his feet he strode quickly through the crisp stubble. Gander drove up at the moment, the binder clattering as it came. The young teamster saw his father through the corner of his eye, and his chest swelled with manly pride. Not for an instant did he deflect his attention from the job in hand. He cracked his long whip over the backs of his four bays and by they went on the half-run, the binder snapping out its great sheaves of golden wheat and its drive-chains singing in the hot afternoon. Just as it passed Jackson it tripped another sheaf; the ejecting arms swung upward; the needle ploughed the resilient stalks until its polished point protruded through the knotter, for all the world as though it were sticking out its tongue at its lord and owner; the compressing finger came up; the cord tightened; the beak, with two threads of twine in its jaws, made its revolution, too quickly for the eye to see, and the knot was tied; the knife cut the string, and the sheaf fell on the carrier. Then the loose chatter of the packers, as, the strain for a moment relieved, they thrust fresh wheat into the loop of twine left by the needle when it receded into its sheath. It was done in a second, or, at most, two; every six or eight yards around that half-mile field the operation was repeated, and a boy of ten was the magician who slew those serried ranks of wheat in less time than a score of grown men with aching backs swinging cradles in the days of his grandfather. An industry which has been so mechanized can spare a Jackie now and again – and does.

There was a glow of pride in Jackson Stake's eye as this young farmer drove past; he followed him for a moment with his glance, then turned to his stooking. A stoop, a grab with his bare hands into the waists of two sheaves; a swing of the elbows and the back which brought them into upright position, heads together, butts slightly tapering out, in the form of an inverted V; then a swift, sharp, downward stroke, planting them firmly in the stubble. Around this nucleus other sheaves were set in a circle; butts out, heads tapering in, to turn the rain; not less than eight, not more than twelve, and father and son moved on to the next. By the time all the field was cut it would be a sea of stooks, ready for two or three weeks of curing in the autumn sun and rain, and then for the thresher. A business this which lays heavy tribute of risk and labor upon its devotees; which rewards them sometimes handsomely, sometimes sparsely, sometimes not at all; but which has in it the elemental fascination of the soil.

The Jacksons, senior and junior, plied their work without another word. To the father no further discussion seemed necessary. Jackie was restless, and a bit ungrateful; when he was older he would realize the advantages of having a home he could call his own, in foul weather as well as fair.

"I'm ready to do what's right with Jackie," the elder Stake assured himself. "The far quarter can be his when he marries, an' a team, an' the use o' the machinery until he can buy his own; but I'm not tellin' him that – not jus' now. No use startin' foolish notions. Time enough. An' if the crop comes off all right I'll slip him a little cash after threshin'; maybe a twenty-dollar bill to do as he likes, an' no questions asked. I don' blame him for bein' sore, held up there at the door o' the hall; dang it all, when I was his age I'd 'a' bust my way in, but times is different now. Wonder who the girl was? He didn't say, did he? Well, Jackie's gettin' along; eighteen now, but it seems like yesterday I walked the post road to Plainville for him, an' Susie." Over the gap of years the advent of his firstborn came back to him, poignant and overwhelming, and a mist which was not from the red rust of the wheat sent the sea of stooks swimming before his eyes. "Dang it all, I'll make it fifty, if the crop comes off, so help me!" he promised himself.

But he didn't make it fifty dollars, or twenty dollars, or any other sum, when the crop "came off." For on Friday of that week Jackie drove to town with cash for two hundred pounds of twine, and a boy from the livery stable brought the team home, saying Jackie had taken the morning train to Winnipeg.

FIVE

After Jackie left the farm such work as Gander could do was even more in demand than it had been before. He finished cutting the crop, with an occasional "spell off" from his father, who was now obliged to hire a man in place of Jackie, and found him much less efficient. When the stooking was finished Jackson Stake and his hired man stacked the sheaves from a strip of the earliest cutting, in order to clear a space where fall ploughing could be started in case wet weather should interfere with threshing. In the stacking process Gander was of no great assistance; the sheaves were too heavy for his slim arms, but he made himself useful in other ways about the farm. He could drive to Plainville for supplies; keep the wood pile replenished, and have the horses' mangers and oat-boxes filled when they came from the fields at noon and night. And he lent a hand, somewhat less willingly, to his mother in the house. He regarded domestic service as beneath the dignity of a man. His sister Minnie, now a ruddy-cheeked girl of seven, was a better dishwasher than he – and was welcome to the distinction.

Threshing was a great event, as always it is on those farms where grain growing is the major occupation. Several times had Jackson Stake been on the verge of buying a thresh-ing machine of his own, but always he had been deterred by the vigorous opposition of his wife, who insisted that a new house must take precedence over any such investment. And when Susie really insisted, Jackson, who was not without stub-bornness on his own account, had the wisdom to temporize, with the result that the machine was not bought, nor was the house built.

"I'd think you have enough machin'ry debts as it is," his wife would say to him. "An' a threshin' machine, of all things! What you know about a steam engine? Mos' likely blow it up, an' then where'd you be?"

"Guess I'm kind of accustomed to a blowin' up," Jackson would say, in his droll good humor. "An' look at the threshin' bills I got to pay! Enough to build a new house every two or three years." He flattered himself that this was a diplomatic touch.

"Well, I don' see that those that's got machines are build-in' many houses on what they save. There's Bill Powers; been runnin' a thresher ever since we came to the country, an' what's he got? Nothin' on his place but a mortgage. Better hire Bill again an' save your money."

Bill Powers was the chief thresherman of the commu-nity. He had graduated from the old horse-power days into the steam-engine class in the early nineties, and was now wearing out his third machine, which, with the assistance of his home-stead quarter, carried the accumulated mortgages passed on by its predecessors. Bill's credit was a matter of high finance on a small scale. He bought oil, grease, and belting from the Square Deal Hardware Store by giving orders, payable after threshing, on such comparatively solid farmers as Jackson Stake. He had little trouble with men leaving him during the rush of the season because he never had enough money to pay them off;

how he managed at the end of the term no one seemed to understand. But he was a good thresher; he took all the wheat out of the straw; he wasted nothing; he cleaned up after the sets as conscientiously when the farmer was away as when he stood at his elbow; he gave sixty pounds to the bushel and a little over – it was said of Bill Powers that his "thresher's measure" was always better than the elevator weight; and in fifteen years' threshing with steam he never had had a fire. Jackson Stake had fallen into the way of engaging him each year, after the annual debate with Mrs. Stake on the buying of a threshing machine had been settled in the negative.

It was late at night, near the end of September, when Powers' outfit moved on to the Stake farm from Gordon's, a mile or two to the south. Mr. Stake and his hired man were helping their neighbor with his threshing, and Gander was at home filling mangers and, in his small way, getting ready for "the gang." His mother, also, was getting ready, but in no small way. The "cook car," in which the thresher feeds his men, was an innovation in those days not yet adopted by Mr. Powers, although he had so far fallen in line with the march of progress as to carry with his outfit a caboose in which the gang slept during the all too brief hours between quitting time at night and starting time the following morning. The result of such an arrangement was that the farmer's wife had to be ready, frequently at short notice, to feed eighteen or twenty additional men, each equipped with the most ravenous appetite, and to feed them well. To feed the threshers well was a matter of honor among the farm women, and in this culinary competition Mrs. Stake excelled. It never had been said of Mrs. Stake, nor would it, while she had power to bake and boil, that she had failed to rise to the occasion of the threshers' visit. Indeed, so established was her reputation that it was the fixed policy of the Powers gang to get to Stake's as soon as possible, and to remain as long as circumstances would permit.

This year Mrs. Stake was placed at a special disadvantage. It had been understood that the threshers would move to Loudy's from Gordon's before coming to Stake's, but an insurrection which had been simmering in the gang for some days came to a head that very afternoon. Mrs. Loudy's reputation for cooking was at the opposite pole from that of Mrs. Stake's, and, while the mill was stopped for a few minutes for the repair of a broken belt, a knot of men gathered around Powers and reckoned that they'd move to Stake's as soon as they had cleaned up at Gordon's.

Powers scratched his ear with a hand black with engine oil as he received this ultimatum.

"But gosh, boys!" he expostulated, "I promised Loudy I'd go there next, and he's got everythin' ready. Can't hardly pass him up now."

"Nothin' doin'!" said the spokesman of the gang. "I threshed at Loudy's last year, an' I cut 'em off my visitin' list, from that time, henceforth. Nothin' doin'!"

"That's right!" said another. "Salt pork she fed us; doesn't seem to know there's a butcher shop in Plainville. Send 'er that word, Bill, an' let's move to Stake's to-night."

"But Mrs. Stake ain't ready," Bill argued. "Ain't lookin' for us for three days. 'Tain't fair to Mrs. Stake, boys, to stampede in on 'er like that."

There was a laugh of derision at this defence. "Huh! You'd think you didn't *know* Mrs. Stake, to hear you talk. Send 'er word now, an' I bet she'll be all set for us by mornin', with fresh beef an' pungkin pie for to-morrow's dinner, or I'll eat your overalls – an' they don' look none too appetizin'."

"An' what'll I tell Mrs. Loudy?" Powers pleaded. "It's kind o' rotten on her."

"Not a bit more rotten than the grub she set out for us a year ago. Tell her you hear they got some fine juicy quarters o' beef at the Plainville butcher shop, an' the boys has decided to give her two or three days more to make her prep'rations."

Powers gave in, as a man must who isn't in a position to pay off his mutineers, and a spare hand was sent with the word to Mrs. Stake.

"Well for the soul or sake o' me!" that good woman exclaimed, when the man in the door announced that the threshers would pull over from Gordon's that night. "What d'you think I am – a hotel?"

"Sure, mum, it'll be all right. The boys says, 'Leave it to Mrs. Stake,' they says. 'She won't be stuck.'" And with this little speech he departed, leaving Susie Stake torn between pride in her well-earned reputation and misgivings over how it could be maintained on such short notice.

So the afternoon had been a busy one for Mrs. Stake. She was fortunate in flagging a messenger to town as he went by on the main road and sending in an order for supplies, which would be delivered late that night. In the meantime she attacked her baking, and the preparation of her vegetables. When Gander came in to supper he found a plate of potatoes, with two fried eggs on top, thrust at him. He ate it off a corner of the wood box, the table being fully occupied with his mother's activities.

Gander had just cleaned his plate when a tap came at the door; not a man's knock, but a hesitating, gentle little tap.

"Well for the soul or sake o' me!" Mrs. Stake exclaimed, for the fiftieth time that day. "Ain't I got enough without visitors?" Then, her sense of courtesy righting itself, she began scraping her doughy hands on the back of a knife. "Open the door, William," she commanded. "What you sittin' there gawkin' about?"

Gander opened the door and beheld a mite about his own size, or smaller, in the wedge of light from the table lamp. It was Josephine Burge.

"Hello, Jo!" said Gander. "Come in."

Mrs. Stake peered at her caller. "Why, if it ain't little Joey Burge! My, but it's late for you to be out! Are you all alone?"

"Yes'm," said Jo, wriggling under Mrs. Stake's gaze, and slipping her arm about Minnie, who had left her potato-peeling and edged up beside her. "If you please, Mother sent me to say she'd come over in the mornin' and help you, if you like."

"Well, now, I declare, that's right good o' your ma. That's what I call neighborly. These con-suffered threshers come plunkin' in on me without a moment's notice —"

"That's what Mother said, when she heard," the little girl agreed. "And she sent me over —"

"All by you'self? Ain't it pretty dark?"

"Yes'm. Tommy couldn't get away, 'cause my father's helpin' at the threshin', and he ain't home yet. So I came. I know the road well, and it'll be moonlight goin' back."

"Well that's a right smart girl. You won't have had your supper?"

Josephine hesitated. "Well – some," she admitted.

"Guess you could get a couple o' these buns inside o' you, without bustin'," Mrs. Stake suggested, "'specially if they was greased with a dish o' corn syrup." She broke two fresh brown buns from a great panful, poured some golden syrup in a saucer, and drew the little girl up to a corner which she cleared on the table. Any supper in which Josephine already had indulged had no difficulty in making way for the new arrivals.

"Threshin's a powerful hard time on women," her hostess commented, as she resumed the kneading of a panful of dough. "The men hire lots o' help for threshin', but the women jus' got to hitch up an' go to it. I'm waitin' till Minnie grows up – if she don' light out about the time she's some use, like most o' them do. Well, it's a God's goodness o' your ma to come over to-morrow. Thank her kindly for me, an' tell her I'll save some odds an' ends for her to do, or maybe she better bring her fancy work. Maybe we'll both do a little fancy work between meals, eh, Joey?"

The little girl smiled suitably at this sarcastic humor, and finished her second bun. Mrs. Stake was too occupied with her work to notice that the second bun had been finished, and presently Josephine wriggled to her feet.

"Well, I guess I better be goin'," she said.

"Yes; your ma'll be uneasy if you're late. William'll run home with you for comp'ny. Get your hat, William, an' run home with Joey, an' don' stay."

"Can I go?" piped Minnie. "Can I go, Ma? Can I, Ma?"

"You're too small; you couldn't keep up," said Gander. He liked his sister Minnie well enough, but he had a mature instinct that this was no occasion to encourage her presence.

"Yes, you're too small," their mother dismissed the subject. "'Sides, I need you here. Skip along, now, William, an' hurry back. An' tell your ma I'm ever so much obliged." It was understood that the closing sentence was intended for Josephine.

The two children were at once on their way, running lightly through the groves of poplar and willow that shut the farm buildings from the highroad, picking their steps deftly in the darkness. It was not until they emerged on the road allowance that they drew up to a walk. Gander had a feeling that this was a time for speech, but he had no idea what to say.

He was not a romantic boy in the sense of being a worshipper of heroes and heroines. The few books which the Stake household afforded were without interest to him; his little sister, only seven years old, was already a better reader than he. Gander hated school, and he hated books, but he loved horses, and machines, and he suspected that he loved Josephine Burge. But he had no words in which to express his sentiment – he had no models to copy. And, after all, what need of words? He reached out and took Jo's hand in his, and again they ran on together.

When they stopped for breath a full moon was shoving a blood-red segment over the crest of the world. They paused to look at it, and then turned their eyes to the glow from burning straw piles on all quarters of the horizon, for in this way, for lack of a better market, do the farmers lavish their humus and nitrogen into the air.

"They look like moons, don't they?" said Josephine.

"Yep; a little," said Gander, and again they ran on together.

Presently the long, sharp note of a thresher's whistle cut across the night.

They stopped to listen.

"They're through at Gordon's," Gander remarked. "They'll be movin' now."

"They'll be comin' up this road, won't they?" Josephine asked.

"Yep; I guess."

"They'll see us, won't they?"

A pause. "I guess."

"Do you care?"

"Nope."

"Neither do I."

Then they walked, and Gander felt his tongue unloosed.

"Guess I won't be goin' to school no more," he remarked.

"No more? Any more." Josephine was not quite a hater of books. "Why?"

"Jackie's lit out, an' I got to work."

"I heard about that. Will he come back?"

"Dunno. He can stay, for all I care."

This was a confidential discussion, of great interest, and Josephine waited for her companion to continue. About the Burge's table the going of young Jackson had been analyzed, with no very satisfactory conclusions. As Gander did not speak she led him out.

"But you have a hired man now. He can do the work, when the threshin's over, an' you can go to school."

"Hired men ain't much good," said Gander. "'Sides, I don' want to go to school."

"I wish you would. It's – it's lonely at school, without you."

This confession silenced both for another hundred yards. "Maybe I'll go a little while in winter," Gander conceded.

They could now hear the panting of the steam engine, and the voices of men carried curiously distinct through darkness now thinning in the ruddy light of the rising moon. As they crested a hill they saw the black caterpillar of the "outfit" stretched before them, Bill Powers walking ahead with a lantern, on the lookout for stones and badger holes, and the engine following solemnly a few yards behind. The highroad was little more than a prairie trail, with ruts too close for the wide-geared trucks of the engine, so that one side ran on the road and the other on the virgin prairie sod. The light from Powers' lantern glinted on the front wheels of the engine as they wobbled drunkenly but irresistibly along their uneven course. A sharper exhaust snorted out as they struck the grade of the hill, and Gander and Josephine drew over as far as the field that bordered the road to let the outfit pass by. Here they could watch unobserved. Their boast about indifference to public opinion had been sheer bravado.

The straw-wagon drew up beside the engine and Gander could dimly observe the fireman shoving straw into the fire-box. It was his ambition some day to fire an engine, and even his devotion to Josephine could hardly hold him from running up and climbing on board. But while he wrestled with temptation the opportunity moved on.

Behind the engine came the separator, and behind it, the caboose. Behind that again was the water-tank, and one or two supply wagons; quite a train, as it moved solemnly along that lonely road, here and there a point of metal catching the moonlight and picking itself out in brilliance against its somber background. The steady pant of the exhaust, the rumble of the wheels, the voice of Bill Powers raised occasionally in caution or direction to his engineer – these were the accompaniments of that mechanical procession which on the morrow would thresh in a dozen hours the wheat to feed a hundred families for a year. Only two or three men were about; the others still were having supper at Gordon's, and the absence of human attendants heightened the dramatic ghostliness of the scene. And although Gander was a boy not touched by the romance of books here was something that stirred him deeply – the romance of machinery, of steam, which, at the pull of a lever, turned loose the power of giants! He watched until it had gone over the hill.

"I'm goin' to run one o' those, some day; you see if I don't," he whispered to Josephine, and his words were the confession of a great and secret yearning, as that of a young artist who gives his dearest friend a glimpse of his ambitions.

"'Course you are, when you're a man," said Josephine. So that was settled.

At the Burge gate Gander stopped. "Guess I won't go no further," he said.

"Won't you come in?" Josephine invited him, feeling that that was the proper thing to do.

"Nope. Guess I'll skip home. Maybe I'll catch up on the outfit."

They hesitated. "Wish I could go over to-morrow, with Mother," she confessed.

"Wish so, too. P'raps you can. . . . Night, Jo."

"Night, Bill."

She moved toward the house, and he watched her little figure as it silhouetted across the square of light from the kitchen window. Then he turned and ran to overtake his other love.

SIX

Gander's prediction that his school days were at an end proved to be accurate. As soon as the ploughs in Jackson Stake's fields of brown stubble were stopped by the freeze-up the hired man was paid off and turned at large. What might become of him through the winter months of unemployment was no concern of Jackson Stake's; possibly he would drift into Winnipeg, where, after his money was spent, a compassionate city would see that at least he had something to eat. In any case one doesn't – or, in those days, didn't – pay thirty dollars a month to any man after freeze-up. The practice of paying for labor of any kind was a new one to Jackson Stake, and he took to it rather badly; by a second year he would be more ready to "dicker" for help through the winter months on a board and lodgings basis.

With the going of the hired man Gander's help about the farm became indispensable. His father was now hauling wheat to the elevators at Plainville; the sloughs in the pasture had dried up, and with the approach of winter the stock needed additional attention. The November mornings opened gray, with a spray of light filtering through frosty mist; mid-days were sunny, but with a chill nip in the air, and night came early. Each morning the stock was turned out to feed in the straw piles, which they browsed into the shape of huge mushrooms, or single-storeyed Chinese pagodas, burrowing under the sides in answer to the joint attractions of food and shelter. At the approach of dusk Gander and Queenie would set out across the fields, rounding up the milch cows and the younger stock, but, except in the threat of storm, leaving the steers and the spare horses to shift for themselves. There was something about these November days, with their stillness, their silence, and their forecast of winter, that would have stirred a nature more romantic than Gander's; to him they were merely part of the routine of the farm, a routine in which he found a sort of placid enjoyment, particularly in contrast to the more deadly routine of the school, from which it enabled him to escape.

It was not all work, of course. On afternoons when he was not needed about the farm he went skating on the lake, his thin figure a pathetic suggestion of loneliness, thinner than ever in its contrast with the great expanse of ice and the hills sprinkled white with snow and hoar frost which shouldered up from the lake to the prairies beyond. Yet Gander was not lonely; never in all his days on the farm and the prairie did Gander know the pang of loneliness. This was his native environment; he was no more lonely on these prairies than is the coyote or the badger.

Once in a while Tommy Burge and Josephine would join him on the lake, but Josephine had no skates, and Tommy, with the blindness of big brothers, saw no reason why he should lend her his. Gander's position, in such circumstances, was a difficult one. If he urged Tommy to lend his skates he ran the risk of being suspected of showing preference for the company of a girl, which was a very black suspicion; if he lent his own, Tommy and Josephine would go skating off together, while he sat on the bank, a victim of misplaced gallantry.

"How'd you like to watch for rabbits down this run, Porridge?" Gander would suggest. "I saw tracks there yesterday, an' you might catch one, if you had a snare."

Tommy would look at his sister's skateless boots, and understand. "You catch 'em, Gander," he would say. "I ain't got any snare."

Gander would finally compromise by lending Josephine one of his skates, and then the two would stride off together, each sliding on one foot and using the other as a propeller. Occasionally the foot with the skate would develop more speed than the one without, and a collapse would ensue – a collapse which would bring the two youngsters into unconventional entanglements. Laughing, they would lie on the ice until its cold began to penetrate them; then, steadying themselves upon each other, they would scramble to their feet, and slide off to their next catastrophe.

There were days, too, when Gander went shooting rabbits, partridges, or prairie chickens with the new breechloader which his father had bought him; he knew every track in the fresh-fallen snow, and wandered up and down every coulee and ravine leading into that part of the lake which lay not far from his father's farm. A gun under his arm and a dog at his heels gave him a sense of confidence and companionship such as he found in nothing else. Once in a while he would raise a fox or a coyote, but never really within shotgun range, although he always emptied a cartridge or two on general principles. He was looking forward to the time when he would be able to persuade his father to buy a forty-four rifle, such as was pictured in the mail order catalogue which hung beneath the clock in the house, and which he consulted almost every evening.

When wheat hauling was finished Jackson Stake had little occasion to be away from home, and a lull developed in the farm operations. There really was no reason why Gander should not then have gone back to school, had he been so disposed – but he was not. He even could have gone without any sacrifice of his dignity, as it was the practice of the big boys of the community to go in winter, and Gander now counted himself a big boy, although he would not turn eleven until the spring. But he had cut a season's crop, he had taken a man's place, and one who has done that is no longer a child. On one pretext and another he managed to stay at home, and his father, never strict in matters of this kind, was glad enough to accept his help with the firewood and the stock.

By this time the Stake farmhouse had been enlarged by two additions, built at the rear and sloping up to the eave of the original roof. As the original eave had been none too high, and a slope must be provided for the roof of the addition, the back wall was not more than five feet from the floor, so that Mrs. Stake, who was tall for a woman, when she worked in these little rooms had to move about in a very stooped position. But there was space for a bed under the sloping roof, for a window in the gable end, and a wooden box or two for belongings. The only warmth in winter was through the door which communicated with the main part of the house, and was left open at night in the somewhat optimistic anticipation that the heat from the kitchen stove would force its way outward in the teeth of the cold which poured in through the thin roof and about the frosted window.

Jackie and Gander had slept in one of these little lean-to rooms, and their father and mother and Minnie and Hamilton in the other. When Jackie left, Minnie was promoted to his room, but with the concession to Gander's advancing years of a separate bed, home-built of a two-by-four scantling and pieces of an old packing box, in the opposite corner from Gander's. So much for the preservation of the conventions, which, let it be confessed, were frequently shattered when the frost would send Minnie wriggling out of her blankets to the warmth of her brother's long legs and arms about her.

One night, near the approach of Christmas, Gander, who usually dropped to sleep as soon as his head was on the pillow, lay planning a rabbit snare which he proposed to set in a run-way down by the lake. His mother sat by the table in the living-room, darning socks, and his father smoked beside the fire, with his chair so arranged as to promote convenient expectoration into the open ash-pan of the stove. They had been sitting in silence for some time, and Gander had just reached the point where his snare was about to tighten upon its first victim, when his mother spoke.

"I've been wonderin' about our boy, Jackson," she said, and the tone of her voice brought Gander back from his jungles. His mother was a practical woman, who seldom dallied with sentiment, but there certainly was something in her voice now as though she had been thinking of a little baby. Once in a while she used to speak to Gander that way, before the work of the farm and the care of the other children became so pressing. Gander lay still, his ears alert.

"I've been wonderin' about our boy," his mother said. "He's been gone since August, an' not a word."

There was silence for a minute, and Gander could hear his father drawing on his pipe, and the tick of the clock on the wall:

"I reckon he has our address. He knows where we live."

"Maybe he hasn't got any money to come home with."

58

"Maybe not, but a husky chap like him should be able to raise the price of a stamp, anyway. He was goin' away where there's lot o' money. Maybe he's got so much now he's forgot all about us."

There was another period of silence. At length Gander's mother spoke again:

"It don' seem right to let him go like that. It's cold weather now, an' not many jobs, I'm thinkin'."

"He can come home when he likes," her husband returned. "Only I ain't doin' no coaxin'."

"Jackie won't come home beggin'. He'd starve first. You done not too bad this year, Jackson, an' I was thinkin' you might go down to the city for a day or two an' look aroun'."

There was a long silence. Then:

"It wouldn't be the first cold trip I took for Jackie, Mother. Do you remember?"

"I do." Gander started in his bed; his mother's voice sounded so nearly like a sob.

"An' this is all we get for it. As soon's they're able to git out, they git. It don' seem worth while."

"I'd give him another chance, if it was me."

"So I will – any time he asks for it."

There was another silence so long that Gander fell asleep, but the next day he thought of it. Jackie had slid readily from his mind. He never had liked his brother, mainly because, with all a child's intensity, he resented Jackie's attempts to "boss" him. It was born in Gander's blood to take orders from none – a quality in his nature which was to determine his course in more important matters than anything that related to his brother. The obeying of orders clashed with his sense of independence. He loved to work in the fields with his father, for there they worked as man and man; Jackson Stake was much too wise a driver to let this colt feel the rein. Perhaps he had learned something from his experience with his first-born. Or perhaps it was that Gander appealed to him differently.

Gander reacted toward his father perfectly. They were friends and chums together. That was one reason he feared the intrusion of Jackie's return. Again, Jackie's desertion of the farm seemed to hang as something of a quarrel between his father and mother, and Gander was his father's partisan. His mother had been losing her grip on him ever since the night when she had failed to enthuse over his shooting of the wild goose – when the plucking and dressing of the goose had loomed bigger in her imagination than Gander's triumph in shooting it. Besides, his mother was disposed to give orders.

For a day or two Gander lived under a fear of losing the status he had gained, but he heard nothing more of the trip in search of Jackie, and the danger passed away.

So another season came and went. Gander, although without a man's strength, was able to take a man's place in the driving of a team and the management of most of the farm machinery. He drove a seeder in the spring, up and down the moist, black fields; up and down, up and down, up and down. He drove a plough in the summer-fallow; a mower in the long prairie grass about the sloughs in haying time. It was a man's life; a life that thrilled him with the joy of accomplishment. If he was being robbed of his childhood he was content to be robbed, for in its place he was being given manhood before its time. When he saw other boys of his own age going to school he regarded them with pity and contempt. A poor business, that, for one who could drive a four-horse team!

His little sister Minnie was quite different. She loved school, she was bright at her studies, and she had a habit of using Gander as a yardstick by which to measure her progress.

"Do you know the difference between a noun and a pronoun?" she demanded of her brother one evening at the supper table.

"Don' know as I do," Gander admitted, without apologies.

"Huh! Teacher'd call you a dunce."

"Would she?" said Gander. "Well, I know the difference between a Deering an' a Massey-Harris across a fifty-acre field, an' I bet she don't, an' you can tell her that for me."

"You mustn't be impident," his mother rebuked him. "Let the teacher learn Minnie all she can."

"Yes, let her learn Minnie all she can," Gander flared back, "an' let her learn somethin' herself, too. I bet she don' know a Clyde from a Perch'ron."

The contempt in Gander's voice stirred his father's usually slow-moving cerebration.

"I don' know as William is so very far out," he said. "I've noticed that the boys an' girls that goes to school until they're fourteen or fifteen gets themselves eddicated *off* the farm. Jackie went pretty steady, an' he's flew his kite. Minnie here is bright at school, an' she'll likely do the same, about the time you're figgerin' on havin' a hired girl an' not havin' to pay out no wages for her. William —"

"An' that's about the only kind o' hired girl I'll ever have, it looks to me," Mrs. Stake interrupted. "One that don' cost no wages."

"Well, maybe. We'll see." Jackson was capable of almost any obliquity to escape a clash with his wife. "As for William, while I'd like for him to know the diff'rence between those words, an' all that, I want him with me here on the farm, an' maybe when he's my age he can offer a roof to some o' them eddicated fellows that can't get a job in the city. 'Course, a fellow should be able to read an' figger, even on the farm, or some o' them sharks'll leave him holdin' an emp'y sack at the end o' the year, but these pronouns, or whatever it is, what does it matter about them?"

"Me for the farm, anyway," said Gander. "I want to stick with Dad."

Jackson Stake rubbed his fingers through the lad's hair. It wasn't often that he so far forgot himself. "You bet!" he said.

Fifteen years later his college-bred son-in-law, Minnie's husband, was writing magazine articles on How to Keep the Boys on the Farm.

The summer Gander was twelve his father hired a man for the season. He was introduced as Bill, and perhaps that was one of the reasons for the friendship which sprang up between himself and young William Stake. It was one of Gander's secret ambitions to be called Bill; William he despised, as being sissy and stuck-up. The boys and girls of the neighborhood called him Bill, but his father and mother called him William, and he irked under it as if it were an offensive epithet. Once in a great while his father called him Bill, and then he knew that they were man to man together, but such experiences occurred only at rare intervals.

Bill, the hired man, was slight and wiry of stature, with heavy creases showing through the ruddy stubble on his face, brows that hung well over his pale eyes, and hair thinning to a poor stand on top. Jackson picked him up one June day in Plainville, and for a year and a half he was a fixture on the Stake farm. He carried his worldly belongings in a grain sack, and dropped into the life of the place with ready adaptability.

"Where'd you get that spec'men?" the farmer's wife demanded of her husband.

"Found him holdin' up a corner o' the Palace hotel,"

Jackson explained. "He said he knew all about farmin', so I asked him out to give me a few lessons."

"But where'd he come from? Who's his people?"

"Dunno. Didn' ask for no pedigrees. But he seems at home with horses."

"Well, let's hope he's all right," said Mrs. Stake. "But I'd like to know somethin' about him. Why didn' you get some one we know?"

"Of course he's all right," her husband assured her. "If he ain't I'll tie the can on him, quick. An' you can't get anybody you know, no more. 'Tain't like it use to be, when you could always hire one o' the neighbor's boys. There don' seem to be the loose help round home, like there use to be. When I was a boy I hired out with a neighbor, but now, I guess all the young fellows has gone to the city – or gone homesteadin'. What us farmers is goin' to do for help I dunno."

"Oh, 'us farmers' 'll get help, all right, even if we have to hire men that's maybe nothin' but hotel bums. But how about us farmers' wives? Tell me that, Jackson. How about *us*?"

Jackson backed away, mentally. "Oh, you'll manage. You're a dandy manager," he told her. "'Sides, Minnie's gettin' to be a bit o' help, ain't she?"

Susie Stake swept by to the stove, as though she could spare no more time with such a trifler. The years, which so often are generous to the feminine frame, were leaving Mrs. Stake, each in its turn, a little more angular than it found her. This had been particularly so since Jackie's disappearance. After a long silence he had written to his mother from the head of the lakes, where he said he was working in a grain elevator, and expected to get on a boat in the spring. Months later he was heard from in Kingston, and now, for months, no word at all. Even Gander had noticed that his mother's dark hair seemed to draw back further from her brow, and that there were threads of white in it.

She turned from the stove as suddenly as she had gone to it. "Where's he goin' to sleep?" she demanded.

"We can fix him up in the grainery for the summer, an' if he's all right he'll have to bunk with William when the cold weather comes."

"William? Minnie —"

"Well, we'll have to get her out o' the room. Should be out, anyway. William's too big a boy now."

"Guess we'll pretty near need that new house won't we?"

"Well, if the crop comes off —"

By all the tests to which Jackson Stake subjected him, Bill seemed to be "all right." He knew how to harness and handle horses, and, more remarkable still, he was able and willing to milk. Mrs. Stake qualified all her objections to the new man when she found him willing to milk. He was less at home with machinery, in which sphere Gander was able to lord it over him, but he picked up instructions readily. He was gentle with the children, and never fell into worse language than did his employer. He showed no disposition to go to town, and Jackson Stake, scenting his weakness – a weakness from which he himself was not entirely immune – so planned the work of the farm as to keep Bill's feet out of the paths of temptation. Altogether he seemed a very satisfactory man.

But there was one angle of his life of which Jackson Stake and his wife knew nothing. It was an angle disclosed only in his confidences with young William, and the boy, with the instinctive curiosity of his years, kept his secrets well. Life on a mixed farm, where stock raising is combined with grain growing, is lived close to the fundamentals. Gander, from his own observations, and from the conversation bandied about among the farmers' boys at school, had long since outgrown that uninformed condition sometimes described as innocence. His mind was groping into new experiences, instinctively, but blindly; instinctively, because he was a healthy human being, and blindly, because those who should have guided him were restrained by shyness from turning a single ray of light upon his path. Working from what he knew, he was speculating vaguely upon the unknown.

His speculations were given point and piquancy by the confidences of the elder Bill. The man was old enough to be Gander's father, but was, apparently, unmarried. He explained this to Gander by pointing out that no married man was wanted on the farm, and, so far as he could see, no children were wanted anywhere, so what was a man to do? If a man was well off, and had a home of his own, of course he could get married; but if he was just a hired man, what was he to do?

He answered that question to his own satisfaction, while Gander's little soul went surging within him. There had been no great show of religious teaching among the Stakes; yet religion, and with it a code of strict moral ethics, was the unwritten background of their existence. Just as they hid their sentiment from each other, and held it a weakness to show any sign of family affection, so also they concealed their religious life, still and deep, behind a mask of matter-of-factness. Yet they knew good from evil, and no Stake had ever called evil good. Gander knew this, too; but here was a man who opened to him a life which, although it shocked his principles, had the appeal of fascinating adventure. Bill's exploits lost nothing in the telling, and Gander was stirred between horror at his revelations and admiration of a courage which placed all the conventions at defiance.

"Human nature is human nature, wherever you find it," the hired man would defend his philosophies. "Ain't it Kipling or somebody says 'The Colonel's lady and Judy O'Grady is sisters under their skins'? But the Colonel's lady has a fine house or a suit in a swell apartment, and Judy O'Grady is maybe a workin' girl, like I've seen hundreds of 'em in the cities, with nothin' to call home except a bit of a room in some cheap lodging-house. Believe me, they're all alike, but they don't all have the same chance. They've set up a system by which a man or a woman that's got a home can be decent and respectable – although they don't all do it – but what about us folks that haven't got any home? Take me. I'd like a home as much as anybody, but likin' don't put any shingles over my head. If I was to go to your dad and say, 'I'm thinkin' of gettin' married,' what'd he say? Don't you know? I'll tell you. He'd say, 'All right, Bill, I guess I can let you go by the end of the month.' So I'd get a wife, but I'd lose my job, and how are you goin' to keep a wife when you haven't got a job? But that don't change my nature any – nor hers either. You see, your father and mother are awful nice people, but it's them, and folks like them, that's really responsible."

Gander didn't accept all this argument; his foundations were too solid for that. But Bill became something of a hero in his eyes; a sort of moral Wild Wester at war with things as they are. It is the province of youth to protest, and Gander's sympathies were with his friend.

The crop "came off" as usual, but the new house was not built. With the approach of cold weather a third lean-to was added, to which Minnie and little Hamilton were assigned. Bill shared the other room with Gander. There they slept together in a temperature which condensed their breath on the thick quilts that covered them. In the mornings they would reluctantly burst from their warm beds. The hired man would climb into his stiff clothes with amazing alacrity, puffing and blowing

GRAIN

with his exertions. Then he would take the lantern from the
kitchen wall, light it, and for a moment watch the vapor fade
from the globe. Then out into the crisp, starry morning, the
snow creaking beneath his feet. Gander, having not yet
attained to this hardihood, dressed more slowly behind the
kitchen stove.

Meanwhile his education went on apace.

SEVEN

During the next year or two Gander stretched up into a lanky youth, lean and sinewy, stooped with his early labor. Under a thin face his Adam's apple became the feature of his long neck; it jumped and gulped and hopped about with prodigious activity. When Gander swallowed the mechanics of the operation were almost as visible as if his dark skin had been transparent.

"Sometimes," said his little sister Minnie, "it looks as though Gander was going to swallow that lump in his neck." But, for all its ramblings, it never failed to return to its place.

About this time he discarded the braces, which from his early childhood had performed an important office, and adopted a belt instead, as being more in keeping with man's estate. The change was not entirely a happy one, as Gander was singularly hipless at this stage of his development. He learned to make up for his structural deficiencies by walking with a peculiar hitch designed to hold his overalls in place.

It was also about this time that he acquired the nickname with which he was henceforth identified. Gander attended church services in the schoolhouse with the other members of the family, partly because of the unobtrusive but stern religious background against which his life was set, which took church-going for granted, and partly for the opportunity of a half-hour's chat with the other boys of the neighborhood before or after service. And there was always the exchange of a glance, and perhaps a word or two, with Josephine Burge.

Church services were held in Willow Green schoolhouse every second Sunday at three in the afternoon, and it was the custom of the little congregation to assemble about half past two and fill the period until the preacher's arrival with the gossip of the neighborhood. The farmers, after tying their horses, would gather on the shady side of the school building, and, half squatted on their heels against the board wall, or leaning on their buggy wheels, discuss the crop prospects, the need of rain, the prowess of the Plainville baseball team, and the maladministration of the municipal council; while within the stuffy room their wives and elder daughters exchanged confidences about the latest babies, the prices charged by the Plainville stores, the bargains which might be had from mail order houses, and the numerous unsuccessful attempts to establish a Sunday school at Willow Green. All of these attempts had failed owing to the fact that no farmer in the neighborhood was prepared to assume the duties of Superintendent, which involved the making of prayers in public. The religion of Willow Green district was too subjective for the making of prayers in public.

Upon the arrival of the preacher, dusty and hot in his clerical garb, the men filed in, and the school teacher detached herself from the knot of adolescent girls which had gathered about her, and proceeded to press the dilapidated organ into service. The preacher announced the opening hymn, and then everybody stood up and sang.

Everybody sang. That was the remarkable feature of the service. There was no trained talent to bring home to those farmers and their wives, their sons and their daughters, the fact that they could not sing. So in blissful ignorance of a truth which would have been obvious to any cultured congregation, they raised their voices – and sang. Not all in the same key, to be sure; occasionally not all to the same time, and sometimes not all to the same tune; but all in the same spirit. Culture had not yet demanded in those rural districts its severe price of contempt for the untrained.

In this exercise William H. Stake's song rose as high as any; higher, sometimes, for he was just at the stage where his voice, unruly as any prairie broncho, plunged and bucked into unexpected and involuntary cadenzas. These unpremeditated flights of song were a source of some embarrassment to William, but it was a peculiarity of the case that he never was sure just how far his vocal broncho had bolted from the beaten path. After silence for a few lines he would venture forth again, gently at first, but gathering confidence as he went, until once more, in a sudden evil moment, his note went honking off over the heads of the congregation.

It was Dick Claus, the mark of whose exploded ink bottle might still be defined through the thin whitewash on the ceiling over the stove, who christened him. "Did you hear young Bill Stake?" he said, as the boys gathered for an after-meeting behind the school at the close of the service. "Honking like a gander."

"Hello, Gander!" they greeted him, as he joined their group. William's Adam's apple fled for cover, and his long neck twisted in boyish confusion. The name stuck. By the time he was eighteen only the older generation remembered that Gander Stake ever had been called William.

The church services and occasional social events in the community brought Gander into intermittent contact with Josephine Burge. He had not yet reached the age when he might boldly set out to Josephine's house to call upon her; the fires of a boy's heart, at fourteen or fifteen, seldom smoke so openly. But he found excuse once in a while to call on Porridge Burge, if only to borrow a wrench or a clevis, the return of which, by the good fortune of fate, gave occasion for another visit the following day. Tommy usually received his guest in the tool-shed which his father had recently built, and which afforded good cover for the smoking of that porous cane to be found in broken whip stalks. And it almost always happened that for some reason or other Jo had to seek something in the tool-shed during Gander's visit. Tommy regarded these inter-ruptions with true brotherly blindness, but Gander knew.

He began to be conscious of a yearning to be alone with Jo Burge. To meet her at church, or at one of the summer picnics, or to talk with her in the tool-shed under the chaperonage of Tommy, was only tantalization. He had no clear idea of why he wanted to be alone with her, and less of how it was to be accomplished, as he was not of an inven-tive mind except in his experiments with machinery. But he knew that the mere presence of Josephine – alone – was something very much to be desired. Working about the farm, harnessing his horses, shuttling up and down the black fields on his sulky plough, the figure of Josephine Burge flut-tered before him, beckoning, beckoning. He remembered the wisdom that Bill had poured into his young ears, and wondered what Jo must think of him.

It was Bill's theory that women are born to be mastered; that they recognize the master and obey him, but for those who are afraid they have only contempt.

"You mind Eve?" Bill had said to Gander. "She played for Adam with an apple – not that one you're always choking over, but a fresh one out of the garden. A pippin, I guess it was, or maybe a spy. Adam took it, and so got us all into a lot o' trouble. But suppose he hadn't. Suppose he had said, 'Eve, you know better than this. I'm surprised at you. Tut! Tut!' What would Eva ha' done? She'd ha' give him the stoney stare, henceforth. Put him down for a dub and flounced out o' the garden to hunt up a he-man of her own."

Gander reflected on this. "Of course, she thinks I'm a dub," he would say to himself. "And I am."

Fortunately for Gander he was unable to consult Bill in his dilemma. After a year and a half of steady work the hired man had suddenly announced that the white lights were calling him and he must be on his way. Jackson Stake jocularly professed some misgivings as to the color of the lights, and parted with him regretfully. He had been a good man. He had visited Plainville only two or three times in that year and a half, and even then had managed to come home sober. The farmer argued with him, and offered to increase his pay.

"It's pleasant of you to make the offer, Mr. Stake, but it's no good," Bill answered. "If you were to offer me the farm it would be just the same. I'm a bird of passage, and I've roosted here longer than most places. I'd like to stay, but I can't. That's the way I'm built."

Gander had been sorry to see him go, and yet he was conscious in his own heart that the man's influence over him had been evil. His parents knew nothing of this; Gander had kept his secrets well. But his whole viewpoint on life had changed. The spiritualism of childhood, never strong in Gander, had been obliterated in the stark realism of life as he now saw it through eyes that he believed to be mature. Yet he was shy, and ashamed of his shyness. According to his new light it was the measure of his weakness. The prize was for the bold, not for the shy. Girls loved to be mastered. Jo —

It seemed strange to Gander that he never had discussed Jo. For some reason he could not bring himself to mention Jo to his friend Bill. There she was, in his mind, but while he thought of her he talked of others. And in this simple distinction, without knowing it, he belied all Bill's theories. Jo he kept to himself, held apart, as one different, superior. Jo was for him; for no one else. And he had not the courage to assert his right. That was why he despised himself as he turned black furrows in his father's field, and blacker thoughts in his own mind.

The opportunity of Jo's companionship came in an unexpected way.

Gander had overheard another discussion between his father and mother concerning the missing boy, Jackson. Not much had come to his ears, but he had known from his mother's voice that there were tears in it – a thing almost unprecedented – and his father had spoken with unusual harshness. Gander had lain awake for some minutes that night, worrying about this domestic problem. In the morning he noticed that strained relations appeared to exist between his father and mother; they spoke with unnecessary civility across the breakfast table, and as Gander slowly thought this matter over his anger at his erring brother mounted higher and higher. For nearly two hours Josephine Burge was spared the attention of his imaginings.

A day or two later Jackson Stake suddenly announced that he and his wife were going to the Brandon fair.

"Yes, sir, Bill," he said to Gander; one of the rare occasions on which he called him Bill, and the boy's heart bounded – "Your mother an' me are goin' to take in the big show. We've held this old homestead down pretty steady, an' we're goin' out to see the white lights, as Bill used to call 'em, for ourselves. We'll be away a couple o' days, an' we'll take Ham with us, because he can't very well be left, an' you an' Minnie'll have to run the farm. Think you can do that, Bill?"

"You bet we can. The summer-fallow's just finished, an' Minnie an' me'll make it go all right." Gander's heart was glad to see the smiles back in his father's face; for a day or two they had been strangely missing. This idea of going to the Brandon fair was certainly a new one for Jackson Stake, who seldom travelled further than Plainville. The boy was too young to recognize the strange currency in which domestic peace offerings are sometimes presented.

"Yes, the summer-fallow's finished," his father picked up his thought, "but this long spell o' dry weather has left the pasture as bare as a barn wall. I reckon if there's nothin' else doin' you might let the stock out on to the school section an' herd them there while we're away. It'll give them a chance to fill their ribs again. Minnie can stay over at Fraser Fyfe's durin' the day, an' you an' her'll be at home together nights an' mornin's."

For some strange reason it seemed to please Jackson Stake to spend the fifty dollars involved in the trip to Brandon. The farmer was usually close in money matters; he was on record as saying of himself that he was so close he would "bust a rib if he swallowed a flax-seed." But when he spent he spent freely, and this was to be one of the occasions. He whistled an old tune of the lumber woods – what was left of it – as he harnessed a team to drive to Plainville, where he and his wife would take the train. Susie Stake went grimly, as though she was making a concession but was prepared to see it through. Gander was important with the responsibility of the farm, and Minnie danced gleefully over the prospect of long days spent with little Elsie Fyfe.

To Gander and Minnie the house seemed very silent that first night, and they behaved as seriously as any little old couple. Minnie washed up all the dishes and put them in their place; she was now a girl of eleven or twelve, with hair a little darker than red, and a complexion that would be one of her hazards by-and-by. Gander went twice down the mangers, to see that the horses were tied, and even after he was half ready for bed went out again to make sure the granary door was hooked and that there was no danger of the mosquito smudge blazing up if the wind should rise during the night. In the morning Minnie cooked porridge as well as her mother could have done, fried a couple of eggs, and made toast in front of the kitchen fire.

"Wish you'd put me up a bite o' lunch, Minn," Gander told her. "Dad said to run the stock over on the school section for a day or two, the pasture's got so dry, an' I'll have to herd 'em there, account o' the neighbor's crops. Guess I won't bother comin' in at noon, an' you can stay over at Elsie's until it's time to get supper."

"All right." She made four more slices of toast, boiled two eggs hard, mixed a spoonful of pepper and salt in an empty pill box, cut off a healthy slab of cheese, wrapped the lot together and put it in the lunch bag she used when going to school. It was midsummer holidays now, and the bag was out of use.

"I'm not sending any water, Gander; it would get too hot, and tea would get too cold." She laughed gently over this paradox, as though something funny about it had touched her imagination. "You'll be riding one of the horses, I suppose, and you can gallop over to Burge's, or some of the other neighbors, for fresh water when you want it."

Yes, Gander had thought of that. But he hadn't said any-thing about it.

When his lunch was ready he took it from his sister's hand. He didn't often look at Minnie, but in some way she held his eye this morning. She was so smart, so neat, so com-petent. For the first time in his life it occurred to Gander that Minnie was pretty. Funny, wasn't it, one's sister being pretty? Now Jo Burge; he knew Jo was pretty, but then she was Tommy's sister, and two or three years older than Minnie. He wondered if Tommy thought that Minnie was pretty. Could it be possible — Gander's heart suddenly thumped very sharply, and his Adam's apple jumped in panic. Could Tommy think of Minnie as he was thinking of Jo?

Gander saddled one of the work horses, his father having taken the drivers to town, and set out in the clear, bright morning to round up the stock toward the vacant school section. Minnie washed her dishes – not neglecting the porridge pot; swept the floor, made up Gander's bed and her own, placed water in the pans for the chickens, and then, having put on a clean calico dress, went singing down the road to Elsie Fyfe's. Her mother had arranged before she left that Mrs. Fyfe would look after the milch cows, taking the milk in payment for her trouble, so Minnie had no responsibility in that connection.

Meanwhile Gander rounded his stock toward a gate in the far end of the field opening on to the school section. School sections, as every Westerner knows, are tracts of land set aside to create an endowment fund for the support of the public schools – an unique and unexplained exception to the policy of frantic exploitation of the people's domain. The school section bears no necessary relationship to the location of a school; country schools for the most part are built on the corner of some settler's farm, on an acre of land bought or donated for the purpose. Now it often happened that the school section remained unsold after the neighboring land had been taken up, and it consequently afforded choice grazing range for the herds of the surrounding settlers. It was so in this case. It was also so that the school section lay directly south of Jackson Stake's, and directly north of the farm of Martin Burge.

Gander, riding one of the sober work horses, rounded his herd of lazy cows and obstinate steers toward the gate at the south end of the pasture. Queenie before this time had gone to her reward and her successor, a mongrel pup supposed to answer to the name of Gyp, was too distracted by gophers and the smell of a fresh badger hole to be of any assistance. But Gander had all day before him. He rode forward and back over the close-cropped pasture, brown with the midsummer drouth, slowly edging his stock to the southern end of the field. Near a clump of willows he raised a mother prairie hen which went whirring with curious flight over a ridge immediately ahead while her chicks darted for cover among the willows; a minute later he saw the mother gliding confidently back to the willow clump, where she rejoined her excited but obedient family. There evidently had been careful rehearsal of the proceeding to be followed in such an emergency.

Gander edged his stock to the corner of the field and finally crowded them through the gate. Then, as it suddenly dawned on their slow comprehensions that they were being led – or, rather, driven – into green pastures, their tactics were as suddenly reversed; with necks outstretched and nostrils dilated and their long tongues like little scythes whipping the green tufts of grass into their jaws they sampled the verdure of the school section, and, liking it well, broke into a run. Over a ridge to the southward they stampeded, and, by the time Gander had again rounded them up, they were half way across the section. Here they fell into a riot of feasting, and the boy knew that, for the present, they would need little more attention. The nearest cultivated crop was half a mile away, and, the cattle now having been quietened, were likely to gorge themselves for an hour or two, after which they would lie down and re-chew the morning's takings with placid deliberation.

It was now that Gander began to put into effect the plan which had been slowly forming in his mind. Half a mile south lay the homestead of Martin Burge, and, somewhere about the house, or in the fields, was Josephine, his daughter. Gander proposed to take a chance on the behavior of the herd for an hour or two, and seek her out. When he found her he would boldly invite her to come over to the school section and help him watch the cows. The prairie was carpeted with flowers, and under the clumps of willows it was cool and drowsy. True, Tommy might be in the way; he so often was in the way; but this time he must stand aside. Gander would tell him so, in as many words, if it came to that.

The school section lay in gentle swells culminating in low ridges. Gander turned his horse's head to the southward and rode over the next ridge. As the slope on the other side came into view it revealed a herd of cattle dotted along its grassy sward. Evidently some other settler was taking advantage of the free range. And, a quarter of a mile away, was another herd-boy on horseback.

Gander's pulses were thumping and a slow rage was gathering in his heart. Was he not to have even the school section to himself? He resented this other presence; it interfered with his plans. Everything seemed to interfere with his plans, even his most careful plans. Virtue was being thrust upon him; intolerably thrust upon him.

From somewhere it came into Gander's mind that forces which he did not understand persisted in overriding him. His independence was being challenged, his right to manhood denied. He seemed to be under orders. He knew that his friend Bill would have scoffed at any such idea. Yet it held him – and exasperated him.

He was for going back over the ridge and making a long detour, when he saw that the other boy had noticed him, and was riding in his direction. Retreat would now be too obvious, so he rode slowly on to the southward.

The other boy's horse broke into a gallop, and in a minute or two they came up together. Then they looked into each other's face, and Gander saw – Josephine Burge!

EIGHT

Jo was dressed in a blouse and knickers, with a broad straw hat drawn over her head. She was riding astride and wearing knickers at a time when both these practices were still considered strictly masculine. Gander's eyes fell from her face to the curve of her leg about her pony's ribs, to the boot in her stirrup, and he felt the color gathering under his own sunburned cheeks. She was wearing a pair of brown stockings; there was a hole in one, through which her white skin shone like a silver dollar.

"'Lo, Bill," she said.

"'Lo, Jo."

"Herding?"

"Yep."

"So am I."

Then they looked at each other again, and Gander marvelled how Jo had grown since he last had seen her. True, she sat low on her horse; she was only a little body, at that; but there was a look of maturity about her that Gander never had seen before. Perhaps it was the loose blouse, the knickers —

"They're Tommy's," she said, as though in answer to his thoughts. "Too small for him now, of course, but handy for me, when I'm on horseback. Of course, I didn't expect to meet anyone, but when I saw it was you I didn't mind – very much. Do you?"

Gander could see that there was a color in Jo's face, too, for which the burn of the prairie sun could not altogether account.

"'Course not," he said.

"Besides, they're safer," she went on to justify her costume. "And more modest than skirts, when you're riding astride, anyway. In a ladies' magazine I take, it says they're quite the thing, but of course the people around Plainville don't know that, yet."

How grown-up she was! A ladies' magazine she was reading! Gander read nothing. Presently it dawned on him that this girl might not be clay in his hands. More likely she would make clay of him!

She stepped her horse up closer. "Where are your cows?" she asked.

"Just over the ridge."

"And where were you going?"

"Oh, just ridin' around." Gander's bold purposes had seeped from him like water from a sieve.

"Let's go and look at them," she suggested.

They rode up over the ridge, and Jo's pony, being lighter on his feet than Gander's sturdy horse, pranced into the lead. With Jo a few feet ahead Gander studied the little figure from another angle. Her hair was gathered up under the crown of her straw hat; her neck was straight and supple; her body swung free at the waist with every motion of her mount. Here was the great day of his imaginings, when he and Jo should be alone, just their two selves together. And he could think of nothing but the commonplace.

"Dad and Mother have gone to Brandon fair," he explained, "and I thought I'd run the stock on the school section for a day or two. The pasture's as bare as a barn wall."

"Yep. If we don't get rain soon it's all day with the crops."

How matter-of-fact she was!

They had reached the crest of the ridge. "See, we can watch both herds from here," she said. "Let's get off and sit in the shade of the willows."

Just what Gander would have suggested, if he had had the courage. Old Bill was right. . . .

She threw herself lightly from her pony, and dropped the reins at his feet. "He'll stand," she said. "Will yours?"

"'Course. Too lazy to run away," Gander answered, with a nervous laugh.

She looked slimmer, but taller, when he saw her on her feet. Yet when he stood beside her her head came little above his shoulder.

They sat in the shade of a clump of willows, while the prairie breezes fanned their faces, and the cattle drowsed in the pastures below, and patches of sun and shade, like a great quilt of the Creator, drew slowly across the waving grass and the dimpled wheat-fields in the distance. For a while they talked of their school days, and the crop prospects, and then they fell silent.

When the sun seemed directly overhead Jo arose and stretched herself.

"Come to our place for dinner," she invited.

"Got my dinner with me," Gander explained, indicating his lunch bag. "Guess we could make it do for two," he added, and wondered if she noticed the catch in his voice.

"I'd like to," she said, "but they'll be looking for me at the house. Won't you come?"

"Nope."

"Why?"

Then it burst from him. "Because Tommy'll be there, and when he knows I'm here he'll want to herd this afternoon, and I don't want him. I want you."

The speech was not finished before Gander was trembling with the temerity of it. She *must* know, now.

"Tommy's ploughing," she answered, as though nothing epochal had been said. "I can't plough, but I can herd, so I'm sure to be here this afternoon. Won't you come?"

But Gander was irritated that she should pretend not to see the significance of his words. "No. Guess I'll just eat my grub here. But I'll keep an eye on your cows, and you can bring me a bottle of water when you come back, if you like."

The breeze had died down and the summer afternoon lay blisteringly hot when Jo returned. She dropped from her horse and handed Gander a bottle. "Fresh from the well," she said.

"Thanks, Jo."

"And you see I came back, after all."

So she *had* understood!

"Cattle giving any trouble?"

"Nope. Too hot and drowsy."

"It *is* hot, isn't it?"

Gander noted that she had changed her stockings. The silver dollar was no longer in evidence. And she had drawn her blouse lightly about her throat with a ribbon of red braid. Gander appraised her as beautiful – and she had made these changes for him! He rather wished that he had worn something better than his farm overalls.

He drank eagerly from the water bottle, for he was thirsty with his lunch and with the heat, and then they sat in the shade of the willows, edging around to the east as the afternoon wore away. The crystal sky of the morning deadened to an opaque blue in which thunder-clouds slowly began to shape themselves.

"Might have rain to-night," Gander remarked.

"Uh-hum; hope so," she agreed.

"You talk like you were 'most asleep," he told her, somewhat curtly, annoyed that she had no conversation for him, and equally annoyed that he had none for her.

"I am – pretty near," she said.

The cattle began to stir about, and Gander drew himself to his feet. She rose on one knee, as though to join him.

"Never mind, Jo," he said, with something like kindness in his voice. "I'll move 'em around to the other side o' the ridge, an' perhaps they'll settle down again. You have a sleep, if you want to."

She took him at his word. When he came back he found her stretched in the lengthening shade. She had thrown her hat aside and taken his lunch bag, stuffed with grass and leaves, to make a pillow.

He slipped up quietly, uncertain whether she was asleep, and sat down beside her. Her hair, released by the removal of her hat, hung loose around her head; a strand or two curled about her neck. Little beads of moisture had gathered on her forehead, for the day was very hot. Gander studied her fair face more intently than ever he had done before. There were tiny points of freckles about her cheek and nose; not the big flakes which had gained her brother the sobriquet of Porridge, but little points which seemed to shine through the clear skin, as though they were under it, not on it. She was surely asleep;

her chest rose and fell in steady rhythm, and her lips, slightly parted, trembled gently with the current of her breath.

For a long time Gander sat beside her, wondering if she really was asleep, or if this was a subtle feminine play to test him. Leaning low over her face he stooped until almost he had touched her lips. Yet he did not touch them; something seemed to hold him back. He rose impatiently to his feet, and walked aimlessly about among the willows; coming upon his saddle, where he had thrown it upon the grass, he fussed with its straps and girth without knowing he did so, buckling and unbuckling, lacing and unlacing. When he returned to the girl she was sitting up.

"Guess I fell asleep, Gander, eh?" she said, as she drew her hair into some kind of order, for she had not yet put on her hat. "You're a good boy to look after me so well."

"Oh, that's nothin'." He could think of nothing else to say.

The clouds were thickening in the west, and the sun was tempered by a screen which now reached well overhead. The stock were straggling over the next ridge.

"They want water," she said. "We'll have to drive them to water or they'll make for the grain fields."

"Yes," he agreed, slowly, knowing that, after watering, it would be time for each to work homeward.

They saddled their horses, and the girl was astride as soon as her companion. Then, the broodings of the day for the moment crowded out of mind by the operations in hand, Gander again became the dominant and efficient man of the farm.

"We'll work 'em over to the southeast, Jo; there's a slough here, if it ain't all dried up. Then you can cut your herd out, an' they'll be close to home."

"Good!" She dug her heels into her pony and was off at a gallop down one side of the ridge. Gander took the other, and in a few minutes they had the herd moving stolidly to the southeast. When they smelt water they broke into a run, but the slough proved to be almost dry; inside the circle of rank grass and rushes was a broad belt of soft mud, etched with the light footprints of snipe and plover and the heavier trafficking of a family of muskrats. The little sheet of water in the centre lay scummy and green with stagnancy, but the herd bolted knee-deep into mud, from which they drew their hoofs with a suction that popped in the still air like corks. Gander's horse was impatient for the water, too, but his rider held him back.

"If you get in there you'll never get out," he said. "You'd bog to the flanks. Besides, 'tain't fit for a horse to drink. You'll be home soon, an' fill up at the pump."

The cattle took their time, and the horses edged toward each other, until the boy and girl again sat close together. Gander was conscious of the seconds, the minutes, of opportunity slipping by, and he powerless to arrest them.

Suddenly a drop of water struck his cheek.

"Rain!" they cried, looking quickly in each other's face, and the joy in their voices was wholesome and clean. "It's coming!"

The sun was now completely obscured, and clouds were scudding overhead, with patches of serene blue shining tranquilly through their turmoil. On the prairie not a leaf moved. Every living thing stood silent for the gestation of the storm.

Then down came the wind. Gander first saw it raising clouds of dust from the summer-fallow, a mile away; then spirals of leaves from the clumps of willows on the ridges. Yet where he sat it was as still as death.

"Jo," he said, "are you my girl?"

She drew her hat from her head, perhaps in anticipation of the wind, and her fair hair flung loose about her neck.

"Bill," she answered him, simply, "I've always been your girl."

He stepped his horse toward her, but the next minute the blast hit them. Her hair was all about his face, and what he said she did not hear.

The cattle swung out before the storm and the two riders in a moment had work on their hands. They were off at a gallop, rounding up the milling herd and crowding them back against the wind. A few great drops splattered on Gander's shirt; his shouts were whipped from his mouth unheard. Yet for the moment he was happy, and Jo was not uppermost in his thoughts. Here was rain, rain! Rain, the first love of every farmer; the bride of every dry, thirsty field; the mother of every crop that grows! Gander was a farmer. All his instincts were rooted deep in the soil.

With some difficulty they got the herd in motion, and then the girl, with expert horsemanship, cut her own cattle from the moving mass. They came up over a ridge again, and faced the sun, blazing in their eyes. The wind had died as quickly as it had come; the clouds were blown into a thunder-bank, vivid with pink and mauve, floating like a mighty iceberg in the eastern sky; the blaze of intense lightning flashes lit it with sharper color from time to time, but the promised rain had vanished in thin air.

The girl and boy drew up again together, and Gander's jaw was grim and set. There was something fearful and majestic about him as he gazed defiantly at the empty sky; defiantly, perhaps, at God.

The girl watched him for a moment as he sat launching his soul against the inevitable. She, too, was rooted in the soil, and knew something of the mocking tragedy of rain that threatens but does not come. It was as though the heavens flirted with the earth, arousing her hope and passion, only to draw away in cold and beautiful disdain.

"I know – I know," she murmured to herself. Then her sympathy suddenly mothered him. Riding close she threw her arms about him and kissed him on the cheek. The next moment she was galloping her cattle toward their own gate.

Gander rode slowly homeward, a medley of mixed emotions. The sun seemed to come out hotter than ever, but he was afraid his cheeks burned not entirely of the sun. He was too young to be long caught in despair over the fleeting rain; his protest had been a sort of reflex of his father, rather than a cry from his own heart. His thoughts again hung about the girl, and he was ashamed of his own timidity. She had even dared more than he! He was a coward, and she would think of him always as a coward. No, not always! To-morrow! To-morrow she should see!

He was unusually silent as he ate the supper that Minnie set before him. He was wondering if Jo had been asleep; if she really had been asleep. "I don't believe she was asleep," he told himself. "I don't believe it. She was – she was –" He could not disentangle the meshes of his own confusion, but he felt that he had been mocked. Not exactly that he had been mocked; that he had mocked himself.

As he did his evening chores he noticed that the sun sank behind a solid wall of indigo, bordering it for a minute with a ribbon of gold which reddened into brass and copper to the north and south. Overhead a tattered banner of high cloud glowed in slowly changing colors long after the prairie lay under a greying mist of twilight.

Gander went to his room, and Minnie to hers. For a long

while he lay, belittling himself, straining at the leash, unseen and not understood, which the inherited virtue of generations had flung about him. "To-morrow," he promised. "To-morrow. I've been a coward, a coward, but – to-morrow!"

He awoke suddenly with the crash of thunder in his ears. Sitting up in bed, he looked through his little window into a world of utter blackness, but black only for a moment; it was suddenly split with light that shone far out on the prairies, and even revealed the wheat-fields rolling in the rising wind. Then came the rain; not a scattered drop or two, but a blast of rain, lashing the window, trampling the roof, battering the tin chimney, flogging the walls and eaves – a very flail of rain. With a great sigh Gander sank back in his bed. Rain! Rain!

Then it lulled a little, and he could hear the sibilant drip of water from the roof – a drip and patter that seemed to accentuate the silence. It was for a moment only; the walls of his little room again leapt at him out of the darkness; broken fragments of lightning fled through the sky; the crash of thunder shook his window as though it would tear it from the sash. Then down came the rain more terrific than before. And so it went on, and on. After each lull, a crash; after each crash a flood of rain, gradually lulling for another crash. Gander lay and thought of the fields, drinking, drinking, under that downpour; already the water would be gathering in the pasture, running in little rivulets, winding about the roots of the willows, dripping into gopher holes, filling the cracks of the drouth, healing the hurt prairie. And, some way, it seemed to heal more than the hurt prairie, because Gander was at peace.

Quietly, from under the muffled roar of the rain, came a voice almost in Gander's ear. "Gander, Gander, are you asleep?"

He was wide awake again in an instant. "No, Minn; what is it?"

"I'm afraid, Gander. It's an awful storm. I wish Daddy was here."

She was standing beside his bed; a flash of lightning revealed her little figure, her night-dress, her hair hanging in braids about her shoulders, her brown eyes big with alarm.

"It's all right, Minn," he said, reassuringly; "it's a big storm, but it's just what we want. I bet the fields are runnin' in water."

"But the lightning is – very close. I counted the seconds. It's – it's very close." Then, mustering her courage for her big request, "Gander, can I – may I – get in with you?"

"I – I guess so. Of course. Come along."

He made room for her, and she slipped under the blanket beside him. Her arms went up around his shoulders; he could feel the beat of her frightened heart. "I'm all right, now," she said, presently.

Then she lay still, her little frame trembling against his, but in the frequent flashes he could see that her eyes were wide. And, just as he thought she was falling asleep, she suddenly sprang up in bed. "Gander!" she shrieked. "There's a man at the window! I saw a man at the window!"

Gander felt a strange creeping up his spine and into the hair at the back of his neck. "Nonsense!" he said, in as steady a voice as he could. "You're scared, Minnie. You're seein' things."

"I saw a man!" she said. "I saw a man! Gander, I saw him right there at the window!"

Whatever Gander would have said was cut short by a knocking at the door; a boisterous, insistent knocking. Gander drew his sister down and crawled out over her. She was trembling and he feared that, perhaps, she felt him tremble, too. But he was the man of the house, and the duty was his.

"Lie still, Minnie," he said, "an' I'll see."

Gander had years ago outgrown the effeminacy of a night-gown. Without stopping for any dressing he strode into the larger room, found the lamp on the table, and lit it, while the knocking kept up thunderously on the door. Then, suddenly conscious of his bare legs, he ran back and drew on his overalls. The knocking had stopped with the lighting of the lamp, but as Gander again walked across the floor he could hear his heart thumping above the drumming of the rain. He threw the door open. The figure of a man in a dripping oilskin coat and felt hat, pulled close down on his head, was limned in the wedge of light that thrust its way into a darkness slant-ingly streaked with rain.

"Well, William," said the man, "I hope I didn't scare you. Are you all right?"

"Oh it's you, Mr. Fyfe. Come in! Yep, o' course, I'm all right."

"Of course," said Mr. Fraser Fyfe, shaking the water from his coat as he stood inside the door. "I figgered you'd be all right, but the wife got a bit uneasy when the storm broke. Rainin' cats an' dogs, eh, Gander?"

Gander always liked his neighbors better when they called him Gander. It didn't sound so juvenile as William.

"Yep. But it's just what we want. I hope it's rainin' at Brandon. It'll kind o' cheer Dad up a bit."

"You bet it will. Cheer us all up a bit. Well – you're all right, eh?"

"Right as rain," said Gander, without noticing the appropriateness of his figure of speech.

"Minnie, too?"

"Yep. She's all right." Gander would not have liked to confess that she was in his bed, but his heart was beating steadily again.

"I looked in at the window, but I didn't see any light, so I figgered you were all asleep," Mr. Fyfe remarked. "Well – guess I'll be going again."

Gander's duties as host came upon him. "Won't you sit down? Won't you stay till the rain is over?" he urged.

"Guess not. I'm a bit too wet in spots for sitting down. And I hope the rain won't be over till morning."

"Hope so, too. It was awful good o' you to come over, Mr. Fyfe."

"Oh, that's nothing. I knew you were all right, but the wife got uneasy. 'Fraser,' she says, 'I'm worried about those children over at Stake's.' 'Children!' says I. 'Gander's as good as a man, and scared o' nothing.' But she'd got it into her head, and you know what women are – or do you, Gander?" Mr. Fyfe's eyes twinkled under his dripping hat.

"I guess I do – some."

Mr. Fyfe hesitated, his hand on the door.

"Well, guess I better be going," he reminded himself, after a pause. "The wife'll be worried about me, next. Women are great worriers."

"I can lend you an umbrella," Gander suggested.

"Nope. They catch the lightning. I'll be all right. Needed a bath, anyway. So long, Gander."

The farmer drew the door open and slipped out into the storm. Gander watched from the window until a flash of lightning revealed his neighbor ploughing his way through the half mile of mud and water that lay between the two homesteads. Then he went silently back to bed.

Minnie again drew him down beside her, her soft cheek against his. "Gander," she whispered, "I'm so proud of you. You're so brave."

"Huh! Guess I'm not very brave. It was Double F that was brave."

"You are, too. He said so. I heard him, right there in the kitchen. He said you were scared of nothing."

She lay silent for a few moments, then, wrapping her arms about him again, "It's fine to have a big brother, that's scared of nothing," she said. And in his arms she fell asleep.

But Gander lay awake, thinking.

The storm had spent itself when they arose in the morning. The sky was as clear as silver, and the air washed clean and sweet with the rain. Gander fed his horses and then stood for a long time unconsciously watching the play of light on the wet leaves.

"Guess I won't need to turn the stock out to-day," he told his sister at breakfast. "The rain'll freshen up the grass in the pasture, an' I want to do some work on the mower. The knives are to sharpen an' there's a new pitman-rod bearin' to fit. We'll want to jump into the hayin' as soon as Dad gets back."

"Can I help?" Minnie demanded, bright with the prospect of her brother's company for the whole day.

"Well, I *might* let you turn the grindstone," he conceded.

NINE

The next turning point in Gander's life was in 1914. He was then eighteen years old; six feet tall when he straightened up, which was seldom; with a fuzz about his cheeks and lips that called for occasional removal, and an Adam's apple protruding from his thin neck like the knuckle of a bent fore-finger. The hitch which he had acquired in supporting his overalls had been permanently incorporated into his gait, and, although his voice no longer showed any tendency to break forth on honking episodes, the name Gander was as much his as though it had been branded on him with iron. The community had forgotten that ever he had been called William.

The new house had been built. The very year after his visit to the Brandon Fair, Jackson Stake announced that, crop or no crop, he was going to have a new house for his old woman. He was beginning to call her "the old woman" now, a term which, on his lips, carried no suggestion of disrespect, but was rather an appellation of endearment, a safe sort of sentimentalism carefully camouflaged with a coat of transparent harshness. And Mrs. Stake was getting along. She was nearing forty-five when the house was built, and farmers' wives are sometimes old at forty-five.

"You've got this ol' hen-house pretty near tramped into the cellar," Jackson had remarked one night as he watched his wife shuttling steadily back and forth between the stove and the kitchen table. The knots in the board floor were coming up higher with the years. "Dang it all, we'll build a new house this summer, whether school keeps or not!"

"I'll believe it when I see it," said Susie Stake, who had ceased to be an optimist.

But her husband, while slow to make up his mind, was resolute in carrying out a decision finally taken. The spirit which had tamed his section of wild scrub and prairie land into one of the most fruitful farms of the Plainville neighborhood had in it a dogged perseverance akin to stubbornness. For years he had been on the verge of building a new house, and it was his wife's scepticism of his good intentions, much more than any appeal she ever had made, that finally shoved him over the edge. The next day he ordered the lumber, and the following week the carpenters were at work. Before the season's wheat was ripe it stood complete, a frame box with four corners and a roof, a little to the north of the cabin which had sheltered Jackson Stake and his wife during all these years, and the numerous lean-tos which had marked their domestic husbandry. The lean-tos were dragged to various corners of the yard for use as chicken houses and hog pens. The farmer had intended using the central part as a granary but the sills were found to have rotted away, so the idea had to be abandoned. It is one thing to live in a house with rotten sills, but quite another to risk the year's harvest in it. The logs which had been hewn and built into place back in those days when life lay all ahead were torn from their plastered chinks and cut into firewood. By and by the old cellar itself filled up, and another landmark of the pioneer had vanished forever.

For a few months Susie Stake revelled in the freedom of her new house. There were two good-sized rooms on the ground floor, divided by a stairway which led to the second story. The southern room was used as a kitchen and general living quarters, but the northern one was reserved as a family parlor, to be entered only on special occasions. Upstairs were four bedrooms; square, boxy apartments, each equipped with four walls, a roof, a floor, a door and a window. In these commodious quarters Susie Stake, for the first time in her married life, felt that she had breathing space. Her foot took on a somewhat lighter tread, and once in a while Jackson would surprise her singing as she trained her flowers, set in tomato cans in the southern window. On such occasions the farmer would harrow his thinning hair with his great fingers and bask for a moment in a pleasant glow of virtuous accomplishment.

But the new house created new needs. For example, there was the furnishing of the parlor – always called simply "the room." Mrs. Stake never had been given to much entertainment; her companionship had been with the members of her family, and with her cows, her chickens, geese, ducks and pigs. But the new house forced social obligations upon her. Neighbors who for years had been content to inquire for her health at Willow Green schoolhouse on Sundays now found their friendship quickened to the point of paying visits. A new and comparatively pretentious house in a prairie district is a social factor of as great importance as a new bride in any feminine circle. It is to be investigated, scrutinized, commended or criticized as the occasion seems to warrant. Susie Stake's house was not her house alone; it belonged to the community.

It was this that made the new needs. The log cabin never had seemed bare, but "the room," even when decorated with two enlarged crayon portraits of ancestral Hardens and a calendar from the Plainville garage, seemed unaccountably empty. The friendliest of conversations sounded hollow against its plastered walls. It was cold and uninviting, and it could be cured only by further expenditures.

One by one these were wormed out of Jackson Stake. First a carpet, which cost him eleven dollars and seemed an outrageous extravagance when linoleum, which cleans up better after muddy boots, could have been bought for eight; then a parlor suite – pronounced "soot" until Minnie, at sixteen, discovered the mistake, and with much mortification set the household right on so delicate a matter – a parlor suite with birch mahogany arms and brightly patterned upholstery and crimson furbelows that hung close to the carpet, and a rocking chair with springs that squeaked until Gander said he guessed it wanted a shot of grease in the differential; then a polished oak centre table on legs as spindly as those of a young calf, on which to set photographs and Minnie's copy of "Songs of a Sourdough" and a china creation spelled v-a-s-e but the pronunciation of which, in 1914, had not been definitely settled in the Stake household.

"It's not the first cost – it's the upkeep," Jackson one day confided to his chief friend and chief rival, Fraser Fyfe, in the shade of the horse-stable. "Jumpin' jack rabbits! I've paid out more money – It's like one o' them new-fangled automo-billy-goats that cost two cents a mile for gasoline an' the rest o' your bank roll for incidentals. I figgered when I built a house I would be at the end of it. So I was, but not the end I figgered. An' now Minnie's raisin' a war-cry for a piano. Huh! You'd think farmin' was an industry, instead of a pursoot."

"Pursoot is right," Double F agreed, amiably. "I been pursooin' it for twenty years. That is, sometimes I'm pursooin' it, and sometimes it's pursooin' me. And just when I figgered I'd got the crittur by the tail what gets into you but you must build a house, and now ain't I hearin' mornin', noon, and night, 'Well, if Stakes can build a new house I don' see why we can't. Ain't you as well off as Jackson Stake? Don' you figger you're as good a farmer as Jackson Stake?' It got so bad with us I had to promise to put in a telephone, when the gang came along here diggin' holes, so that now the women can tell their troubles to each other, an' give us men folks a chance to do a bit o' work between times." Double F blew a whiff of tobacco smoke from his pipe and contemplated the harshness of his lot with some complacency.

So the seasons had worn away, each bringing its new need, and each new need, when supplied, creating other needs in its wake, as is the way with a civilization which grows more complex with each accomplishment. And at eighteen Gander, lanky and competent, found himself again faced with a problem of high importance.

It was a hot day about the first of August that Fraser Fyfe came strolling across the fields for a word with his neighbor. The wheat was already taking on the copper and gold of harvest, and the prairies lay bathed in the ripening sunshine. The lazy clank of Jackson Stake's windmill came down from the tower above the water trough as the blades stirred irresolutely in the noon-day breeze.

"I wonder you wouldn't put in a 'phone of your own, an' save me these long walks, an' me a busy man," Double F announced himself. "But I suppose you're still savin' up for the piano —"

"It's not that, Neighbor. I wouldn' be so unkind as to deprive you o' your one excuse for seekin' a little upliftin' comp'ny. What's the news to-day? Mrs. Gordon burn her biscuits again? The young lad was tellin' Gander that since they got the 'phone his mother burns most every batch o' biscuits; when she gets listenin' in on a juicy conversation she knows nothin' more until the kitchen's full o' smoke."

"Well, it's more than biscuits burnin' this time, I'm thinkin'. The news from Plainville is that there's a war on."

"Who with? The Germans? I seen somethin' about that in the paper."

"Yep. They're goin' to go to it. They were for bustin' into Belgium an' England said 'Stay out,' an' they didn't, an' so there you are!"

The two men lit their pipes the better to digest this momentous news.

"'Twon't last long," Jackson Stake prophesied, when his pipe was going freely.

"I give 'em three months," Mr. Fyfe allowed.

"Yep. Now-a-days, with our inventions, an' everythin', you can kill 'em too quick to keep it up long."

"Three months I give 'em," said Mr. Fyfe, with finality.

It was typical of their British outlook that it did not occur to either of them to so much as wonder what the outcome would be. They took that for granted.

"They're goin' to send men from Canada," Mr. Fyfe continued.

"Well, it'll be a good trip, but it'll be all over before they get there."

"That's so," said Mr. Fyfe. "I give 'em three months." Then, looking his neighbor in the face, "Jackson, what do you reckon this is goin' to do to the price o' wheat?"

Jackson Stake's mouth slowly opened as the really significant part of the news began to dawn upon him. "Jumpin' jack rabbits! Yes! I remember my father tellin' about the price o' wheat the time o' the American civil war. Two dollars a bushel, I think it was. . . . But this won't last that long. It'll be over in three months."

But for all his mercenary outlook, something deeper than the price of wheat was stirring in the farmer's veins. He was opening and closing his great fists until the veins stood out like whip lashes on the backs of his hands.

"Yep. I give 'em three months. But that's the wheat season. You can't tell what's goin' to happen in three months."

The two farmers discussed their crop prospects in the light of possible record prices for wheat, and, when Mr. Fyfe at last had gone home, Jackson carried the news into the house.

"Double F tells me there's a war on," he announced. "Jus' got the word from Plainville."

His wife made no answer. She was busy kneading dough with her strong, lean fists.

"I said there was a war on," her husband repeated, somewhat annoyed that his important news had produced so little effect.

"I heard you," she answered. "I suppose it's among the Board o' Directors over Mrs. Burge gettin' first prize for butter at the Plainville Fair. I heard talk there was goin' to be doin's about that, an' her husband on the Board."

"No, Mother, this is no butter scrap, but a real war. With Germany."

Mrs. Stake continued her kneading. "Germany," she remarked, between punches. "I've heard about them. There was a German family lived near us when I was a little girl. Nice folks, too, but he drank too much beer, although I'm not sayin' only Germans do that." She paused, and Jackson had a feeling that hostilities were threatening much nearer home than Europe. "Well, it's a pity they couldn't settle their troubles some other way," she concluded.

Jackson opened his mouth to suggest the possible effect on the price of wheat; then closed it again. He had promised Minnie that if the crop sold for a dollar a bushel he would buy a piano, but that was when there seemed no possibility of such a price. Perhaps the less said about it the better.

"Well, think I'll run into town an' get the mail," he said, after a silence. "There ain't much doin', an' I'm kind o' interested in the news."

"Well – don' get anythin' else," his wife cautioned him.

In the yard he met Gander.

"Hear the news, Gander? There's a war on, with Germany."

Gander swallowed a couple of times and hitched his overalls into a more dependable position. "What about?" he asked.

"Dunno. Somethin' about Belgium. Double F was tellin' me."

"England in it?"

"Yep. Double F says it'll be over in three months."

"Less'n that, I guess," said Gander. "Don' suppose we'll hear much about it, this far away."

"Oh, the papers'll have it all. I was jus' goin' into town to get the mail. Come along?"

"I was goin' to do some rivetin' on the binder canvass, but I guess it'll keep. The crop's comin' in pretty fast. Give me time to clean up a bit?"

"Sure." The farmer surveyed his lanky son with amusement. There was a fuzz of down on his dark cheeks, and his hair, long over-due a visit to the barber, clustered thick about his ears. "Sure. Make yourself pretty. I had it, too – at your age."

The boy shaved at a broken mirror hanging over the wash bench in front of the house, put on a clean shirt, which he drew together at the neck with a gaudy tie, dressed himself in his Sunday suit, blacked his boots. These preparations took time, and before they were finished his father became impatient.

"Come on, Gander, come on!" he said. "The war'll be over before we get to Plainville."

"Be a good thing if you had some o' his trouble," Mrs. Stake remarked. "You look like the day after an auction sale."

Jackson laughed, good naturedly. He had long since outgrown the nonsense of changing his clothes, except for Sunday services or on special occasions, like Fair Day.

They hitched the drivers – two light-footed four-year-old bays – to the buggy and went spinning into town as the afternoon sun swung well over the wheat-fields. The smell of the ripening grain was in the air; its rich green ranks, already coloring into copper at the middle of the stalk, swayed gently in the breeze, while other ranks, far from this peaceful scene, rushed to their red harvest overseas. On the way they talked of the war, as something distant and impersonal; something to be settled in Europe. But it had its practical application, too.

"It'll likely boost the price o' wheat," Jackson confided in his son. It was impossible for him to keep this important prospect entirely to himself. "I mind my father tellin' about the price o' wheat the time o' the American civil war. Two dollars a bushel, I think it went to."

"Gee! If it would do that again!" said Gander, and for the moment lost himself in the contemplation of such possibilities.

As they neared Plainville they became aware that the traffic on the roads was unusually heavy. Every converging trail had its string of buggies flying their pennants of grey dust. Two or three times they had been overtaken by automobiles, which were now crowding into the prairie districts, although as yet they had by no means become the universal means of locomotion. That was another war-development which neither Jackson Stake nor his son, nor many a wiser man, foresaw.

Cresting a ridge, the cupolas of the wheat elevators at Plainville came into view, and down the long road between stretched a procession of buggies and automobiles. The whole country-side was crowding into Plainville. Jackson Stake drew his reins tighter; held his whip with a sharper grasp. . . .

They found the streets of the little prairie town lined with buggies and motor cars; the livery stables full; every hitching post occupied. They tied their team to an abandoned land-roller in a vacant lot and pressed through the crowds that had gathered around the telegraph office and the telephone exchange. All sorts of rumors were afloat. There had been a naval engagement; the German navy had been sunk; the German hosts were held on the borders of Belgium. Farm women and men, youths and girls, mingled on the street, but for once they were talking about something other than the weather and the crops. There was an air of excitement, of high spirits, of bantering, and of unconscious boastfulness. It was infectious; it swept through the crowd; it caught Jackson Stake and Gander, and set them cheering boisterously when a number of youths paraded an effigy of the Kaiser down the street mounted on the most decrepit nag the community could produce, and with a disused copper kettle on its head for a helmet. They trailed the figure into the Roseland Emporium and demanded a sauerkraut cocktail – a flight of humor that was wafted from lip to lip through the appreciative throng.

As Jackson and Gander worked down the street they came upon another group gathered about a barrel from which some one was making a speech. "Believe me, men," he was saying, "This is as much our fight as it is England's. The Germans have got to be stopped somewhere. You all agree to that. Now *I* say, stop them in Belgium. Better fight them in Belgium than in Plainville. Eh? Yes" – in answer to an inquiry which Jackson did not hear – "I'm taking names. I've authority here" – he held the yellow sheet of a telegram aloft – "and I'm enlisting the First Plainville Company. What's that? Over in three months? Yes – it will be over *here* in three months, if every one stays at home. That's right – sign your name there – official forms later." Some young men were writing their names on a sheet. There was something grim about the set of their mouths; they didn't seem to be thinking of a three months' holiday.

Gander's eyes met his father's. "Who is he?" the older man asked.

"Why, that's Lee, the tailor. Presses suits, and that kind o' thing." Gander's Adam's apple was leaping at its leash.

The man on the barrel paused in his harangue, and his eye met Gander's.

"Hello, Gander," he said. "Want to sign up?"

"Haven't thought about it, yet," Gander parried.

"Well, think about it. It's something to think about."

Gander slipped out of the group as soon as he could. At the edge of the crowd he came upon Tommy Burge.

"'Lo, Porridge."

"'Lo, Gander."

Then the conversation lagged. With so much to talk about, they had nothing to say. Both were beginning to think.

At Sempter & Burton's store he met Jo Burge. She was a young woman now, supple and close-knit, with fair skin and eyes and wisps of light brown hair showing under her summer hat. She greeted Gander cordially.

"This is exciting news, Gander. They're enlisting men already. Don't you think that's wonderful?"

"It'll be all over in three months," said Gander.

"Yes, I suppose so. But just the same, it's fine to see men answering the call. It makes us feel that we're in it, and doing our share."

For some reason his meeting with Jo gave Gander less pleasure than he had hoped. He was pleased with the care he had taken in shaving and dressing, but there was a hollowness about it all somewhere. Jo was good to look on now, and Gander never had lost the attachment which had been formed back in those days at Willow Green school. He suspected that Jo had not lost it either, yet to-day for some reason she seemed to place him at a disadvantage. There was a light in her eyes which he could not fathom or understand.

In the dusk father and son drove silently home together.

TEN

The months that followed were difficult months for Gander. They were a period of self-searching and indecision. For the first time in his life he began to read the newspapers, but found in them only a jumble of conflicting reports; of overwhelming losses inflicted upon the Germans, who, nevertheless, continued their advance; of heroism among all the Allied forces, and unspeakable brutality on the part of the enemy. The First Plainville Company had been raised and away, with Lieutenant Andy Lee at its head; a second company was now recruiting. Discussions before the church services at the schoolhouse on Sundays had switched from crops and cattle to the theatre of war.

It was at those services that Gander felt the eyes of Josephine Burge heavy upon him. As circumstantial reports of the atrocities in Belgium increased, so did those pale eyes seem to bore deeper within him. Jo met him cordially, as before, but there was a new, deep gravity in her manner, and Gander knew that she was expecting great things of him. Perhaps she was not deeply in love with him, if at all; but she cared enough to hope he would play the hero, as other young men of the district were doing. The realities of war had not yet been brought near enough home to put the fear of death in the hearts of young women. But it was already lurking in the hearts of mothers, and, perhaps, of some fathers.

Gander had become conscious of that, too. He had surprised his mother watching him with an unwonted wistfulness, and one day, after a silence at the table, and quite apropos of nothing, she said, "I have lost one son already." Gander's father had looked across the table but had not answered. Minnie regarded Gander with eyes eager to light up with hero-worship.

The companionship between father and son deepened in those days. They spent much time together, but little conversation. As, one by one, young men of the neighborhood responded to the call, the strain upon them tightened. The three months which Fraser Fyfe had stipulated with so much finality failed to see the war at a close, and the spirit of adventure which had animated some of the earlier recruits was slowly giving way to deeper emotions. Jackson Stake no longer read the head-lines of the paper to the assembled household after supper, but pored over them by himself in the secrecy of the horse-stable or the granary. And often, when the day's work was done, he would sit down by Gander's side and the two men would smoke in silence while the dusk gathered about them. At length Jackson, rising slowly to his feet, would draw his hand across his son's shoulder with the faintest gesture of caress before he knocked the ashes from his pipe and went to bed.

For shelter Gander fled to his work. The sudden call for men had created a shortage of harvest labor, and Gander attacked the ripened fields with more than his usual vigor. He had fed and brushed and nursed his eight big horses into prime condition before the heavy load of the binder fell upon them; he had tightened every nut, oiled every bearing, before the call of the red grain swept them into the harvest. The summer had not been a favorable one for wheat, and the crop was light, so Gander and his father undertook to harvest it without hiring any help. Gander was still the teamster and the binder driver, as his knack lay along those lines, and his father stooked after him. As Gander would approach the part of the field in which his father was working he would note how the big frame stalked among the sheaves; bending, grasping, straightening to a half-erect position, planting the sheaves in place; then on to the next, and the next, and the next. The sun blazed down upon them; the smell of oily dust came up hot from the binder bearings; the white line of sweat crept over the flanks of the big horses. If he dismounted for a minute or two to straighten out a tangle in the twine or remove a trouble-some straw from the bill-hook of the knotter, the iron seat was almost unbearably hot when he returned to it. Yet he found occasion, more than in any previous harvest, to stop as he drew up beside his father and exchange a word with him.

"Well, Gander, how's she goin'?" Jackson Stake would say, resting his hands on his kidneys and twisting his back for relief.

"Not so bad, Dad, not so bad, but she's thin as black bristles on a Tamworth hog. Not more'n eight bushels to the acre; maybe ten, in spots. Like to drive a round or two?"

"No – you go ahead. Spoils my voice, shoutin' at the horses. Besides, it's too hot up there. I like it better down here, where it's cool."

Sometimes he would persuade his father to spell off with him.

"Dad, I'm not a kid any more, an' you keep shovin' me over on the easy job. Rest your back for a round or two an' I'll take the crick out o' mine sagaciatin' a few o' these sheaves into position." Then Jackson would take the lines and, cracking the long whip over the horses' backs, drive off in a great clatter, while Gander threw himself impetuously into the stooking. But by the time his father had gone the second round he would stop his horses and climb down from the seat.

"Guess you'll have to take it, Gander," he would say. "Never was any good drivin' a binder. Either I've got my nigh horse in the standin' wheat, or my off one is trampin' through the stooks. They know me, an' they run on me. I bet that off horse has et a peck o' wheat out o' the stooks in the las' two roun's. Can't afford to lose so much wheat as that, Gander."

Then Gander's Adam's apple would crawl up into his throat and choke the words of affection he would have liked to say, and his father would draw his arm across his shoulder in that way he sometimes did. And that was all. But both of them understood.

In the middle of the afternoon Minnie would bring sandwiches and tea in a basket. She would watch from the house until Gander turned the far corner of the field; then, when she saw his reel glittering in the sun on the homeward stretch she would leave in time to intercept him at the nearest corner. Gander would set the basket on the top of the machine and tell Minnie to hop on to the frame behind, where she would steady herself by clinging to the arm which supported the wind-break. It was a never-failing fascination to her to watch the bright knives shuttling in the wheat, and the ruddy stems falling on the canvas and being swept up the elevator to the deck. . . . When they reached their father they would stop, and, throwing up an extra high stook for shade, sit down on the warm earth and eat and drink together.

"I was just thinking," said Minnie one day, as she chatted to the accompaniment of the busy eating of her father and brother, "I was just thinking as I rode up on the back of the binder that the wheat was Germans and the knives were the Allies. It was great fun watching them topple over, in whole regiments. And where a big green weed would stick up out of the wheat I would say, 'That's a German officer, a captain, maybe, or maybe a colonel, but just you wait! Your time's coming.' And then the knives would snip him off, and he'd fall with a flop on the canvas, and get swept up out of sight, and when I'd look back after a little there he'd be lying, tied up in a sheaf, full length on the ground. And once I saw a great big weed, higher than all the others, and I said, 'Here's the Kaiser,' but we just missed him – he was outside the swath. Can I go 'round with you again, Gander? We'll get him next time."

"Sure – I guess you can, if you want to. But it's pretty hot."

"Yes," said Minnie, thoughtfully, "but not as hot as it must be in France, with all those heavy uniforms and everything to carry. I suppose I'm too big a girl now for make-belief, Gander, don't you think? But I like to feel that – that – *some* of us – is – is cutting 'em down."

Gander was struggling with his tea, while his father stared into the blue haze of the harvest sky. So even Minnie felt it!

Then Jackson Stake expressed a hope that had been forming in his heart; a hope behind which he could shelter his self-respect – and Gander.

"Perhaps one of us is," he said, "or will be, soon as he can get over. I wouldn't wonder that's what Jackie's doin'."

Minnie drew her clasped hands up before her young breast. "Wouldn't that be fine!" she said. "Wouldn't that be fine!"

The harvest season drew by, and threshing was upon them. One day early in September Bill Powers, seated in his lop-sided buggy, drew up in the Stake farmyard. It was the noon hour, and Gander and his father were sunning themselves on the edge of the water trough beside the windmill, for the summer's heat was over and the day was only pleasantly warm. Powers had driven from a farm some miles south, where his outfit was at work. There was chaff on his faded felt hat and engine grease on his overalls.

Powers' horse edged to the water trough and Gander slipped his check-rein to let him drink.

"Well, how's the Powers?" Jackson greeted him. "You won't be one o' those wild European Powers we hear so much about these days?"

The red line of a grin sliced across the dusty stubble of Powers' face. "No, but I'm about as wild as if I was," he said. He extracted a pair of long legs from the diminutive box of the buggy, and, thrusting them over the side, alighted by the simple process of straightening them.

"Come in an' eat," Jackson invited. "Gander an' me has pretty well cleared the boards, but I reckon the missus can drag out a bite o' somethin'."

"Nope – thank 'ee the same. Got to get back." Powers stood for a moment without further speaking, as though he had a weighty matter on his mind but did not quite know how to present it.

"How's the crop runnin'?" said Jackson.

"Poor. Threshin' out poor. No money threshin' this year, an' wages goin' up, an' men not to be had. I tell you, Mr. Stake, this war's got to be more'n a joke. My best men's gone, an' I lost another last night. You know Dick Claus? Has been firin' for me for two seasons, an' I always used him well, an' stood likely to raise his pay. By another year I might ha' let him run the engine himself. Well, he's been actin' kind o' absent-minded lately, an' yesterday I had to say a word or two to him,

decent, though, as I always do. You can't have a fellow firin'
an engine an' his mind not on the job – you know that,
Mr. Stake. Dick was over to Burge's on Sunday – he's been
chasin' that Burge girl a bit, an' he hasn't been the same since."

Gander felt a strange sensation creeping up his back, and
his heart quickened its beat, but he hoped his face gave no sign.

"Well, he jumped it las' night," Powers continued.
"Shoved in the last forkful o' straw before quittin', an' then
handed me the fork. 'You take it,' he said. 'I'm done. From
this on you poke your old garbage-burner yourself. I'm done.
The next pokin' I do'll be at a German – with a bay'net.' An'
this mornin' he beat it for Plainville, to sign up. Course, I gave
him my blessin', even if he did miscall my engine – as good a
steamer as ever lugged a separator up a prairie trail; you know
that, Mr. Stake – we got to win the war, an' I gave him my
blessin', but I thought he might ha' stuck till after threshin'.
The Germans'll keep, but this weather may blow up wet any
time. Garbage-burner!" Mr. Powers twisted his mouth into a
protest of disgust.

"Well, I guess they got to have the men," Jackson Stake
agreed, with a gesture of resignation, "but it's a bit hard on us
farmers, with our crops out, an' everythin'. Gander an' me took
ours off ourselves this year, an' saved a wage bill that'll come
handy. You can't tell what's goin' to happen, these times."

"That's what I came to speak about," said Mr. Powers.
"Gander's got a handy way with him, an' now your crop's in
stook I thought maybe I could get him to fire for the rest o'
the season. What you say, Gander? I'll give you the same's
I was givin' Dick, an' him with two years' 'sperience."

Gander's heart thumped again, but with an altogether
different emotion. If the thought of Jo Burge could make that
heart quicken its beat, so too could the prospect of firing a

steam engine. Short of actually driving an engine, and perhaps, some day, having one of his own, to fire one was his greatest ambition. Yet even in that epochal moment he had a thought for his father.

"It'll depend on Dad," he said. "If he thinks he can get along —"

Jackson Stake was harrowing his hair with his thick fingers – an unfailing sign of cerebral activity. "I guess I could manage," he said, "if only we were threshed. But if I don' get threshed Gander an' me were thinkin' o' stackin' a field or two so we could get along with the ploughin'. You see, Bill, that's how it is. Now if you was to pull in here to-morrow Gander could start with you at once."

So Jackson Stake drove his bargain with Bill Powers that his threshing should be done the following week. With the possibility of the "outfits" working shorthanded, Gander was a good pawn to play, and his father played him to the best advantage.

Firing Bill Powers' straw-burner opened a new world for Gander, a world of great activity and accomplishment, in which the throbbing of the steam exhaust for a time beat down that inner throbbing which could be quietened, but could not quite be killed. It was a hard life, to one who weighed his work, but Gander did not count it hard, because he loved his engine and delighted in its company. Powers, who seemed to sleep only upon odd occasions, wakened the boy at four each morning. Even at that hour the lantern was already burning in the caboose. Gander would stretch his stiff muscles, then thrust his legs out of the bunk and follow them into the narrow aisle, cluttered with the garments of the other sleepers. Finding his own clothes, he would climb into them quickly and silently; quickly, because the atmosphere of the caboose, although stale with insufficient ventilation, was sharp with the nip of the autumn night; and silently because noise had a way of bringing upon his head the frank and personal expletives of those fortunate members of the gang who were permitted to sleep until the lazy hour of five o'clock. Then, out into the tingling night air, with the stars blazing a million points of fire upon the sleeping earth, and away through the crisp stubble to "the set." Generally he found it by his prairie sense of direction, or, if the moon still hung in the west, by the temporary trail made by the grain wagons. There it lay, a blacker hulk against the darkness, inexpressibly silent and weird in its repose. Gander's first act was always to place his hand on the boiler, as one might reassure a nervous horse. By the same half-caressing touch he gauged the coldness of the night and the temperature of the water. Then, having lighted his lantern, he cleared the fire-box and ash-pan.

"Well, how's the old girl the smornin'?" Gander would say, as he raked the ash-pan clean. "Ready for another day's run? I bet we are. Water pretty low, eh?" as, holding the lantern close to the glass, he distinguished the dim line of the liquid inside. "She'll go up again when she gets hot. Ready for a bit o' fire?"

Selecting a small armful of straw from the dump beside the engine he would set a match to it and thrust it into the fire-box; then, as it burned up, add more, being careful not to choke his fire before it had found a draft. Those first moments, when the flues were cold and the smoke oozed back as from a stubborn kitchen stove, were sometimes the most trying of the day. But if the fire was properly nursed the heat would soon create its own draft, and away it would go. It was fine to see the smoke beginning to roll and billow out of the short stack overhead.

Then came long minutes of gentle stoking, coaxing the fire to its maximum heat, and, between times, studying the stars or the waning moon. Sometimes Gander wondered what those same stars, looking down in Europe, saw, but he was not imaginative, and he had a man's job on his hands, and was content. After a while a welcome, sizzling sound, as from a mighty tea-kettle, would proclaim that the fire had found its teeth. Then another long wait, and, just as the first flush of dawn crept up the eastern sky, the steam-gauge would begin to register pressure.

From that on was easy. As soon as he had steam pressure Gander would turn on the blower, which creates draft by making a vacuum in the smoke-stack. Under this impetus the fire would spring to new life, licking up greedily the straw which Gander pressed, almost continuously, into the fire-box, while the hand on the steam-gauge crept slowly around the dial. By the time dawn was throwing the shadows of the stooks across the stubble Gander would send forth a shriek from his whistle, choking at first with the cold in its larynx, but rising quickly to a clear, high note which pierced the morning silence for miles around. It was his word to the world that he was ready for another day's business.

It was Gander's pride to be first to sound his whistle in the morning. Other firemen, firing other engines off somewhere through the grey dawn, heard that challenging whistle, and said to themselves, "Gee, Old Bill Powers is cuttin' 'er out early these mornin's," while Gander grinned in satisfaction and warmed his back against the boiler.

Powers would be the second man at the set. He usually arrived about the time Gander was ready to whistle, and with a word such as "Nippy the smornin', Gander," or, "How's the old gal takin' 'er milk the smornin', Gander?" he would reach for the battered teapot filled with machine oil which was warming against the smoke-stack, and stride off with it to the separator, where he filled the oil cups, adjusted the belts, raked out accumulations of chaff and seeds, and generally put the mill in order for the day's run. Meanwhile Gander urged his pressure up to a hundred and thirty pounds, which was the limit allowed by the exacting Government inspector on a boiler not as youthful as it once had been; injected as much water as could be carried without danger of foaming, filled his cups with oil and tallow, and sent another shrill blast into the morning air through which the sunlight was now sifting from great fan-shaped streamers overhead. The men by this time had had their breakfast, and their horses came jingling out from the barns to take their places on the bundle wagons, the grain wagons, and the tank wagons in which water was hauled from the nearest pond. The fields awoke; "the outfit" shook off its slumber like a giant aroused from sleep.

After the first few days, Powers, finding Gander competent and eager, left him practically in charge of the engine and gave his own attention mainly to the separator. It was a great hour when Bill said to his young fireman, "All right, Gander, you start 'er the smornin'." The drive belt had not yet been put on, but Gander had watched the careful Powers run his engine idle a few minutes every morning to warm the bearings before applying the load and to clear the cylinder and valve-chest of the night's condensation. With infinite pride and responsibility he climbed to the driver's position, and, throttle in hand, gently eased the first gush of steam into the cylinder. There was a wet hiss from the rear cylinder-cock; then, almost imperceptibly, the driving-arm began to lunge forward, the eccentric heaved on the shaft, the governors began to rotate, the idle fly-wheel stirred into motion. Then a pause at the end of the stroke, and Gander's Adam's apple jumped in panic lest he had misgauged the exact amount of power needed, and had suffered the humiliation of being stranded on dead-centre. But the flywheel furnished the necessary momentum; the crank swung slowly by the point at the end of the stroke; the steam entered the forward end of the cylinder; the wrist-pin bearings clicked almost imperceptibly with the reversal of the pressure, and the driving-arm lunged backward with a sharper and accelerating hiss. She was away! Gander let her ramble gently for a few revolutions, while the exhaust beat its pleasant tattoo inside the stack; then slowly gave her more steam while he watched the quickening fly-wheel and knew the thrill that comes only to those who hold great power in the hollow of their hands. Jo Burge? This – this power – this mighty thing that sprang at his touch – this was life!

Two men ran out from the separator, reeling the great belt between them, as firemen lay a hose along a city street. Gander stopped his engine, mounted the fly-wheel, wrapped a grain sack around the belt and the rim of the wheel, and, throwing all his weight on it, while men strung along the belt toward the separator like knots on the tail of a kite added their strength to his, drew the great rubber ribbon around the wheel.

Powers was standing by the engine, making no interference, but ready for instant emergency.

"All right, Gander; let 'er go. Remember, you've a load on now, an' don' rip out my separator bearings."

Gander blew a short blast on his whistle as a signal for the men to take their positions; then gently opened the throttle. The steam roared from the cylinder-cock, but there was no answering lunge of the driving-arm.

"You got a load, Gander; you got a load!" shouted Powers. "Give 'er juice!"

Gander opened the throttle further. The driving-arm thrust forward; the great belt drew taut on its lower side, while the other flapped prodigiously, almost to the stubble. The arm took its stroke – and stopped.

"Dead-centre, lad, dead-centre," said Powers, sympathetically. "Never mind, I sometimes do it myself. Here, you fellows!" he shouted to some of the crew who were looking on, enjoying Gander's discomfiture, "take a pull on the belt!"

"Maybe if you'd just call Gander off we could run the whole thing with the belt," one of the wags suggested. "We got as much horse power as that ol' soap-kettle, anyway."

"Have you?" said Powers. "We'll see, before night. I bet Gander'll give you a wet shirt, when he gets 'er goin'!"

The men pulled on the belt until they swung the crank off dead-centre, and Gander, nettled by their taunts, took no chances this time. He opened the throttle, and the crank came back with a bound.

"Easy, Gander, easy; you'll throw your belt!" Powers shouted to him. But the belt held; the engine was in motion; the separator was in motion; the knives of the feeder began to whittle the sunlight now glancing across them; a puff of chaff went rocketing out of the blower; chuck-chuck-chuck sang the exhaust in the smoke-stack, and Gander again was captain of his soul.

The engine steadily quickened its stroke and a roar came up in a mighty crescendo from the separator at the other end of the belt. Presently it struck its gait, and Gander knew that it was the governor-valve, and not the throttle, that now controlled the speed.

Meanwhile the spike-pitchers had mounted their wagon-loads of sheaves drawn up on either side of the feeder. Between them was the feeding-table, along which traveled slats with projecting spikes (hence the term "spike-pitcher") designed to drag the sheaves under the revolving knives which cut the bands. When the hum of the separator showed that she had "hit her gait" Powers gave his men a signal, and the spike-pitchers dropped their first sheaves on the table. Up the incline they went, like miniature logs into a sawmill; under the knives which snapped their bands of binder twine; into the teasing arms which tousled the straw out of its lumpy mass so that it might feed steadily into the cylinder; then into the cylinder itself, where rows of whirling teeth racing through rows of stationary teeth stripped the wheat and chaff from the stalk and sent all back into the body of the mill, the straw and chaff to be eventually blown out through the stacker, the wheat to be elevated to the weighing device, weighed, and dropped into the big, tight wagon-box standing beside the mill to receive it.

It was not until the first sheaves struck the cylinder that the real load came on the engine. The belt flapped; the rhythmic chuck-chuck-chuck of the exhaust suddenly deepened to a roar which sent ashes and soot hurtling from the smoke-stack overhead. But the sensitive governor-valve responded to the strain, feeding more steam to the piston, so that in a moment the engine had automatically adjusted itself to the load and the mill ran on smoothly with only a hoarser hum as the separator swallowed its first great gulp of chaff and straw. Working quickly, with an easy, systematic swing and a dexterity with the pitchfork which comes not without practice, the spike-pitchers dropped their sheaves on the feeding-table in two steady streams, heads forward, each head touching the butts of the sheaf in front, so that the load might be continuous and even. Out from the great iron funnel at the back of the machine roared a cyclone of straw; up from the internals of its digestive apparatus arose a cloud of dust. Chaff and straw and dust – they poured into the still morning air, catching the glint of fresh sunlight, trailing their mottled shadows across the brown stubble.

And some grain. It rattled down the iron tube; it plunged in half-bushel gusts into the waiting wagon-box, bright and clean and resonant, singing as it danced on the hard boards. . . . Chaff and straw and dirt – and some grain!

In a few minutes the first pair of bundle-wagons were emptied; the drivers shouted to their horses and pulled out to the fields to reload, while the next pair of wagons, which had been awaiting their turn, drew into position and the procedure was repeated. Bill Powers' "outfit" was well away on its day's run.

Gander was down again, stoking straw into his firebox, when Powers lolled around the side of the boiler.

"Good enough, Gander," he said. "You got 'er hummin', anyhow. Don' forget your breakfas'. I'll stoke while you eat."

Gander had quite forgotten the pail with his morning meal which one of the crew had set beside the engine. Why not? This was Gander's day of romance. Not that he knew it for that – but who knows Romance when he meets her in the daily round?

ELEVEN

Josephine Burge learned of Gander's appointment to the position of fireman on Powers' outfit with somewhat mingled emotions. The part she had played in the resignation of Dick Claus from that position was never clearly understood by the community, and Jo offered no enlightenment. All that was known was that Dick had developed a habit of spending his Sunday afternoons and evenings on the Burge homestead, and that after one such visit he suddenly threw down his stoking-fork and enlisted. The community was disposed to credit this increase of the Allied forces to Josephine Burge rather than to any special patriotic impulse operating in the bosom of Richard Claus.

But whatever had been Jo's part in bringing about Dick's enlistment it was an unexpected development that Gander should so promptly step into the shoes vacated by his rival. Not that Gander had ever recognized in Dick a rival for Jo's affections, but Gander's attitude toward Jo was too ill-defined to admit of very clear thinking. At school they had played together, preferring each other by some law of natural selection which neither understood nor tried to explain. When

Gander left school and threw himself into the work of the farm the girl had occupied only a small part of his thoughts until the hired man Bill had kindled his imagination along new and dangerous lines. That spark had been quenched, or, at least, subdued, by his curious reaction to the trust and hero-worship of his sister Minnie during the storm that night when they were alone in the house together. Gander was not a deep psychologist, but he had been unable to escape the conclusion that Jo was Tommy's sister, just as Minnie was his sister.

This new point of view kept him away from the girl during the following years, except when they met for a few minutes at church, or on the more rare occasions of a country picnic or other social event. He was shy in her presence; at times she even suspected that he avoided her; yet he seemed pleased when they met and his eyes were bright even though his tongue was dumb. Back in his memory he carried that word of hers, "Bill, I've always been your girl." Some day, he supposed, he would ask her to make that promise good, for his simple mind accepted it as a promise for the future as well as a declaration of the past. In the meantime he was tremendously busy with other things – and Jo could wait.

She waited. When Gander did not return to the school section that day after the storm, Jo, with the intuition of her sex guessed that it was not because he didn't care, but because he cared too much. Well – she too, perhaps, had cared too much. She tried to school herself to an attitude of indifference, an attitude which she sustained rather well in Gander's presence, but from which she slid ignominiously in the privacy of the prairies when she wandered them after the cattle, or when she took long walks by herself, for she was a girl with a taste for solitude. One thing gave her assurance: If Gander paid small attention to her, he paid less to any one else. He was wrapped up in the affairs of the farm.

She was accustomed to hearing her father sound his praises.

"That's a great boy, that Gander Stake, as they call him," Martin Burge would say at the supper table, over his plate of pancakes and syrup. "'Specially since young Jackie lit out, Gander's comin' up strong. Drives a seeder or a binder like a man, he does, an' no nonsense about runnin' to town two or three times a week."

"That's one to me," said Tommy, who was not without the gift of frankness. "Well, I guess Mr. Stake knows how to get a man's work without payin' a man's wages."

"Thomas!" his mother reproved him. "You mustn't speak ill of Mr. Stake."

"Oh, I didn't. I think he's very clever."

"Wish I had some of his cleverness," said Mr. Burge.

"Well, none of your family has run away yet, anyhow," said the irrepressible Tommy.

Mr. Burge found this a poser. It was hard to defend the management which had cost his neighbor a good farm-hand, and that right in the midst of harvest. Mr. Burge cut a lusty pancake in four, cleverly doubled the corners of one quarter in upon themselves with his fork, drenched the mass with syrup, and downed it while he gave his thoughts an interval in which to collect themselves.

"Jus' the same, Gander'll make a good farmer – a darn good farmer, Tommy."

"Well, I'm glad of that – for Jo's sake," said Tommy.

"Mind your business," his sister suggested to him. But the color rushed to her face, so she rose to replenish the pancakes from the stove. "That's an awful hot fire, Mother," she said, when she returned with the smoking cakes.

With the outbreak of the war Jo wondered whether Gander would enlist. Nothing was further from her hopes than that anything should happen to Gander, but in those early stages the risk of casualty was considered small. The whole neighborhood shared Double F's opinion that the war would be over in three months; but to wear a uniform and march away with bands playing was an heroic gesture. . . . It was yet too early in the struggle to see anything heroic in raising wheat. Jo was proud of Gander, but she was not blind to his defects. He was awkward; he was shy; the boundary of his world was little further than his father's farm. Enlistment would change all that. Like any honest girl, she was not satisfied that she alone should be proud of Gander; she wanted other people to be proud of him. She wanted to see the stoop taken out of his back, the hitch out of his gait, the drag out of his legs. Then, when the papers began to glare with reports of atrocities in Belgium she wanted the heroic in Gander to well up and send him rushing to arms, to the defence of womankind, to the defence of Josephine Burge! Gander's heroism did nothing so spectacular. He went on working fourteen hours a day in the harvest field, associating with his father a little more closely than before, and trying to keep the war out of his mind.

In all this it is not to be granted that Gander was essentially less patriotic than other young men who responded to the call. Any analysis of patriotism may lead to dangerous ground, and nothing more will be said than that Gander was happy in his home, that he saw no occasion to break away from it, that he was attached to his father, his sister Minnie, his younger brother Hamilton, and, in a lesser degree, his mother; that he loved the farm horses and machinery, and that, after all, the war was away in Belgium, or some such place, which was in Europe, or Asia, or some such place; Gander was not very sure of his geography, but of this much he was sure, that the Atlantic ocean lay between, and the British navy ruled the Atlantic ocean, so what was there to worry about? With Gander, as with most others, it was a matter of perspective. He was not lacking in courage, or in a spirit of readiness to defend his home; if an enemy battalion had appeared on the road allowance that skirted his father's farm Gander would have faced them single handed with his breech-loading shot-gun. He might even have marched into Plainville to resist their landing in his market town. But Belgium? Gander was unable to visualize a danger so remote.

In the meantime, his activities were so centralized upon the firing and driving of Bill Powers' engine that the war gave him no great concern. Its chief visible effect was the number of boys, his own age or younger, working on the outfit. Already there had been a thinning out of the classes from twenty-five to thirty-five years old, and youngsters not long out of school were stepping up to take their places. Some of these openly looked forward to the day when they might enlist, and hoped that the war would not end too soon; but most of them, and particularly those who were already eighteen, or nearly so, showed a reticence about discussing the matter at all. Something inside was troubling vaguely, and they found an opiate in work.

Gander fired for Bill Powers for the remainder of the season, with only one incident that seems worth recording. That occurred when they were threshing at Martin Burge's. Gander, although hired as fireman and drawing fireman's wages, was practically engineer; old Bill gave little thought to the power end of his plant except when moving from set to set or along the country roads from farm to farm. Then Gander fired and Bill handled the engine. To make a Y turn, couple on to a separator, and pull out across the fields without a foot of wasted motion is not learned in a day. Gander never failed to thrill with pride in his boss when, the moment the belt was thrown, he manoeuvered the engine through that sharp turn in the shape of a Y, backed up to the separator, calculating his distance and momentum to a nicety at the risk of his life – more than one engineer has been crushed to death between separator and engine as the price of a moment's misjudgment – coupled on, and was away almost before the pulleys had quit revolving or the last gust or straw had been blown from the stacker. Powers was greasy, and bent, and masked such real features as he must have possessed behind a dust-filled black stubble of beard, but he was the only man aside from Jackson Stake in whom Gander ever had caught a glimpse of the heroic.

It was about ten in the morning when they pulled in to Burge's. Martin Burge had cut his pasture fence in two places to save a detour around by the farm buildings and the consequent loss of valuable time, and Powers navigated his craft over the bare pasture, down the side of a shallow gulley, across its hard gravel bottom, up the other bank, through the temporary gate in the barbed-wire fence, and into the hundred-acre wheat-field of Martin Burge to which it gave admittance. The bundle teams, having taken a short cut by means of a culvert which could not be trusted to support the engine, were already in the field loading up; their reddish-green masses rose against a background of transparent sky like bronze tents silently heaving in the morning breeze. Now and again the voice of a driver to his team came across the field clear above the patter of the exhaust and the sluff of the wheels in the soft earth.

Martin Burge walked ahead, indicating the route to a favorable location for the set; Bill Powers stood at the throttle, the steering wheel in his hand, the front truck of his engine jerking from side to side like a mighty caterpillar, yet following a course that was almost direct; Gander stoking with straw from a wagon drawn alongside and with one eye on the water-gauge and the other on the steam; behind them the great hulk of the separator dragging heavily in the soft soil of the cultivated field; behind that again the caboose with two or three men riding, enjoying a brief respite from their morning labors or turning the moments to account by drawing together rents in their overalls with darning needles and wrapping cord. At a suitable spot Powers stopped; the caboose was uncoupled and left standing in the field; then engine and separator moved on again to the place indicated by Mr. Burge. Here Powers again slacked back while the separator was uncoupled; then, reversing his Y manoeuver, swung his engine out, around, and quickly into place. Meanwhile two men ran out from the separator with the belt, measuring the distance to the spot where the engine should stand, but Powers, from long practice, had judged it almost as well with his eye. Without a wasted motion he brought his engine to the stop, swung the belt on to the fly-wheel with the last impulse of its dying momentum, and shouted to his fireman, "All set, Gander. Let 'er go!"

Gander touched the whistle cord and gently opened the throttle; the first two bundle wagons, already loaded, drew up beside the feeder; the blades began to revolve, the spiked slats to slide up the incline, and a moment later the high whine of the threshing cylinder deepened to a roar as the first sheaves were gulped into its iron jaws. Gander, observing that his engine had taken its gait, dropped down from the throttle, replenished his fire, and walked around to the front of the boiler in a mood of casual inspection. It was then he noticed that the pitcher on the left-hand bundle wagon was young Walter Peters, who had brought a team over from his father's farm that morning to reinforce Powers' somewhat depleted staff. Walter had been one of the little boys going to school when Gander left it; he was not yet more than fifteen or sixteen, slim and straight and willing, but without either the weight or the skill for a spike-pitcher. His parents were ambitious to make a doctor of him, because (so they thought) medicine gives a much easier living than farming, and he had been attending high school in Plainville until called home to help with the threshing. Gander watched him for a moment, noting that, while not altogether unskilful with his fork, he was flustered with the responsibility of his position, sometimes getting two sheaves at once, and occasionally missing his thrust altogether.

"Must speak to Powers about him," Gander suggested to himself. "Not heavy enough for that job. Put him drivin' a grain team, or somethin'." But at that moment the boy, having thrust the head of his fork under the band of a sheaf, so that it became caught in the cord, threw fork and all on to the feeding-table. Realizing the damage that would be done to the machinery, and the shame which would engulf him for such a blunder, he lurched forward frantically for the fork, now floating up the carriers just beyond his reach; lost his balance, and himself fell on the moving sheaf! There was a chance that the carriers would stick with this extra weight, but the lad was light, and they swept him up toward the knives like straw for the threshing.

Gander's decision was instantly taken. It was impossible to stop the engine in time; before he could so much as reach the throttle the boy would be chopped to pieces. But the great belt was rushing by within a yard of Gander's arm. To hurl himself upon it, with his whole force striving to run it off the flywheel, was the work of an instant. It whirled him from his feet, carried him for a moment like a leaf on some dark and rapid stream, then suddenly leapt from the wheel and fell like a serpent writhing in the stubble. At the same instant the spike-pitcher on the opposite wagon, who had seen the accident and had his wits about him, threw a sheaf cross-wise straight into the blades. Choked with this sudden load, and with its power cut off, the separator stopped like a ship upon a rock. Some one reached a hand to Walter and he climbed sheepishly back on to his load.

"Mustn't take a chance like that," said one of the older men, severely. "You'll make a sausage machine of old Bill's straw-hasher."

Meanwhile Powers, who had observed the latter part of the accident, came rushing as fast as his crooked legs would carry him to where Gander lay entangled in the belt. "For God's sake, Gander, are you killed?" he cried.

Gander dragged himself clear of the belt and staggered to his feet. "Nope, I guess not," he announced, when he had rubbed some of his more prominent protrusions. "Guess I'm all right; jus' kind o' lost my wind for a minute. How's little Watt? Did he get hurt, at all?"

Peters, described as "little Watt" as a hang-over from schoolday recollections, but now as tall as Gander, came up beside him.

"Thanks, Gander," he said, extending his hand. "That was awful decent. I hope you didn't get hurt."

Gander, now feeling the more sheepish of the two, grasped the proffered hand. "Oh, that's nothin' – I'm all right," he said. Then, as an outlet for his embarrassment, "Come on, fellows! Give a heave with this belt! We've lost about twenty bushels' time already!"

At noon Gander found himself the hero of the hour. He had not quite forgotten that they were threshing at Jo Burge's home, and he drew on a less soiled smock and raked the chaff out of his hair before going in to dinner. Mrs. Burge and Jo were at work in the big kitchen; Mrs. Burge poring over the stove and a side table on which great stacks of food were piled; Jo waiting on the men. She looked neat and trim in her plain house dress, with her fair hair drawn in a mass at the back of her head, and the little points of freckles peering through her white skin. She smiled at Gander as he slouched to a place at the table, but did not speak; she was too engaged in serving hot tea into the great cups that sat by the thresher-men's plates.

"Well, we got a hero among us," said one of the gang. "Gander, get up and be presented with the Victoria Cross, or whatever it is a man gets for being a fool an' livin' through it."

Gander humped himself over a full plate of beef and potatoes, while his Adam's apple jumped from his shirt band to a sheltered position between his jaws.

"'Twasn't nothin'," he said. "Anybody 'ud o' done it."

"That's what I read in the papers," said another. "These great men in the war – all modest as school-ma'ams."

Gander, and some of the others, wished they would keep off the war for a bit.

Bill Powers waited until the banter had subsided, so that his pronouncement might have a proper hearing. Then:

"Well, all I got to say is, in thirty years' threshin', it's the quickest thinkin' – an' doin' – I ever seen." And, having spoken, Powers slashed into his meat with knife and fork, as though to indicate that the last word had been said.

But it hadn't. "Shucks!" remarked another member of the gang, "I've run that belt off, myself, as often as there's hair on Hector."

This brought Bill to arms. "You have, eh? From where? That's what I'm askin'. From half way down to the sep'rator! Anybody can do that, when you've got room to run, an' lots o' purchase on it. Huh! I've seen the wind blow it off, if you give it sweep enough. But ten feet from the fly-wheel – that's diff'rent! If he'd gone under that wheel he'd been jus' like a fly under your foot —"

"Or in the soup," suggested another.

"I guess it's young Watt here would have been in the soup, an' cut good an' fine at that," said the first speaker, "if that head-piece of Gander's had been as empty as it looks. I'm for the Victoria Cross! The presentation'll take place to-night, an' Miss Burge'll pin it on our hero's gallant breast – won't you, Jo?"

The rapid development from "Miss Burge" to "Jo" in a single sentence was typical of the threshers' conventions. During a visit of the threshers a farm girl is, ex-officio, a member of the gang.

Then Jo spoke. "Maybe he'll wear a real V. C. there, some day, for all you know." And for some reason that brought the banter to a close.

But after dinner she found occasion for one word with Gander. "That was a brave thing, Gander," she said. "I'm very proud of you."

And what was the Victoria Cross to that?

Meanwhile the Germans were forcing their way across the Yser.

TWELVE

When the threshing season was finished Gander went back to his father's farm with a pocketful of money and a promise from Bill Powers of a raise in wages next year. The crop had been light, and, even though the threshing gangs had been somewhat short-handed, or, to be more exact, had consisted of a larger proportion of boys and youths than usual, the "run" was completed by the time the first snow was flying in November.

Gander found his father nailing a hinge to the door of the cow-stable. All summer the door had managed with one hinge, on which it teetered forward and back in the wind, but the approach of cold weather demanded a door that could be closed, and Jackson Stake was busy making his repairs. He had been unable to find screws to fit the hinge, so he nailed it up with four-inch spikes, which he drove home with a hearty wallop, muffling the sound of his hammer under the body grunts with which he accompanied it. He was so intent on his work that he did not notice Gander's lank form at his side until he had driven the last spike home.

"There!" he said, approving his job. "That'll hold 'er till

there's whiskers on the wheat." Then, looking up, "'Lo, Gander! Through?"

Gander drew his feet a step or two nearer. "Yep. Closed down the smornin'."

Jackson surveyed his tall son, darker of complexion than ever with six weeks' engine grease ground into his skin. He looked stouter, too, but this may have been because he was wearing two suits of overalls, as the most convenient way to bring them home.

"Get your money?"

"Yep."

"All of it?"

"Yep."

"Huh! Old Bill mus' be pickin' up. I was holdin' back a bit of his threshin' money in case he didn't come through."

"Yep," said Gander. "Old Bill told me that, but I says to him, 'You settle with me, an' Dad'll settle with you,' an' I got it right here in my pistol pocket."

For a minute the two men measured each other, but presently Jackson's face softened into a smile. "'S all right, Gander," he said. "You earned it; you can keep it. Buy yourself an automobile – or some clean underwear."

The point as to who should own Gander's wages had not troubled the boy until the big handful of greasy bills was counted out to him. Then he began to wonder. If he had stayed at home he would have worked for his father for nothing, except, perhaps, some new clothes at the end of the season. He would have taken that for granted. But money in his pocket – to hand that over, that was different. He had been framing arguments all the way home – and his father had capitulated without attack.

"Course, if you need the money, Dad –" he began, but his father stopped him.

"No, I don' need it – no more'n a rabbit needs a run-about. I guess maybe I made a mistake with Jackie that way, an' I don' wan' to lose no second boy, if I can help it."

Gander felt his Adam's apple becoming unruly. He was suddenly ashamed of his misgivings.

"I'll stick to you, Dad," he said, "till the cows come home."

"Yep, I kind o' figger you will," said Jackson Stake. It was the most intimate talk the two ever had had together, and it filled them with a glow of domestic affection that held them in silence for some minutes.

Gander's father was the first to speak.

"Better run up an' see your mother," he suggested. "She's been missin' you – both o' you – a lot lately. An' say, there ain't no law against a hand-out to *her*, you know, if you're so disposed."

The boy shuffled off toward the house. He was fond, in a natural sort of way, of his mother, but he had no sympathy with her lamentations over his brother Jackie. Not that she often spoke of him; it was a name little heard in their household, but he seemed to be continually present in her mind, crowding from her life such happiness as she might have saved out of her drudgery. Gander thought this unreasonable. Jackie had gone – let him go. Gander counted it good riddance; he wasted no goodwill on Jackie, who had been over-disposed to exercise the authority of an elder brother. He came to understand, too, that his mother blamed his father for what had happened, and Gander was a partisan of his father's. Still, if a hand-out would help —

He found his mother baking; she seemed to be always baking. Minnie had gone over to Elsie Fyfe's on an errand; Hamilton was out with a horse and stone-boat hauling in fallen branches from the poplar groves for fire-wood, so the two were alone in the room.

She did not look up; evidently she thought it was her husband who had entered. The muscles of her strong arms rose and fell as she kneaded the dough; the hair on her temples was thin and gray.

"Hello, Mother! Always bakin'!" said Gander, with an effort at amiability.

Susie Stake looked up quickly. As her face and hair whitened with premature age her dark eyes seemed to grow sharper and darker; now they caught and held Gander as on two tines of a fork.

"Well for the soul or sake o' me!" she said. "I thought it was your dad. Are you done threshin'?"

"Yep. For another year."

"Get your money?"

"Yep."

"Well, that's a wonder. I was figgerin' Old Bill Powers 'ud try to do you out o' it."

"Old Bill don' seem to have no Rockefeller reputation 'round here, but he came through like a Government check," said Gander.

"Well, I'm glad o' that. It'll be a nice help to your father."

"Not partic'lar. He ain't gettin' it."

Mrs. Stake rubbed the dry dough from her hands and sank on to a chair beside the table, as though this sudden information was too weighty to bear standing.

"You mean you ain't goin' to give it to him?" she said at length. "Are you goin' to light out, too, like Jackie?"

"Jackie! Jackie! You're always thinkin' o' Jackie!" Gander exploded. It was not often he spoke to his mother like this, and he was surprised to see her face soften, just as his father's had, when he stood his ground.

"Now you talk like a Harden," she said. "Your dad's too easy-goin', an' too set, when he's set. . . . Well, what if I do think o' Jackie? He's my son. An' las' night I saw him, in a uniform, with blood on his face —"

Mrs. Stake's mouth began to twist strangely, and Gander, not knowing what he did, or why, crossed over to his mother and drew his arm about her shoulder.

"There, now, Mother," he said. "I ain't goin' to light out, whatever happens."

Her strong arm reached about his waist, and held him in a gesture of affection.

"Minnie's got it next," she said, after a silence. "Nothin' 'll do but she mus' be a stenografter. Bound to go to high school at Plainville, an' then on to a bus'ness college at Winnipeg, an' I'm thinkin' your father'll let 'er. After me —" The poignancy of her broken hopes for Minnie filled her throat. "I always figgered Minnie'd stand by me, but no! Says she's fed up on milkin' cows! Too much of a lady for a farmer's daughter; that's the way with them all, when they get a bit of eddication. Says that now we're at war, everybody should be doin' somethin', an' I says, 'Well, how about milkin' cows? I guess the soldiers wants butter, more'n they do stenografters,' but o' course she wouldn't listen to that. She's like her father; when she's set she's set, an' I reckon she's goin' to bolt."

Gander had nothing to say. But presently he reached into his hip pocket and drew out a roll of greasy bills. He thumbed them over clumsily until he came upon one for twenty dollars. He drew it out, folded it into a heap, and pressed it into his mother's floury palm.

"Wha's that for?"

"For you – jus' for you."

"Why, Willie, I – you –" He felt her form trembling beside him.

"Guess I better go an' help Ham with the wood," he said suddenly, and slouched through the door.

He found Hamilton hauling a load of short poplar poles on the stone-boat with old Nigger, the least ambitious of all the farm horses. Hamilton brought his steed up with as much flourish as he could muster, and surveyed his brother.

"Well, you didn't blow 'er up?" he remarked.

"No, not yet."

"I guess you're an engineer now, eh?"

"Well, I wouldn't say that, but I can make 'er snort a bit in a pinch," said Gander, modestly.

Hamilton started the horse, and they drew the poles into the yard.

"Did you hear about Freddie Gordon?" he asked, when they had finished unloading. "He's joined up."

"Hadn't heard," said Gander.

"A lot of the fellows are joining up, so Double F says, now that threshin's over."

Gander made no reply.

"Gee, I wish I was old enough!" said Hamilton.

Hamilton was of a sturdy design, more the pattern of his father than of his mother. He was fair, as were all the Stakes, but the Hardens were dark. He had an old fur cap pulled about his ears, and a very holey pair of woolen mitts on his hands, through which his bare red fingers gleamed in the cold, but he was a very resolute-looking little figure as, his eyes full on Gander, he repeated, "Gee, I wish I was old enough!"

Gander resented that look. "If you was maybe you'd have to stay home an' help Dad, an' it's me that'd go snipin' Germans," he retorted.

"Huh!" said Hamilton.

Gander did not see Minnie until supper time. He spent the remainder of the afternoon helping his father put the cow-stable in shape for winter, and feeding and renewing acquaintance with the farm horses. When the two men went into the house the table was set for supper, with the big lamp which Mrs. Stake had won as a special prize at the Plainville Fair shedding its yellow light up and down the well-laden board. Gander observed Minnie working by the stove, and noted how tall she had grown even in these few weeks, and how her dress seemed to be taking shape from the young womanhood which it covered, but he took his seat at the table without remark. Mr. Stake confided in his plate a blessing which grew more hurried and less articulate with each passing year; helped himself to fried eggs and potatoes, and passed the platters on to Gander.

Gander was in the midst of his second gulp when two hands closed gently about his neck and a forefinger pressed his Adam's apple, much as one might pull a trigger, and with somewhat similar effects.

"'K out, Minn! You'll choke me," he spluttered, when he had recovered from the involuntary explosion which almost wrecked his supper. "Shouldn't do that!"

"Big brothers, when they come home, shouldn't ignore their little sisters," said Minnie, as her warm hands drew Gander's straight hair down about his ears. Minnie was the one member of the Stake household who thought it no shame to be affectionate. She leaned over and pressed a kiss on Gander's forehead. "There!" she said.

Gander laughed off his embarrassment, but after all, she was his sister, and he liked her. The meal was half finished before there was time for further discussion. Farms are busy places, and the kitchen table, three times a day, the busiest place on the farm.

"Ol' Bill have much trouble about help?" Jackson Stake inquired when the eggs and potatoes were cleared away, and he was about to attack a second course of strawberry preserves and toast. "This fracas over in Europe makin' much diff'rence?"

"Nope – not to speak of," said Gander. "Lots o' men, such as they are. Youngsters, mostly, but, as Bill would say, a good boy's a better horse than a poor man. We made a good season's run, though, if we are kids – most of us."

"Next year's when we'll be short of men," Minnie observed.

"It'll be all over before that," said her father.

"That's not what they're saying in Plainville. Double F was in to-day, and he says they're talking of three years' war – says that's what Kitchener is figuring on."

"Double F ain't much of a judge," Jackson Stake remarked. "When he first come across with the news he was tellin' me it'd be over in three months, sure as Sunday. Now it's three years."

"At any rate," Minnie persisted, "Double F says the young men are all signing up, and what are we farmers going to do about next year's crop? He's worrying over *that* already."

"Well, it's somethin' to worry about," her father agreed. "But I reckon it'll be over before then, and what's the use puttin' the country to the expense o' shippin' all our young men over there jus' to cheer at the Kaiser's funeral, an' then come back again? More to the point to stay home an' work the farm."

"An' milk the cows," Minnie's mother suggested.

Gander took no part in this conversation, and Minnie dropped it at that point. They were busy with thoughts of their own.

THIRTEEN

T he following day Gander began hauling wheat to the elevators at Plainville. During the threshing season, and owing, perhaps, to the prospect of a rising market, Jackson Stake had hauled out only a few loads in order to meet his need of ready cash, and had then gone on with his fall ploughing. But now the ground was hard with frost and bleak with a thin fretwork of dusty snow. On the frozen prairie trails the rattle of an empty wagon could be heard for miles.

Gander harnessed a four-horse team – three old Clydesdales that had long since lost all but a flicker of frac-tiousness, and young Jim, the colt, who could be counted upon to behave himself in such a preponderance of good company. Jim's first glimpse of the serious side of life had been in the fall ploughing. There he bent a surprised and protest-ing shoulder into his collar, marvelling the while at the strange turn in events which had taken him from the freedom of the pasture field to the irksome monotony of dragging a wholly purposeless device up and down an interminable furrow. But discipline soon ground the imagination out of his soul, as it does to other beasts of burden besides horses, and already he accepted straining on his traces as a distasteful but inevitable procedure.

The horses were harnessed in double tandem, two abreast, and Gander skilfully swung the rear team to position on either side of the wagon-tongue. He slouched about their heads and heels in long, ungainly strides, but there was speed in his gracelessness; in a moment he had the tongue in the neck-yoke, the traces hitched to the whiffle-trees. A word, a touch of the reins, and the four horses moved off as one, while Gander circled them around to the spot where the grain box had been dropped in the centre of the yard after its previous use. Then were puffs, and grunts, and straining of hard muscles while father and son heaved the heavy box to position. Jackson Stake threw two scoop-shovels into the box while Gander, already up over the front wheel, directed his team toward a spot in the field where a straw stack raised its mountainous dome, half crusted with snow, against the grey November sky.

"I'll have to get me some port'ble graineries," said Jackson, who, with as much alacrity as his son, had climbed over the rear end of the box after the wagon was in motion. "Skid 'em around wherever we want 'em."

As they neared the mountain of straw a grain bin seemed to detach itself and stand a little to one side. It was a square box, framed of boards to a height of seven or eight feet, and tied together across the top with strands of heavy wire. Into this the grain had been spouted straight from the separator. When filled with wheat it was covered with a thick cap of straw to keep out rain and snow, and left to stand until a suitable time for marketing.

Beside the bin were two long-haired steers, licking up stray kernels that leaked out between the boards. Jackson Stake threw a shovel at them, as a matter of principle; then got out, gathered up his shovel, and, again with his surprising alacrity, clambered on to the bin. Here the two men turned back the straw until they bared the golden bosom of the wheat below; thrust went the shovels into that chaste embrace; then, singing, the wheat slid into the great box, where it rattled like nails on the wooden floor. Thrust and swing, thrust and swing, went the shovels, while the golden tide slowly rose in the box. The men worked on, without conversation and with the precision of machines, until the box was full; then, when the flood lapped its very lip, they threw their shovels on board, and Jackson Stake, straightening his great frame, rested his hands on his kidneys in a way he had and twisted his back for relief.

"You take 'er in, Gander," he said, "an' don' let them rogues in Plainville rob you any more'n seems necessary."

Gander threw his folded horse-blankets across the front of the load, settled himself into a comfortable, shapeless heap upon them, and snapped a sharp order to his team, which tightened their traces and swung off slowly toward the Plainville road.

It was a long, slow haul to the market town, under a sky curtained with grey clouds and shaking an occasional threatening snowflake in the air, by stark clumps of leafless poplars, along trails rutted smooth with the broad tires of many wagons, through a world in which nature had already hibernated for her long sleep until another spring. As Gander crouched on his blankets, his cap down about his ears, his collar up around them, he, too, might have been a lifeless thing but for the occasional automatic word of command or suggestion to his horses. It was a great opportunity to think, and, in his way, Gander made use of it. He wondered what price his load would bring, and how many bushels he carried in that heaving box. He wondered whether he would spend an hour or two in town; maybe get a haircut at the barber's shop, and pick up the latest gossip in the pool-room. Perhaps, too, he thought a little of that dark cloud which hung over all the world, and even, sometimes, wrapped its noisome mists about his heart. And when he thought of that he thought of Jo Burge, and wondered. Gander had no definite idea about Jo Burge. Still, he supposed that sometime – That would be the natural thing, and Gander lived close to nature. Her beauties may fall upon blind eyes, her harmonies upon deaf ears, but her instincts, unerring, stir in every clod.

As he neared Plainville Gander became aware of other traffic on the road. Now and again an automobile or buggy overtook him, pulled out on to the rough prairie at the side, rutted with tracks made in wet weather and now corrugated into frozen ridges, and went bumping by. Other heavily-laden wagons in front, and still others behind, the faster teams gradually overtaking the slower, but unable to pass, resolved themselves into an irregular procession – the march of King Wheat into the gates of the world.

Gander drew up in the straggling street that skirted the railway track at Plainville. On his right a row of garages, livery stables, implement warehouses, grocery and hardware stores, offices; on his left the huge bulk of the grain elevators, each with its squat little engine-room from which came the intermittent spit . . . spit . . . of the gasoline motor. The air was filled with the dust of wheat; around the elevators were drifts of chaff, in which one or two outlaw cows of the town were browsing; from the railway track came the sound, like rushing water, of wheat being piped into cars for shipment, first to Fort William or Port Arthur, and later to those hiving lands of Europe, now so assiduously engaged in a business of their own, but a business which could not be carried on, for long, without the help of that little red kernel, mightier than siege guns and battleships. . . . Gander straightened into the attitude of a biped and awaited the verdict of the buyers.

They came presently, three of them, from the wagon just ahead. With a great show of competition they clambered up Gander's wheels and dug their hands into his ruddy load, sifting samples through their fingers, turning them over in their palms, smelling them, chewing a few kernels.

"All I can see is a Three Northern," said one.

"Just what I was going to say," said another.

"You beat me to it," said the third, with a gesture of annoyance.

"Then you better get somethin' done for your eyes, all of you," said Gander. "I can see a One Northern, and I ain't wearin' no glasses."

The three buyers laughed as though Gander had perpetrated a great joke. But Gander wasn't laughing. His gorge was boiling within him. He had the farmer's deep-rooted sense of injustice over the fact that whenever he bought he had to pay the seller's price, but whenever he sold, the buyer dictated the figure. His gorge boiled none the cooler for the helplessness of his position.

"Take another look," said Gander to the three buyers, who, for competitors, seemed to him to be on much too friendly terms with each other. "It's a One Northern, or there ain't no such thing."

"No, Gander," said one who knew him. "It's nice wheat, all right, but a little bleached, and you're lucky to get a Three out of it. Rusted, too. I dunno but I was a little rash in offering you Three for it; may not go any better than Four."

"That's what I was thinking," said the second.

"Yep. It's pretty risky," said the third.

"Well, I'll ship it myself," said Gander, with a show of finality. "I'll get a bin an' ship it myself."

"That's risky, too," his acquaintance told him. "The lakes'll be freezing up pretty soon, and if you don't get your car down before the close of navigation you're in for a bump. Besides, I don't know whether you can get a bin."

Gander's inquiries proved this misgiving to be well founded. Individual bins, in which a farmer may store and ship his own wheat, were at a premium. The alternative of loading a car direct over the loading platform, without making use of an elevator, was out of the question; he had no car, and no idea when he could get one. He came back to the buyer who had made him the first offer.

"Guess I'll have to take your price, George, but it don' seem right. That wheat's better'n Three Northern."

"You're all wrong, Gander," the buyer said, pleasantly. "I'll be lucky if I get out on it. But I'll tell you what I'll do. I'll send a sample to Winnipeg for official grading – or you can do it – and if it goes higher than Three I'll pay you the difference, but if it goes lower you pay me the difference. That's fair, Gander."

"Oh, take it!" said Gander, helplessly. This was not his world. He was a producer, not a seller.

Gander drove his team up the gangway into one of the elevators. He guided his four horses with a dexterity that was an art, bringing the great load to position to an inch. This was his world. The load was weighed as it stood in the wagon; the warehouseman touched a lever; the front end of the wagon went up, the rear end down; a trap door in the back of the wagon-box was opened and the wheat rushed out in a golden stream into a hopper under the driveway. It was all over in a minute. Gander got his ticket, good for cash at the bank, and drove on.

He put his team in a livery stable, rubbing down their fetlocks and wiping the sweat out from under their collars before he left them, and then went to the Chinese restaurant to get a bite of dinner. The "Chink's place" was a comparatively new establishment in Plainville. It rejoiced in a painted signboard, No Sing – Wun Lung, which occasioned much local merriment. If the owner knew the reason for the amusement he gave no hint; but it is a good thing to have men come into your place of business smiling. Gander patronized the slant-eyed gentleman with the vocal disadvantages, not on account of the wit in his signboard, but in order to escape the tyranny of tablecloths and napkins with which the Palace hotel insisted on encumbering its guests. Besides, the meals were ten cents cheaper.

Gander was bent industriously over pork and potatoes when two young men in uniform entered and took seats at the next table. He observed them under his eyebrows. Their faces were clean shaven and their hair was close cropped about the ears and up from the back of the neck – a fact that recalled Gander's own need of tonsorial attention. Their uniforms sat upon them snugly, and Gander could not but admit that they probably looked much more handsome than he, in his overalls and smock drawn tight over an old tweed suit which he had put on for warmth. And they appeared to be quite happy. If they were charged with the duty of saving the world from the Germans they evidently were not worried about it. Gander was no eavesdropper, but he would have had to stuff his fingers in his ears – those ears over which the hair straggled and curled – in order to avoid hearing some of their remarks. They seemed to be talking about girls. Yes, there was no doubt they were talking about girls.

No Sing or Wun Lung or both (no one seemed to know whether the name was singular or plural) combined a grocery business with his restaurant, and at this moment, as though to afford a proper setting for the military conversation, two young girls of Plainville came in to buy a can of salmon. Gander had no idea that the purchase of so trifling an atom of commerce could exhaust so much time, so much giggling, so much obvious desire to be observed. He had no delusions as to the audience for whose benefit this performance was presented. In a dusty, fly-specked mirror he could see his own humped profile, his shaggy locks, the long hair about his ears and neck, the fuzz on his lips and chin. . . .

With color rising in his cheeks Gander gulped the remainder of his meal, paid for it, and hurried into the street. The sharp tang of the November air was a tonic and a stimulant. He walked by an implement warehouse and a garage and stopped in front of a barber's shop. For a moment he stood irresolute, then plunged inside and flopped into the empty chair.

"Hair cut?" said the barber.

"Yep," said Gander. "Mow it good and short."

"Military cut, eh?"

Gander wasn't very sure. "Yep," he hazarded.

"Thinking of joining up, maybe?" the barber suggested.

"Well, not to-day," said Gander.

The barber's chair was by the window, where the light was good, and further back were pool-tables, with several young men playing at them, and a fringe of others seated on benches around the wall. Here, again, Gander noticed two or three men in khaki. Suddenly another, in a smarter uniform, came through the door, and as he did so the soldiers in the room sprang to their feet, clicking their heels together, squaring their shoulders, and looking generally as though they had been petrified into an attitude of aggressive immobility.

"All right, men, carry on," said the officer, smartly, and the petrification suddenly ran limp again. Something in the voice stirred Gander's memory, and he studied the officer's face for a moment. It was Andy Lee, the clothes presser! And men springing to their feet, and clicking their heels!

"A little shampoo?" the barber suggested. "Fine to take the dust out of the hair."

"Sure; hop to it!" said Gander, recklessly. He was in the intoxication of his first reaction to the war. Three-quarters of an hour later he walked out of the barber's shop, shampooed, shaved, massaged, scented, and with the pride of his soul somewhat restored.

He made some purchases for his mother at Sempter & Burton's; then, wishing to give his horses ample time to feed and rest, he loitered about the elevators. The gasoline engines fascinated him. They were so like and so unlike steam. Less human than steam, and more mechanical, but still somewhat on the same principle. Thumping faithfully away, without supervision; that was the remarkable thing about them. Gander was looking forward to the day when he would persuade his father to buy a threshing mill, and wondering whether it would be steam or gasoline.

"Still," he said, as though in answer to an argument within himself, "when you got steam you got steam, but when you got one o' these cha-punkers you don' know what you got."

A freight train pulled in, picked up some cars, and pulled out again. Gander watched the huge engine struggling with its load. He caught a glimpse of the engineer up in his seat in the cab, a lever in his hand. That was power for you!

That was life! Sometimes, in the wildest flights of his imagination, Gander thought of himself as a locomotive engineer.

When the horses were well rested he hitched up again and started for home. He was barely out of town when, in a vacant space, he saw four or five soldiers drilling. They were near the road, and Gander, curious, allowed his team to come to a stop. It seemed that four were drilling and the fifth was giving orders. Gander gathered also that the fifth was disappointed in the way in which his orders were being executed.

"Na-a-gh, I didn't say 'Right turn,' I said 'Left turn.' Do you not know one side o' you from the other? Or will I have to tie a string on your fingers? A little silk bow, maybe. Now try it again, and see if you can all turn the same way, for once.

"Left – turn!" The sergeant's voice snapped through the cold air. "Quick – march! . . . Form two-deep! . . . Form – fours! Na-a-gh, I didn't say 'Left turn'; I said 'Form fours.' As you were! *As-you-were!*"

The sergeant's voice indicated, as only a sergeant's voice can indicate, the hopelessness of instilling intelligence into heads so ill-designed to receive it. He explained this in a monologue of some length, while Gander's Adam's apple hopped boisterously about, for had he not at this moment, in spite of the khaki, recognized the bucolic figure of Freddie Gordon? Gander chuckled outright. So this was war? Strutting about on a vacant lot, like a flock of mating prairie chickens! Being told you don't know one foot from another – and proving it! Taking the lip of that fresh guy, and not saying a word back at him! Ha!

At this moment Freddie Gordon, glancing toward the road, recognized the humped figure on the wagon, and Gander, with the most innocent of intentions, sang out cheerily, "'Lo, Fred! How's she goin'?"

Freddie twisted his mouth as though to speak, but before any sound had been emitted the sergeant intervened. "Silence!" he roared. "Silence in the ranks! You're not gawkin' now on the street corner, me-lads, remarkin' on the weather. Shun! As you were! Shun! As you were! Shun! As you were! Put some gimp into it! With the help o' God I'll make soldiers of you yet." The sergeant's voice suggested an imprecation rather than a prayer. "And *I'll* take care of your conversational duties for the time bein', me-lads. Shun!"

The sergeant surveyed his four "rookies," now galvanized into a convulsive attitude supposed to represent attention. Suddenly his voice fell from its note of autocratic command to one of amiability. "Stand at ease! Stand easy! Now I'll just interview our visitor."

He came over to the wagon where Gander, despite a sudden impulse for flight, remained immobile.

"Well, me-lad," he said, in a quite friendly manner, "you seem interested. Perhaps you were thinkin' of joinin' up?"

"Not partic'lar," said Gander.

"It's a great life, and you're a likely lookin' chap."

But Gander was irritated by what he had seen and heard. It clashed with all his ideas of democracy. When Gander worked for his father, or Bill Powers, he counted himself as good a man as the boss. So did the boss. But here was a boss who said things to his men – well, if Bill Powers had said them to *his* men they would have given him directions to his ultimate destination.

"Do you have to learn that new-fangled square-dance before you can kill a German?" said he.

"It's discipline, me-lad; discipline. An army is built on discipline."

"It may be what you call it, but it looks to me like a new kind o' square-dance – an' I ain't much of a dancer," Gander retorted. "Giddap!" He chirped to his horses and left the astonished sergeant standing by the road.

As he wound his slow course homeward through the closing night Gander chuckled more than once over his smart repartee. "I ain't much of a dancer," he would say to himself. "That got him. He didn't know what to say."

But that was all on the surface. Down underneath was a gnawing sense – a sense that he was running away from something, that he was a fugitive, taking refuge on the farm! He actually experienced a feeling of escape from danger as he rumbled over the ridge beyond the school and the light in Double F's kitchen window came into view.

"But I can't do anythin' else," he argued with himself. "I promised both Dad and Mother I'd stick to 'em, an' I guess that's my job."

He felt the air cold on his ears and neck, and turned his collar closer around them. From that he fell to thinking of the girls in the restaurant, and of how obviously they had ignored him, playing their little patter to the two men in uniform. And up through the grey night came a picture of Josephine Burge – Jo of his old school days, of his herding days, of the threshing gang where she had said, "Maybe some day he'll wear a real V. C."

His happiness over the discomfiture of the sergeant seeped from him, and at supper he was more silent than usual. His father attributed his gloom to the after-effects of a tonsorial spree which had cost him a dollar and a half.

FOURTEEN

The first year of the war was the hardest for Gander. Before another season's crop was being threshed the world – the Allies' world, at any rate – had awakened to the quite obvious fact that the war must be won by wheat. Growing wheat became a patriotic duty into which Gander fitted like a cylinder nut into a socket wrench. He could grow wheat, and none of that "form fours" nonsense about it. True, there were still some who refused to see in the growing of wheat the highest expression of service; some even who were frank enough to suggest that the prospect of a high price had more to do with the sudden increase in acreage than had any patriotic motive. But Gander avoided argument and kept on with his ploughing, his seeding, his harvesting and threshing. He, who had been reared on the plains, with himself for a companion, more than ever receded within himself. He avoided company, he avoided discussion, he avoided trips to Plainville. As a matter of custom he continued going to church at Willow Green, but even there sometimes found eyes that bored him through, and sent him home in a tempest of self-excuse.

One of the difficult times was when Tommy Burge enlisted. The Burges gave a party for their soldier son, and Gander, as one of the nearest neighbors and friends of the family, must, of course, attend. He willingly would have denied himself that pleasure; not even the prospect of dancing with Jo Burge could balance the disadvantages under which he would be placed. But he felt he ought to go; he owed that much to Tommy, and he could cover up a little by taking his sister Minnie as his guest.

"Well, Minn," he remarked with forced casualness at noon that day, "how'd you like to go to Burges' dance to-night?"

Minnie, now a girl of fifteen or sixteen, and beautiful even to her brother, blushed pink under her bronze hair.

"I'm going," she said. "With Walter Peters."

Peters! The boy whom Gander had saved from the separator! Oh! So he must go alone.

It was a June day, and Gander worked in the summer-fallow until seven o'clock. Then he unharnessed, fed, and watered his team; had his supper, and went up to his room to dress. As he wrestled with his razor the idea of attending the party became more and more repugnant.

"Darn it all, I don' want to go," he at last confessed to himself. "It's goin' to be a hot night, an' I'm tired, an' I guess I ain't much of a dancer, anyway." The answer he had given the sergeant came to his mind, and he smiled, a little bitterly. There would be a number of fellows there in uniform, and he – he never would be missed. Yes he would! Jo would miss him, and Tommy. . . .

He sat down on his bed, dangling one bare foot over the shoe that lay beside it. He had no stomach for the thing. Why did they have to have a dance, anyway? Why couldn't they just let his friends drop in —

He was still sitting thus when Minnie, her shoulders bare, her bronze hair hanging about her white neck, passed his door. She stopped; held him in her eyes a moment; then came in.

"What's the matter, Gander? Aren't you going?"

The setting sun was blazing through the window, disputing with Gander's little oil lamp possession of the room. In the mottled light his face was a picture of distress.

"I – I don' think so," he said. "I ain't feelin' very gay, to-night. Guess I been workin' too hard. An' I ain't much of a dancer, anyway. You tell 'em, Minn. Maybe I'll run over Sunday."

The girl's hands dropped on her brother's shoulders; she turned his face to hers.

"Gander," she said, "I know what's the matter – and so do you. . . . It isn't so very easy for *me*, either." There was a little gulp in her voice. She withdrew her hands from him and switched out of the room.

On Sunday he went over to the Burges', but Tommy had already gone forward. Jo received him at the door.

"It's stuffy inside. Would you like to walk?" she said.

"Yes – if you would."

They walked out over the school section, now studded with flaming tiger lilies, and if both of them had memories they kept them to themselves. Jo was a tall, straight woman now; not bent with work, as Gander was. The freckles still peered through her white, transparent skin. Gander thought of that day, and of the hole in her stocking that shone like a silver dollar.

"Sorry you couldn't get over the other night, Gander," she opened their conversation.

"Yes," he agreed. "Sorry, too. But I ain't much of a dancer." He hadn't meant to use that phrase again. It just slipped out.

ROBERT STEAD

"You always seemed to me a good dancer, Gander. . . . Tommy was sorry, too."

"Yep. . . . I didn't know he was goin' so soon, or I'd ha' come, anyway."

"He's gone!" she breathed, almost in a whisper. Suddenly she swayed so that Gander caught her in his arms. He supported her, helplessly, wondering what to do. A tremor was running through her frame; she seemed at the point of sobbing. But presently she straightened up, erect, and withdrew herself from his arms.

"I'm all right, Gander," she told him, smiling a little wanly into his face. "Just a little silly. . . . I should be very proud. . . . I *am* proud."

Her head was back now, and the summer breeze was fingering her fair hair. "I *am* proud," she repeated.

"Yes, I suppose so," said Gander, not knowing what else to say.

They walked on, charted only by some strange instinct, until they reached the grove of willows where they had lain in the shade that hot day of the cattle herding. Here the girl paused, toying with the leaves at her feet; turning them over with her toe, as though looking for something. Gander stood beside her, mute. Suddenly she turned about and seized his shoulders in her hands. Her lips were trembling, but her eyes were straight on his.

"There's only one thing could make me prouder, Gander," she said. "You know what it is."

"You mean I should join up?"

She nodded, pressing her lips together hard.

"I'm not trying to tell you what you should do, Gander," she added. "You must settle that for yourself. But *that* is what would make me proud."

"Well, I suppose," said Gander. "But there are other

things, too. They want wheat, an' I'm helpin' to raise it. Besides, I promised my father an' mother not to leave 'em."

"Did they make you promise that?" There was a new note of challenge in the girl's voice.

"Well, not exactly," said Gander, in whose veins honesty flowed like blood. "But, you see, Jackie is gone, an' they worry over that a lot, so I told 'em I'd stick with 'em."

"Hamilton is coming along," Jo argued. "My dad and mother had only Tommy."

Gander did not answer. What could he say to that?

She had dropped her hands from his shoulders, but still stood close to him, her eyes on his. "Gander," she said, "tell me this. Do you really *want* to go?"

Gander found himself being cornered, and he had no gift of argument. But he could be stolid. His strength was the strength of immobility.

"No, I don't!" he blurted out.

"Are you afraid?" He had not known that Jo's voice could cut like that.

"Oh, I dunno," he answered. "Guess I could take a chance with the rest."

Her tone suddenly softened. "No, I know you are not afraid," she added, gently. "A boy who could do what you did – that day at the thresher – isn't afraid."

Gander grunted. "Nothin' to that," he said.

"Then why is it?" she insisted.

Gander considered for a moment. "Well, I'll tell you, Jo," he answered. "I don' know very much about war, but I know somethin' about farmin', an' I figger this is where I belong. An' I ain't much for a crowd; I can get along with two or three, but in a crowd I'm out of it. I guess it's bein' on the farm like I have, I been alone so much —"

"You mean you're shy? . . . Gander, I believe you are."
She laughed a soft, teasing laugh, the first she had laughed that
day, and for a moment Gander had an impulse to belie his
own confession. But he conquered the impulse, and so justified her conclusion.

"You would get over that," she went on. "It would do
you good. And they'd straighten you up, Gander. Straighten
those shoulders of yours. Put some gimp into your step. I've
seen them marching in Plainville, and" – she colored frankly,
now, but faced him still – "and pictured you in uniform, and
thought how good you would look, straight and tall, for you
are tall, Gander, when you straighten up —"

"Oh, I guess I'm all right," he interrupted, sulkily. He
had no desire to hear his defects analyzed.

"It would do you good," she repeated. "You'd get
over – *that* – in a week. And, besides, all the girls like to have
their – their fellows – doing their bit."

The appeal of that suggestion was not to be lightly dismissed. But Gander still held his trump card. He played it.

"Besides, I got too much spirit to be a soldier," he
said.

"Too much what?"

"Too much spirit. . . . I'll explain." Then he told her of
the day he had seen the recruits drilling on the outskirts
of Plainville. "Struttin' like prairie chickens, they were," he
said, "an' that fellow bawlin' 'em out like nobody ever bawled
me out an' got away with it – or ever will," he added belligerently. "Jumpin' on Fred because he went to speak to me. If I'd
been Fred I'd ha' hit 'im a poke in the eye."

She was so long in answering that for a moment he
thought she had found his argument beyond reply.

"So that's it?" she said, at length. "You're too good to take orders? Too big a man to be told what to do? If everybody was like you, who'd stop the Germans?"

"Well, I guess I could stop my share, if it came to that," he retorted, "an' without doin' a square-dance in front o' them."

She was angry now. "Better men than you are doing the square-dance, as you call it, Gander."

"Meanin' who?"

"Never mind."

"Dick Claus?"

"What if I do?"

Gander's fire was up, too. His was a slow fire, but suddenly it blazed up as though swept by a prairie wind. "Well, if you're goin' to be his pardner, you ought to learn his dance," he cried. "See – I'll show you." He seized her by the arm. "Form fours! Form two-deep! Shun! As you were! Shun! As you were!" He suited grotesque movements to his commands, jerking her about until she wrenched herself from his grasp. "That's the way to lick the Germans," he explained.

She ran from him a few steps, then turned and faced him, her cheeks pink, her pale eyes ablaze. She had twitted him with his shyness, but she had no need to twit him now. Something new had broken out in Gander. She read it in his eye, in the twist of his face, in the pose of his body like an animal set to spring. A horror of fear swept her. Her cheeks went suddenly white again, and she tried to run, but she seemed held in a vice. He was coming toward her, this new Gander, this man she never had seen before; coming with slow, menacing strides across the grass. For a moment he held her in his spell; then, with a scream, she regained control of her limbs, and fled across the prairie like a deer.

Gander gave chase, but he was no match for Jo in a trial of speed. He followed her with long, ungainly strides, up and down the ridges of the school section, with little hope of catching her, and with no idea what would be the outcome if he did. Something wild had taken possession of him and egged him on in his madness. Yet even as he ran and marvelled at her speed he recalled that day when, a little girl, he had rescued her from the prisoner's base and led her back triumphantly to safety. They had been friends then. They were friends yet. Of course they were friends. Of course.

That thought seized him. "Jo!" he called. "Oh, Jo! Wait a minute!" But if she heard him she seemed only to run the faster.

As she swept down the slope of a gentle hill her speed was her undoing. Something gave way; her skirt wrapped about her feet, and she fell headlong in the grass. In a few seconds he had overtaken her, and was down on his knees beside her.

"Jo!" he cried. "Jo, are you hurt? Speak to me, Jo!" But she lay as motionless as death.

A great fear suddenly gripped him about the chest. He threw his arms around her, turned her over, raised her face from the ground. A tiny trickle of blood was making its red way across her forehead, now whiter and more transparent than ever he had seen it. He called her name again, but there was no answer; she lay limp in his arms.

In genuine alarm he looked about for help, but the prairie was empty of all except themselves. A hundred yards away a pond lay like silver in the afternoon sunlight, and the sight of water brought an idea which stirred him to action. Gently he laid her again on the grass and started on a run for the pond. Half way there he remembered that he had nothing with which to carry water when he reached it. For a moment he paused, bewildered; then hurried back, raised the girl in his arms, and began to carry her. She was not light, but Gander was strong, and in memory he never knew whether she weighed more than a feather. Her head fell back, and was swinging free; he supposed that must be uncomfortable, and perhaps dangerous, so he raised her higher, and drew one of her limp arms about his neck. Her head now rested against his; he even could feel that trickle of blood against his cheek. . . .

At the pond he laid her down, and, carrying water in his hands, poured it on her face. Presently she opened her eyes.

"Are you hurt, Jo?" he asked, gently and contritely. "You're not much hurt, are you?"

Her eyes looked into his like a child's. "Where am I? How did I get here?" she asked. "Oh, it's you, Gander."

Suddenly recollection leapt up within her. She thrust out her hands as though to shove him away.

"Go 'way, go 'way!" she cried. "Don't touch me! Go 'way!" There was such an abhorrence in her look that Gander shrank before it.

"I won't touch you," he pleaded. "But I'll help you home. You've been hurt."

"Go 'way! Go 'way! I never want to see you again. I'm all right." She arose unsteadily to her feet and drew her loosened skirt about her.

With her first step she staggered, and Gander rushed to her aid, but she shoved him away with her hands. "Go 'way! Go home! I never want to see you again!"

The girl moved off across the prairie, at first slowly, but quickening her pace as she regained control of her muscles, while Gander stood as one rooted to the spot, watching her through a flood of self-abasement.

When she disappeared over a ridge he turned and slowly made his way northward to his father's house.

FIFTEEN

After the incident with Jo Burge, Gander became more than ever a creature of his father's farm. He ploughed and harrowed early and late, and found his companionship with his horses and machinery. From even his father and mother he withdrew as into a shell.

As the months went by and the war, instead of drawing to an end, grew steadily more pressing and more furious, Jackson Stake and his wife thought much and spoke little of Gander. They had no desire that he should run the risk of battle, and they could ill afford to spare him from the farm, but they had a feeling which would not down that in some way the Stakes should be represented, not only in the wheat field, but on the fighting line. Such comfort as they could they took from the thought that maybe Jackie was there, and they read the casualty lists, which now filled columns in the newspaper, with mingled hope and fear. . . .

Not that they were anxious for Gander to go, but it would have been a solace to their pride if he had *wanted* to go, and he showed no such inclination. He worked in the fields all day, and sat about the stables or the blacksmith shop during noon hours and in the long, still summer evenings. He had learned to smoke, and the glow of his pipe, moving about like some disembodied spirit, would come up through the darkness to the room where his father and mother were preparing for bed. Sometimes Jackson would sigh as he saw that sullen point of fire and thought of the strange, stubborn, faithful shame that moved behind it; and then his wife would sigh, but whether for Gander, or for Jackie, or for herself, or for the mystery of life that perplexed and baffled her, her husband never knew. . . . Meanwhile Gander played with his dog, and affectionately cuffed the muzzles of his friendly horses, and went on in the deepening furrow of his circle, round and round.

Not so Minnie. "I'm fed up," she announced one night after milking her eight cows as usual. "I'm through. There must be something in life besides cows, and I'm going out to find it."

"Where did you think you would find it?" her father asked her. "In Plainville?"

"I'll start in Plainville," she said. "I'm going to the Plainville High School, then to Winnipeg to learn stenography."

"That takes money," her father reminded her.

"I know. And you've got the money. I helped you earn it."

"But suppose I don't give it to you? Your mother needs you here."

"I know," the girl answered, more gently, but her firmness was unshaken. "I know, and I'm sorry, but I must go. I really must. You see, it's *my* life, and I've got to live it, and no one else can. And I'm going. If you won't help me I'll – I'll help myself."

With mixed emotions Jackson Stake looked on this child of his, yesterday a baby, now almost a woman. Her eyes were brown, like his mother's had been; her hair was dull gold, deepening to bronze. He harrowed his head, once also bronze, and still with a ruddy hue running through its thinning locks.

"You're a Stake, Minnie," he said. "Go ahead. I'll pay your way."

"And who's goin' to help me about the house?" Mrs. Stake demanded. "An' the everlastin' cows an' pigs an' chickens? I declare to hope I'm run off my feet as it is."

"Yes, that's so," Jackson agreed. "Guess we'll have to hire you a woman – if the crop comes off," he compromised.

So Minnie went to town, and the farm became a place more remote than ever.

In the third year of the war two events of importance touched Gander's life.

The first was the purchase by his father of a Ford car. Crops had been good and prices unprecedentedly high, and the farmer's bank account was bulging. He was in a preferred position for making money, with his land, stock, and equipment acquired when prices were low, and with two farm hands of his own – Hamilton was now doing a man's work in the fields – and no war-time wages to pay.

"A car?" he scoffed, when the dealer first approached him. "One o' them rantin' automobilly-goats? No, sir! Give me a good team, that goes *an' comes back*, an' I'll scare the grease out o' them wind-broken go-humpers so fast you'd think it was a hired man comin' to dinner!"

The salesman was quite undaunted by Jackson's figures of speech. "They're a great time-saver on the farm, Mr. Stake," he suggested. "Why, with one of our machines you could skip into town in twenty minutes, and save your horses —"

"An' feed it on hay, I suppose?" Jackson interrupted. "No, sir! You see, with a horse, I stoke him right on the farm, hay an' oats an' that kind o' stuff, but a gas wagon takes gas, an' they do say as John D. is quite comfortable fixed already. No. I might be on the market for a manure-spreader this fall, if you think you could rig it up that way —"

But a week later, when Jackson's team shied so sharply they broke a wagon tongue as a new Ford went whizzing by with Fraser Fyfe at the wheel, he came home and discussed it with his wife.

"Might's well have one, it seems to me," he argued. "They're gettin' as common on the highways as coppers on the collection plate."

"I could do with a new sewin' machine," said Susie Stake.

"Yes, I suppose."

"Or a little engine to run the washin' machine."

"Yes, that 'ud be handy."

"Or a woman to help about the house – *if the crop comes off.*"

Jackson laughed, but he felt the cut. And he went out and bought a car.

Within a week Gander had ferreted into its innermost parts, without destroying any vital organs. He knew every gradation of its most whimsical mood before his father could distinguish between a cylinder knock and a flat tire.

The other event was the death of Tommy Burge. The telegram was delayed, and the first intimation received by the Willow Green community was the finding of his name among a half column of casualties in the daily paper. There it was Thomas Burge, just like any other name. But it seemed different to the Willow Green people. He was the first of their casualties, and all of a sudden the war jumped from France to Willow Green! There it squatted, horrible among the peaceful farms, licking its chops. . . .

Jackson Stake showed the paper to his wife.

"Tommy Burge!" she exclaimed. "Little Tommy Burge! . . . Poor woman, I must go over and speak her a word in her trouble."

"Yes, do," her husband agreed. "I'll take you in the car."

As they skirted the fields, again ripening for harvest, Jackson and his wife wrestled hard with one disturbing thought. At length the woman spoke:

"Jackson, I feel like a hypocrite," she said. "Me carryin' comfort, when I – when we —"

"Yes, I know. If only Gander – But he's needed on the farm. How could we spare him from the farm, Susie?"

"The Burges spared Tommy." Mrs. Stake was in no mood to excuse either her husband or herself. "I'm only prayin' that maybe Jackie —"

"Yes, maybe he is. Likely that's where he is."

Suddenly the old farmer's face began to twist, and the car wobbled in the prairie trail.

"Suppose you was to find *his* name – there – to-morrow?" he said.

"I'd be a proud woman," she answered. Susie Stake drew herself up more erect, and her black eyes flashed as they had not flashed for years.

The news had preceded them to the Burge homestead. Martin Burge met them at the gate, and wrung their hands without speaking. But he seemed older, and his form was all humped up.

Inside the house they found Mrs. Burge in bed, recovering from a fainting spell, and Jo attending her. "It's Mr. and Mrs. Stake, Mother," the girl announced.

The woman's wild eyes seemed at first not to recognize her neighbors. "Oh, yes, Mrs. Stake," she said, after peering at her as though she were a stranger. "It's thankful you must be, Mrs. Stake, that there's none of yours at this awful war. What did ever my poor Tommy do that he – that they – Oh, God, it's not fair, it's not right! If I could put a mother's curse on those who made the war I'd – I'd —"

"Hush, Mother," said Jo, leaning over and stroking her hair with her fingers. "I'd rather have Tommy there than – some – where they are."

"You're thinkin' of William," said Mrs. Stake. "An' I'm not blamin' you for feelin' bitter. But I've lost a boy, too, an' I know what it is. We're hopin' he's there, doin' his part. Must I give two?"

For a moment Mrs. Burge made no answer, but moaned like one crushed under physical pain. Mrs. Stake came near and stood beside her.

"It's sorry for you I am, my good neighbor," she said. "We've seen this country from the wilderness to what it is, and we've seen many a trouble between us, but never like this. An' to bring our wee boys into the world! We never thought, Mrs. Burge – I'm thinkin' we'd ha' died in it, if we could ha' seen ahead!" Their hands were gripped together now, and the chasm between them had been bridged.

"But it's not fair!" the woman moaned. "It's not fair! It's not just!"

Jo had been going about her work, apparently the most composed of all. But suddenly she ran out of the house, weeping. "Nothin's fair, nothin's just – any more!" she cried.

On the way home Jackson Stake suddenly broke into unprecedented profanity. The car swerved, and, horrified, his wife seized the wheel. "Why, Jackson, whatever do you mean?" she cried.

Jackson brought the car to a stop and then, looking into his wife's face with a calm more terrible than his sudden anger, said, "Susie, I was just thinkin' o' the price o' wheat. Blood money, Susie, every dollar of it!"

The next morning, as though it had been but a moment later, he took up that thread again. "But we have to go on with it," he argued. "They must have wheat. Gander, don't you think we could handle that school section, if the Gover'ment puts it up for sale?"

"I reckon we could, or part of it, anyway."

"Martin Burge an' me often spoke o' buyin' that section between us. Kind o' figgered it would come in handy for you an' Jo. But I guess Martin ain't hardly able to handle it now."

As Tommy's was the first death from the Willow Green district a memorial service was held in the school house. Later, the harvest of war became too plentiful for that. For Tommy's service the little frame building was crowded, and many stood out of doors. Gander was there, sick at heart, but unsurrendered. He was doing his bit, he told himself a hundred times; he was doing his bit. No man was working harder in the fields than he, and wheat was the thing to win the war. Besides – "Form fours!" He heard that derisive voice, he saw those seemingly senseless antics, and his spirit hardened within him. No! No! Not even for Jo!

He caught a glimpse of her as she came out from the service, whiter than ever, but with a new dignity in her carriage, with a great pride in the way she held her head. Jo had never spoken to him since that wild episode in the field. He wondered if to-day she would relax; he even pictured her coming to him and holding out her hand. In his own dumb way he knew how empty the world was, and forever would continue to be, without Jo Burge. Already it had driven him back deeper into the shell of his seclusion. He wanted to tell her what a fool he had been, and that he never really meant her any harm. . . . She was coming toward him, and his heart thumped in his ears, while his persistent Adam's apple teetered in his throat. She was so close he could see the blue veins in her forehead, and the freckle-points peering through her white skin. Her hair almost brushed his face. Suddenly he knew he was ready to do anything for Jo; yes, even to enlist, for Jo. But if she saw him, or, perhaps, because she saw him, she inclined her head slightly away and passed without any sign of recognition. He went home angry and ashamed, more than ever to lose himself in the routine of the farm.

The harvest that year was too much for Gander and his father, even with the staunch help of Hamilton, now a boy of sixteen, whose concern in life was divided between Elsie Fyfe and a fear that the war would be over before he was old enough to enlist. As a source of additional labor Jackson Stake succeeded in hiring in Plainville a farm hand answering to the name of Grit Wilson. Grit was a silent humorist, with a slumbrous twinkle in his eye and a smile enclosed between heavy elliptic creases that bracketed his mouth. He was just the person needed to turn Gander's thoughts from Josephine Burge and to bolster up his sagging self-esteem.

As their acquaintance ripened they discussed the war. "Looks to me you ought to be about military age," said Gander. "Ever had a poke at the Heinnies?"

"Sure, I'm military age; over eighteen and under sixty, and they're crowdin' 'em in on both sides of that figger now, if you're likely lookin'. But I done my bit."

"Been in France?"

"No; never got that far. But I got my papers; flat feet, they call it. Took 'em a year to find it out, an' I don' know it yet, but I ain't quarrelin'. In the army you do as you're told, an' if an officer says to you, 'Wilson, you got flat feet,' you don' argue about it; you go home. An' here I am."

"I suppose you can do all that chicken-dance stuff?"

"What you mean, 'chicken-dance stuff'?"

"Form fours!" Gander shouted the order as he remembered it from the drill that day on the vacant lots adjoining Plainville.

"Sure, I can form fours, but not all by myself. You'll be orderin' me into battalion formation next. Try me on 'Shun'."

"Shun!" Gander shouted, and the new hired man sprang to a military attitude, as though hit by an electric shot. His shoulders came back, his heels together, his waist-line shrank inward.

"Real Kaiser stuff," said Gander. "Now we got an army of our own. To-morrow mornin' we'll attack the barley. Do you form fours for that?"

"It ain't so bad when you get used to it," said Grit, puzzled at the bitterness in Gander's voice. "An' the girls, they fall for you, hard."

Gander grunted, and Grit avoided the subject for the time. He entertained a pleasant and apparently harmless philosophy about women. He regarded them from a distance, but with much quiet amusement. Women to him were like a picture show, to be looked at, laughed at, and forgotten.

By the time harvest was over Grit had become a fixture on the Stake farm. From his own abundant unconcern he innoculated Gander, and, although Grit was a dozen years the elder, the two became close cronies. It was from Grit that Gander learned to laugh at the world. And every time he laughed at the world he felt that, in some way, he was getting even with Josephine Burge.

In the summer of 1918 Dick Claus came home, checked out for tuberculosis. The doctors hoped he would be all right when he got his lungs full of prairie air, and his father deeded him a half-section of land – a generosity which had the double merit of providing for his son and at the same time reducing his own income tax.

The marriage of Richard Claus and Josephine Burge took place in September.

SIXTEEN

Peace had returned. The oppressive drag of the war was suddenly cut loose, like a horse breaking from his whiffle-tree. For a few days the horse ran wild, to the damage of himself and all adjacent property; then Reason – or Habit – bridled him again, and he fell back into his furrow.

For Gander the furrow was that unending routine which encircled his father's farm. It was a routine from which he had no desire to be disturbed. Several times the war had threatened to shoulder him out of his furrow, and he made the war his enemy on that account. Minnie and Jo had tried to prod him out of it, and had succeeded in prodding themselves out, instead. He stuck to his furrow. His life was on the farm, where he left other people alone, and asked only that they do the same to him.

It was the easier to stick to his furrow when he travelled in double harness with Grit Wilson. Grit laughed at the world, and laughter gives a pleasant sense of superiority. Gander could not have worked out any theories of philosophy about it, but he knew that it was a very comforting thing to laugh at the world. It placed the world at such a disadvantage.

True, there were times – times when he met Jo Claus at church at Willow Green, or shopping in Plainville, or at some country picnic in the district, when Gander was not so sure of his mirth. Since her marriage Jo had unaccountably affected to forget that there had been any unhappiness between herself and Gander; she greeted him again as a friend of her school days, without any suggestion that he ever had been more, or less. If Dick knew anything he gave no sign.

"Lucky dog, Gander, old boy," said Dick, when the two met at Willow Green. "When the next war comes I'm going to raise wheat, or make munitions."

There was no apparent bitterness in Dick's remark, and Gander found it hard to answer. Dick was tall, and straight, with a fineness about his features that no one seemed to remember from the old days. But it was pitiable to hear him cough.

"Must come over and see us sometime," Dick continued. "Jo is often speaking about you."

Gander thanked him, but did not accept the invitation. It might not be so easy to laugh at the world from Jo's doorstep. . . .

That evening, as Gander sauntered in the dusk along the trail which ran through the poplar groves, thinking a little of Dick and Jo, a ripple of laughter caught his ear. It arrested him; he could not place the voice. There was music in it – music even to Gander, whose scales all were written in the solid earth, whose gamut was the range of experience on his father's farm. He shuffled quietly away from the road and obscured himself in a group of poplars.

Three people were walking along the trail; he just could outline them in the dying light. There were Hamilton and Elsie Fyfe, but the second girl – who was she? She was chatting gaily, and Gander heard that rippling laughter again, now within a few feet of his place of concealment. They passed by, and he waited until they were well out of sight before moving onward again toward the house.

It was not in Gander's nature to be casually disturbed about women. Jo had been his one love; all others moved on the stage of his life almost unobserved. Not that that stage had been overcrowded; there were not more than a dozen eligible girls in the Willow Green district, but some of these would have regarded Gander's attentions without marked annoyance. Gander had not thought of any of them seriously. Jo had been his, but she had slipped away; that had been the price of his four years of safety. Well, some others had paid another price. Walter Peters, Tommy Burge, for example. Gander had accepted his fate as final; it had not even occurred to him to suppose that he could transfer his affections. He had taken it for granted that he would just go on – and on.

But something in that laughter had dug into strange, unused cells in his being. It was happy, spontaneous laughter – laughter without any ring of bitterness. When Gander laughed it always was in self-defence, as a mask behind which he could take shelter, or at the discomfiture of some person or thing. Laughter was not much heard on the Stake homestead, and it nearly always was at people – not *with* them. This laughter was different, and it stirred Gander more than he knew or understood. He must question Hamilton.

Not, of course, too obviously. He allowed the breakfast opportunities to pass without comment. If Hamilton had anything on his mind he carried it easily, plunging into his porridge and its following course of pork and potatoes with his usual gusto and effectiveness. During the forenoon Hamilton and Grit plied their plough-shuttles up and down the fields while Gander busied himself with grinding the

valves of the Dodge car, which, as a result of war-time prosperity, had displaced the more humble Ford. When the
teams came in from the field at noon Gander set the windmill running; its pleasant clank . . . clank came down
from above as its bright blades slashed the sunlight under
the impulse of the prairie breeze. The horses crowded to the
trough and as each drank his fill he made his way straight to
the stable and to his own stall to investigate the contents of
his oat box. Finding it empty, he thrust his nostrils into the
air in protest; then, enticed by the fragrant hay, he plunged
into his manger, drawing great wisps between his facile lips
and champing with satisfaction.

At the door of the stable Gander met Hamilton and Grit
coming out together, and stepped aside to give them room.
"Two is comp'ny; three ain't," he observed. But Hamilton
made no answer. Gander's first decoy had not drawn fire.

A few minutes later Gander followed, past numerous
obstacles in the yard, to the front of the house, where
Hamilton and Grit were crowding over a wash bench, much
as their horses had crowded at the trough.

"You don' need washin', Ham," his brother told him.
"You was slicked up last night enough for a week."

A basin of graniteware sat on the bench, and a leaky
barrel, half full of rain water, stood at the corner of the house.
Grit had left the basin partly filled with the proceeds of his
ablutions. With a swing of his arm Hamilton sent the dirty
water spraying over the yard with a scientific exactness that
included Gander in the circle.

"Sorry, Gander," said Ham, with mock apologies. "You
should either come in or stay out."

Gander found no ready answer; Hamilton's allusions
had been too indefinite. He washed in silent ill-humor.

Once inside, all hands attacked the meal vigorously and without formalities. With the passage of years and the increasing pressure of farm activities Jackson Stake's grace before meat had become more and more hurried and confidential, until now it was employed only upon those rare occasions when they had visitors. The men slumped into their chairs and helped themselves from well-laden platters. They rushed on with their meal, as though it were something to be disposed of with the least possible delay, and at the first sign of a pause Mrs. Stake dumped great helpings of rice-and-raisin pudding into plates just cleared of meat and potatoes.

They were in the final stages of the pudding course when Jackson Stake himself touched the fuse that was to work havoc with Gander's furrow.

"That's a lively lookin' piece, that niece of Double F's," he remarked to the company in general. "Elsie had better be watchin' out."

He ended with a benevolent smile at Hamilton, and the boy's color flowed up his fair face into the roots of his hair. "Oh, I guess she's all right," he answered, non-committally.

Gander tried to bury his interest in his plate.

"What's her name, Ham?" Grit demanded. "Make us all acquainted."

"I'll introduce you – when she asks me to," Hamilton retorted, with a dignity that, in all the family, was peculiar to himself, and Minnie.

Gander turned over in his mind that afternoon this meagre information as he worked on the car. He was surprised that he should be interested in this strange girl, and his surprise was mingled with a certain boldness – a certain sense of adventure. A hundred times he recalled the outline he had seen of her in the dusk among the poplar groves, and each time that outline seemed to become more enticing. Mingled with it was the outline of Jo Burge; mingled with his happiness was a sadness inseparable from Jo Burge. Without knowing or understanding it Gander was still, at heart, faithful to his first love, and this new experience had in it all the allurements of the illicit. He had felt that, in a sense, Jo must be his, always. It was an ownership which he never would be able to assert, and yet it was a pleasant thing to tuck away in his heart. He knew – don't ask him how – he *knew* that although Jo had married Dick she had wanted *him*. He had nursed that thought, found comfort in it, when no one but himself knew he harbored it at all. It was a delicious secret.

And now that another affection came knocking at his heart he was caught between two fires. Could he give up that secret love? Would it be quite honest to Jo? Gander felt these questions pressing vaguely in his mind, but he did not stop to answer them. He only knew that he wanted to meet that girl with the rippling laughter – then he would see.

"Huh!" he told himself. "Like as not –" But he couldn't finish the sentence.

He completed his work on the car and took it out for a trial spin. Its renewed life seemed to feed life back to him through the steering-wheel, the switch, the gear-shift, through every contact. The hiss of the air in the carburetor, the almost noiseless rhythm of the motor, were music in his ears. Before he knew it he was speeding down the highway that divided his father's farm from that of Fraser Fyfe.

The school section, redolent with memories of Josephine Burge, lay to the southeast; he could see the bluffs of willow and poplar green upon its higher ridges. Under one of those bluffs he and Jo had rested that hot day – that day when he wondered (and he still wondered) whether she had been asleep. Down one of those slopes he had chased her in a madness he never had understood. Somewhere behind those fields he had carried her in his arms. . . . And mingled in his memories of her everywhere was a new joyousness, and something which had to do with laughter.

He drove by the school. Even at the distance of the road he could see one or two wistful faces turned toward the windows, envying him his liberty. He remembered how he had rescued Jo, that first day at school, and how she had fought for him, burying her little hands in Pete Loudy's hair. . . .

He circled the country to the south. The high tide of spring, merging into early summer, was in the air; pennants and spirals of dust marked the slow drag of husbandry on the distant fields. The snow water still lay, bright as quicksilver, in the prairie ponds; about its edges the grass grew a more luscious green; wild ducks were nesting under its emerald canopy. The sky faded into infinite blue distances, bearing on its bosom white puffs of lazy cloud.

Eventually Gander's circle brought him back to the school. Between the school and the Stake homestead the road crests a ridge; Gander thrilled to the power of his car as it raced up the incline. As he swung over the top his brakes brought him up with a jerk. A few yards ahead a girl was bending over the grassy strip in the centre of the trail, in the act of picking some prairie flower which had braved the hazard of many horses' feet. The nose of the car was almost touching her when it stopped.

"Well, I pretty near scored off you," he said, annoyed that she made no move to get out of the way.

She was standing erect now, facing him, with a bunch of flowers in her hand. She wore no hat, and her dark hair, massed about her head, made her face appear very small and winsome.

"Didn't you see me?" she asked. "I was here first." And then sunshine seemed to break from her parted lips, and her voice trilled off into a ripple of laughter. It smote Gander like a blow; his Adam's apple jumped into his throat. This was she, undoubtedly – Double F's niece! And he didn't even know her name!

Still, she had given him a fright. "I might have killed you," he blurted.

She laughed again. "Oh, you are much too good a driver to do anything like that. Aren't they beautiful?" She was holding her flowers toward him.

"Lots of 'em on the prairie," said Gander. Flowers were nothing to him. Then, with sudden boldness, "Better get in and I'll drive you home, or wherever you want to go."

She came around to the side of the car, and as she did so he saw that she was small, as small as Jo, and lighter on her feet. There was more spring in her step. She might have reminded him of Minnie, but Minnie was fair, with bronze hair and brown eyes; this girl was dark, with black hair and black eyes and a round, smooth face of olive-brown skin. She wore a light dress of some pinkish material, white stockings, and little black shoes – much too little, thought Gander, for the country roads.

She raised one foot to the running-board; then she paused. One hand rested on the car door, the other held her treasured flowers. Gander thought he never had seen hands so small and fine. "Not much use for farmin'," he had told himself afterwards, and pondered that point rather deeply.

"You see, we have not been introduced," she explained her hesitation. "I don't know the country very much, but in the city we – *nice* girls expect an introduction."

"Oh, that's all right," Gander assured her. "Everybody knows me. They all call me Gander; Gander Stake."

"Oh, then, I know you, too!" There was something about her eyes most enticing to look upon. "You are Hamilton's brother. *He's* a nice boy. Will you open the door, please?"

Gander knew of no reason why she should not open the door herself, but he did not make an issue of it. For a moment she stood up in the car, and the prairie wind swept her light skirt across his knees. He was conscious of his greasy overalls.

"I'm all grease – been fixin' the car," he warned her. "Don' sit too close."

"Oh, I won't," she answered.

Her manner piqued him. "I didn' mean *that*," he explained.

"Neither did I."

She was much too smart. She was too quick with her answers. For the first time his slow mind began to catch a glimpse of how slow it was. He was afraid to speak lest her reply would place him at a disadvantage. He felt like a mouse under the eye of an agile but tolerant cat; safe while he remained quite still, but sure to be pounced upon the moment he moved.

Gander gave her a sidelong glance from time to time. She was engaged mainly in burying her little nose in the prairie flowers. Unconsciously Gander increased his speed. The speedometer hand crept up to thirty-five.

When it became apparent that he was going to drive on in silence she opened conversation.

"The country is beautiful, isn't it?"

"Oh, I dunno. What?"

"Why, the grass, the trees, the flowers, the fields, but most of all, the sky. In the city we don't seem to see the sky."

"Lots of it out here," Gander remarked.

She laughed, and to Gander it seemed that he had jumped across a great chasm, and landed safely on the other side. They were getting along.

"I suppose you have lived here all your life?" she tried again.

A bit of burlesque humor flashed up in Gander's memory. "Not yet," he answered.

Again she laughed, and Gander felt as though a short-circuit were charging him through the steering-wheel. No; it was coming from beside him; he knew it was coming from the passenger at his side. How dainty she was! How small, and how clean! He was tremendously conscious of his greasy over-alls, and a bit uneasy about the cushion on which she was sitting. That pink skirt – He wondered if he should mention his misgivings. But, while he wondered, they arrived at Fraser Fyfe's gate.

"It doesn't take long, with a car," he remarked, with a supreme effort to make conversation.

"Not when you drive so fast. But I suppose you are in a great hurry. Farmers are very busy people, aren't they?"

Her words tantalized Gander. She seemed to be poking verbal fingers at him.

"But I'm not in a hurry," he protested. "I've all after-noon. Let's go for a drive – somewhere else?"

"That would be nice, but – not to-day. Elsie will be looking for me. I said I would be only a little while." For a moment she sat, waiting for him to open the door. When he made no move she opened it herself, and got out. With her unengaged hand she brushed particles of dust from her dress, giving him an opportunity to speak.

Gander's heart was thumping, but now was the time. He summoned all his courage to his aid.

"If I call you up some day, will you?" he asked, almost choking on the words.

She flashed a look at him from her dark eyes, dancing under long black lashes. Her lips parted; her teeth were smooth and regular and strangely white against the olive brown of her skin. Gander thought he never had seen any one so beautiful.

"Thank you for the ride – and the company," she said. "I think the prairie is very beautiful, don't you?"

As he drove home alone Gander wondered whether or not she had answered his question.

SEVENTEEN

Gander mechanically backed his car into its garage. Then he sat for a long while, the steering-wheel held in a tight grip, thinking.

With Gander, any thinking that broke new ground was laborious effort, and his thoughts to-day were breaking new ground. They were at first much too confused to have any definite trend, but gradually certain points began to emerge. For example, he had not learned the girl's name.

It took half an hour for that fact to crystallize, but when the thought had finally taken shape it landed on him with the impact of a prize-fighter's fist. She had got the information she wanted, without evasion or delay, but she had not so much as told him her name! He felt a sort of helpless resentment, and he condemned his slow wits for refusing to function when he stood most in need of them.

"I'm a dub," he said to himself. It was an important conclusion.

Gander's standards of comparison were such that he had not often suffered by them. When the girls in the restaurant had giggled for the obvious edification of the two men in uniform – that had been one instance, and his hurt pride had sent him to the barber's shop for tonsorial adornment. But usually he felt that he could invite comparison. With Jackie gone he was the elder son; he was practically manager of the farm. He could run a steam engine. He could take a car to pieces and put it together again. He could drive a team of four, six, or eight horses. He knew every oil-hole in a binder, mower, or seeder. He was strong. He could take his turn on a pitchfork with the best of them. He could shoot and ride as well as the average. With all these things in his favor never before had it occurred seriously to Gander that he might make a poor showing in any company.

Yet this strange girl had left him with just that impression. It was unpalatable, and he choked on it a bit, but it had to be swallowed. He had made a poor showing with her. He couldn't analyze it, he couldn't go over their conversation item by item and check up the scoring pro and con, but in some inductive way he knew that she had had the better of it. She was too quick for him.

He had an indefinite sense that he had been acted upon, rather than acting; that she was the superior force. Absurd although it appeared, he gathered the idea that in some way she was stronger than he. He almost wished that he had had an opportunity to show his physical strength. If the car had turned over, for example. Suppose it had pinned her under! How he would have swung it up, his muscles knotted like iron! He would have raised her in his arms, he would have run with her to the nearest house! She would be but a feather's weight to him. And he would set her down, and when she opened her eyes —

It was Gander's greatest stretch of imagination. It stirred him so that he got out of his seat, out of the car, walked two or three times about the garage. That would show her his strength! He felt his pulses throbbing within him. The walls of his furrow were beginning to crumble.

In the garden to the west of the house he saw his mother working, her form doubled over in a gingham dress faded drab with age. He felt a sudden surging of his heart toward his mother. He shuffled over to her, down between rows of currant bushes greening with their spring foliage. She did not hear his footsteps in the soft earth; she was bent over, setting out cabbages.

"Couldn't I do that?" he interrupted her. She looked up quickly, her sharp eyes piercing him, as though she suspected some kind of treachery. She could not recall that Gander ever before had offered her a service. He was playing a joke on her. But he held his ground, steadily.

"I thought you was busy with the car?" she parried.

"Through with it. Could help you a little, if you like."

"Why – why – Willie?" Her old face began to twist. It recalled the day he gave her the twenty-dollar bill.

"That's all right, Mother," he said, with strange gentleness. "I'm goin' to give you a hand. I'm goin' to help you, once in a while."

Still with misgivings, she showed him how to set out the tender plants. Gander crouched on his knees, setting each little stem in place, pressing the soft moist earth about the root with his hands, while his mother watched in a silence and wonder through which happiness was beginning to break like sunshine through a cloud.

Presently, out of this new experience, she felt a disposition to talk.

"You was out with the car?"

"Yep. Tryin' her out."

"Where'd you go?"

He briefly sketched his course.

"See anybody?"

Gander hesitated. He was shy about mentioning the girl, and yet he felt an impelling desire to talk of her.

"Yep. Double F's niece. Out pickin' flowers. Gave her a ride home."

The cabbage plant trembled in Gander's hand; he felt the color tingling in his ears.

"You better not be takin' up with the likes o' her," his mother cautioned him.

"What's wrong with her?" he demanded, sharply. He had an impulse to let her plant her own cabbages.

"Oh, nothin' as I know. A very nice girl, no doubt. But these city girls – they ain't cut out to be a farmer's wife. Did you see her hands?"

"I did," said Gander, defiantly. "An' they looked good to me."

"For plantin' cabbages? Willie, don' be silly! There's good girl's aroun' Willow Green, if you're thinkin' that way. There was Joey Burge —"

Gander sat back on his heels. "Jo's married," he said.

His mother nodded. "Yes. You could ha' had her, but you was too slow. Let her slip away on you. An' if you couldn' catch Joey, you'll never get in sight o' that young minx at Double F's."

In his heart Gander believed his mother was probably right, but he was not prepared to admit his deficiencies.

"Don' be too sure," he said, and went on planting cabbage. But that evening, in the after-glow of sunset, he found himself wandering over the fields, dividing his thoughts between Jo Claus and the little olive-skinned city girl he had picked up on the trail. He watched the light climbing up the sky, touching tatters of cloud into golden flame. She had said the sky was beautiful. For the first time Gander watched it – and wondered.

But other events were soon to demand a share of his thought. The following day he took his turn in the fields, and when he brought in his team at noon a young man, little older than himself, was waiting at the water trough. Something in his look suggested Dick Claus; he had that same fineness of appearance, and with it a self-confidence in meeting strangers which is not often acquired in the furrow.

He came forward pleasantly, and his evident desire to be agreeable put Gander on his guard. That was the way with life insurance agents and other people who had something to sell.

"I'm Cal Beach," he announced. "The new hired man."

Gander surveyed him doubtfully, but Grit, whose head at that moment emerged from among the heaving shoulders of the horses, flashed him a look of good-humored interest.

"Welcome to our city," he hailed the new arrival. "We need an extra man – to do the work."

Gander hesitated. "Didn' know Dad was figgerin' on hirin' any more help. However, he's the main gazabo. What can you do?"

"Not so very much, I'm afraid. I can drive a Ford —"

"'An' it takes a good man to do that,'" Grit chanted from a popular song.

"— and horses a little, and I'm middling strong, and – I've been through university."

Gander had noticed, drawn up by one of the portable granaries, an old Ford, dog-eared and weather-beaten, which he now associated with the visitor. Still, Gander was prepared to admit that many a good man, at some time in his career, had driven a Ford. This new-comer was guilty of a more serious offence. He had gone to a university. Worse than that, he boasted of it!

"An eddicated smart-Aleck," said Gander to himself. "He'll last on this farm about long enough to crank that old road-turtle o' his." Then aloud:

"Sounds all right, all but the last. Don' know as what they learn you in the university'll help much. A man on a farm don' need no D.D.'s, or whatever it is, after his name. What he wants is horse power an' savvy. Well, we'll see. Go down to the barn an' throw some hay in the mangers."

Something in Gander's tone recalled to him that episode on the vacant lots adjoining Plainville – the ordering of the men about by the drill sergeant. Gander had taken the same attitude. He was "breaking" his man. But, to Gander's surprise, Beach showed no resentment; on the contrary, he swung off smartly to the stables to carry out his instructions.

"Huh!" said Gander. "Not much spirit there. About two days on the farm'll fix him."

At the door of the stable Gander came upon a little boy of eight or nine years, sunburned and touzled, with threads of hay hanging about his hair and shoulders.

"Hello, who's the kid?" said Gander. "Another hired man?"

"Yes, sir," the boy answered, respectfully.

"What's your name?"

"Reed, sir."

It was the first time Gander ever had been called sir, and his Adam's apple plunged violently with the shock. It was a wholly unprecedented experience.

Gander's heart warmed somewhat to the child.

"Reed what?" he questioned, more pleasantly.

"Reed Beach."

Gander stroked the back of his long neck meditatively. "You don' mean he's your daddy?" he said, indicating Cal with a jerk of his head.

"He's my Daddy X."

Gander turned this singular reply over in his mind, as though to discover what lay beneath it. Then:

"An' have you been through university, too?"

"Not yet, but I'm going to. Have you?"

"Not so slow," thought Gander. "He's some kid." He ran his fingers through the boy's hair with a friendly scuffle.

"D'ye ever get hungry?"

"Yes, sir."

"Hungry now?"

"Yes, sir, a little."

What a bright kid he was! And how pleasant that sir sounded!

"Well, let's go an' eat. C'mon, Cal."

Mrs. Stake did not join the men at their meal, but waited on the table. She seemed to-day even more straight and stern than usual; the prospect of two extra mouths to feed was an additional grievance which she bore with heavy tread from the table to the stove, and back again.

Notwithstanding the exigencies of eating, Gander managed to give some quiet attention to Cal and Reed during this their first meal in the Stake household. He noticed that both of them apparently were under the impression that knives must be used only for cutting – a limitation that surely would place them at a disadvantage in the tri-daily scramble at meal time. They ate with apparent relish, but Cal, at least, controlled his haste. Gander laid this to design on Cal's part; he probably would drag out his meal hours as long as possible. Well, he knew a cure for that.

Gander and Grit consumed amazingly big meals in an amazingly short time, and as each cleared his plate he got up and went out. They met in the shade of the blacksmith shop, where they were accustomed to smoke an after-dinner pipe.

"I don' reckon the kid is his," Grit declared, after some minutes of silence. "He's too young to have a kid like that."

Gander took his pipe from his mouth and shook his head sagely. "You can never tell," he said. "An eddication is a great thing."

The two cronies snickered at this suggestion, but Gander went on more seriously:

"No, I don' think he's his, that way. Fact, I asked him – the kid – right there in the door of the stable, I says, 'Is he your daddy?' an' he says, 'He's my Daddy X.' Now what do you make o' that?"

"I tell you what it is," said Grit, thumping his pipe into his palm. "It's a mystery, that's what it is. You mark my words, it's a mystery." His slumbering eyes were alight.

"Well, he's a nice kid," Gander conceded, the soothing effect of Reed's deference being still upon him.

It was presently time to hitch up for the afternoon work. Gander got his four horses out like Company on Parade, while he snapped the reins to their bits and affectionately cuffed the muzzles curled up at him as he went by.

The new hired man came over from the windmill, where he had been talking with Jackson Stake.

"Will you show me how to do that?" he asked. "Let me get the system of it into my head. I'll savvy if you give me a chance."

It was the word savvy that won Gander. This was language he understood, and which brought the two men, so to speak, face to face. Besides, it showed that Cal recognized his inferiority. Gander, for all his democracy – or, perhaps, because of it – responded instantly to obeisance. He purred like a cat when his fur was stroked the right way.

"Now you're shoutin'," he said. "See, it's easy –" He led Cal through the labyrinths of lines, showing him the order in what looked like a chaos of leather. Then he chirped to his horses, and they were on their way.

Their road lay along a narrow lane between two sagging wire fences, with moist, ploughed fields on either side. As the two men walked together behind the team, with the little chap holding Cal's hand, Gander initiated them into some of the mysteries of the farm and of the neighborhood. He mentioned Minnie, and even as he did so the thought struck him that Minnie would find a peculiar interest in this new hired man. They were likely to have much in common. Well, he would see.

Gander hitched his team to the seeder, making every movement with quiet, rapid efficiency, and inwardly amused at Cal's abortive attempts to be of service. The field was a mile long, and when the end was reached Gander thrust the reins into Cal's hands. With a few instructions the new man picked up the work readily, and after a round or two Gander was content to let him go by himself while he enjoyed a quiet smoke in the shade of a willow bush at the end of the field and wondered about a number of things, including Cal, and the boy, and Minnie, and Jo Claus, and another girl whose name even he had not learned.

That evening Gander found excuse to visit the home of Fraser Fyfe. He went to borrow a clevis, and that notwithstanding the fact that three unused clevises were hanging in his father's blacksmith shop. As he came up the path he saw two girlish figures in the garden, and Gander, who scarcely knew a rose from a tulip, developed a sudden interest in flowers.

"Why, here's Gander!" cried Elsie Fyfe. "Hello, Gander; you don't often come to visit us?"

"Not as often as some," said Gander, significantly.

Elsie blushed winsomely through a new crop of freckles. "Perhaps you'll do better," she hinted, slyly. "Have you met my cousin?"

The dark girl had paid no attention to Gander's presence; she was diligently setting out geraniums, using a great kitchen spoon for a shovel. But at Elsie's words she turned toward him.

"I think we have met – at least, we have travelled together," and her voice trilled off into a little ripple of laughter. Then, as though repentant, she stuck her spoon in the ground and moved toward Gander, flicking specks of earth from her fingers daintily as she came.

"My cousin, Geraldine Chansley," Elsie announced. "Commonly called Jerry, for short."

The girl's little hand sank softly in Gander's sun-burned fist, but it sent a tingle through his fingers that ran up his arm and agitated the prominent feature of his lean neck.

"Sounds tom-boyish, doesn't it? Elsie shouldn't give away my failings – to strangers."

Gander thought she looked very small and pretty before him. He could have lifted her with that outstretched hand, and yet he was caught in some dumb kind of fright. He choked for words. He was filled with a surging for which he had no expression.

She was ready to help him out. "Are you fond of gardening?" she asked.

The question loosened his tongue a little. "Well, not partic'lar. My garden – you couldn't plant *it* with a spoon. Wheat. Two – three hundred acres."

"It must be wonderful to run a big farm like that." There was real admiration in her voice.

But Gander's panic was again upon him. "Yep," he admitted, "but it keeps you awful busy. Jus' come over to borrow a clevis. Is your father about, Elsie?"

And without waiting for an answer he lurched off through the rows of currant bushes to Fraser Fyfe's red painted barn.

EIGHTEEN

The two new-comers on the Stake farm had been allotted one of the portable granaries in which to sleep, and their first act had been to scrub it thoroughly. That, in itself, stamped them as unusual people. Gander paid the place a surreptitious visit while Cal was in the fields and Reed at school, and denounced it as being effeminately clean. That sort of thing was all right in a house, where there was a woman to keep the dust on the jump, but a he-man never troubled about such matters. Look at their threshing caboose – Bill Powers' threshing caboose! Gander smiled at the droll thought of Cal squirming in one of Bill's over-occupied bunks.

"An' they're he-men, every one o' them," said Gander to himself. "Not like this fellow Cal —"

He stopped at that. It didn't ring true, and Gander, whatever his faults, was a believer in the truth. Generations of Puritan ancestry had woven a fibre into his character that still held taut on most of the fundamentals.

And Gander was fair enough to admit that Cal, in spite of his eccentricities, was measuring up to his standards of a he-man. Cal had followed the team continuously since his first initiation in the oat-field; was on the job in the mornings without being called, and in the evenings, when Gander and Grit thought it no shame to be tired, Cal still had the energy and spirit for a game of ball with Ham and Reed.

Gander stepped into the granary, for a closer study of the habits of this mysterious man. What he found was simplicity and order. The bed on the corner of the floor was as neatly made up as if his mother had done it; the clothing, not in use, was hung on nails about the walls; even the spare tire from Cal's old Ford occupied a place especially prepared for it. Cal had built a little shelf, on which were two or three books. Gander lifted one, and, with difficulty, spelled out the name.

"M. A-n-t-i-n-i-n-u-s," he made it. "Some Dutchman, I guess. Well, he won't learn much about hitchin' a team in that."

It was on Cal's first Saturday night on the Stake farm that Gander had a further glimpse of the man's peculiarities. Gander had gone to town with the Dodge, with the excuse of bringing Minnie home, but in reality in response to that prairie mood which sends every young man into town on Saturday evenings. There the more vigorous play football or baseball until darkness falls; then they line the sidewalks, jostling each other playfully; commenting on the young women who, of necessity or a desire to be observed, thread their ways among them; occasionally breaking into innocuous rowdyism, and, once in a great while, into a fight. Main Street, Plainville, was Gander's Broadway, and the Broadway of all the other youths of the district. Although cruder it was no more sinister than its great prototype, and it contained as much humanity per individual as any street in the world.

During the years of the war Gander had resisted that prairie longing to spend his Saturday evenings in Plainville. No doubt the psycho-analyst would find in that suppressed

desire the explanation of his sullenness, his aloofness, his occasional unbalance, such as had ostracized him from the
company of Joey Burge. But now that the war was over, and
the recruiting posters had been taken down, or were flapping
in tattered remnants from neglected walls and fences, Gander
again felt at ease to move about among his kind.

He found Minnie completing some household purchases at Sempter & Burton's general store, and they drove
home through the closing twilight at a speed that rolled up
the Plainville road like the belt of Bill Powers' threshing
machine. When Gander was driving a car, especially in the
gloaming, the road suggested a belt which he was winding up
beneath him. Sometimes he thought of that incident when he
had saved the life of young Walter Peters, and Jo Burge had
hotly predicted that some day he – Gander – might wear a
real V. C. For a year and a half Walter had been sleeping
somewhere in France.

"If it comes to that," Gander argued to himself, "I
suppose I could claim some credit for him. I gave his life to
his country, in a way."

As he thought of these matters he unconsciously speeded
up his car, until Minnie brought him to earth. "What's the
rush?" she shouted in his ear.

"It's all on your account," he told her. "'Thought you'd
be anxious to see the new hired man."

"So I am," she said, with a touch of that coquetry in
which Minnie was something of an artist.

"You've heard about him, then?"

"A little, over the 'phone. A man and a boy, I think?"

"Yep. Cal Beach, D.D., an' a little gaffer that calls him
Daddy X."

"D.D.? No? Not a preacher?"

Gander slowed up to enjoy his sister's curiosity. "Sure," he said. "A kind o' preacher. Oh, you'll like him, Minn. An' such a swell housekeeper! He'll be puttin' lace curtains on the grainery, next. Him an' the boy sleeps in the other grainery."

"Perhaps he'll set a good example to Grit and you. Your room, until Mother clears it up, looks like the swath of a cyclone. But tell me about the boy. I want to hear about the boy."

Gander, not subtle enough to detect his sister's move to cover her real interest, plunged into a discussion of Reed.

"Well, he's a nice little shaver," he admitted. "About eight or nine, with a bright face and good manners. Mother's all set on him already. She's got him goin' to school, an' to-day he's off playin' with Trixie (the immediate successor of Gyp) over the prairie huntin' flowers an' gophers."

"But what is he? Cal's – Mr. Beach's – son or what?"

"That's the mystery, Minn; that's the mystery. That's what's got us all beat."

"But what does he say?"

"He don' say. I asked him if Cal was his daddy, an' he says, 'He's my Daddy X.' Now what do you make o' that? What relation is a Daddy X? I tell you it's a mystery."

By this time they had reached the trail which leads in from the highroad to the Stake farm. The windows of Fraser Fyfe's house were yellow with light. Somewhere behind those windows, or perhaps in the garden – Gander wondered if his sister had not heard of Elsie Fyfe's cousin. He was eager to talk about her, but too shy and self-conscious to introduce the subject. Gander was not in the habit of taking much notice of girls; if he mentioned Jerry Chansley to Minnie his quick-witted sister would understand, and undoubtedly subject him to her nimble ridicule. And yet, to have a confidant – Minnie, to whom he could talk – seemed almost worth the risk. Twice his lips were shaped for a mention of Jerry Chansley, and twice his courage failed him, until now his undivided attention was required to guide his car around the sharp curves between the poplar groves which sheltered the farmstead from the western wind. As he stopped near the house he was surprised to see a glow of fire at the door of Cal's granary. He ran a pace or two in that direction; then, seeing the forms of Cal and Reed sitting unconcerned in the circle of light, he turned back, wondering.

"What's the smudge for, Dad?" Gander demanded, as he entered the door with an armful of parcels.

Jackson Stake was enjoying his bedtime smoke beside the kitchen range. For his greater comfort he had discarded his boots and was resting his feet, on which his heavy woollen socks sagged in rolls and creases, on the cover of the ashpan, drawn partly open to permit of convenient expectoration. He answered Gander's question without missing a puff.

"No smudge," he said. "Bonfire."

"Bonfire? What's the celebration?"

"No celebration." Puff. "Just a notion." Puff. "Cal an' the kid."

"My land," Mrs. Stake exclaimed, sharply, "can't you let the boy have a fire, if he wants it?"

The readiness with which Gander's mother came to Reed's defence nettled and surprised him. Mrs. Stake was a lonely old woman, although Gander knew her only as his mother, which is often a very partial acquaintanceship. The boy was winding strings about her heart.

"Sure! Let 'em have a good time," Gander retorted. "If they set fire to the grainery or the horse-stable we can all go out an' cheer."

"They won't set fire to nothin'," said Jackson Stake. "Cal'll watch to that."

As Gander went out to put the car away he reflected on the fact that this strange man and boy already had won for themselves champions in the Stake household. His mother bristled at any question of Reed's privileges, and even his easy-going father limbered up in defence of Cal. They were strange people.

"Minnie'll fall for that guy like a boot on a bedroom floor," Gander concluded, as he thought the matter over.

Later in the evening he saw his sister down by the fire, sitting with Cal on one of the cushions of the old Ford. Gander did not mean to be an eavesdropper, but he happened to wander into their vicinity, in the shadow of the granary. All he could gather was not very conclusive. It seemed that Cal had been telling Reed a story, and Minnie had made herself one of the party.

Gander studied his sister, as she sat there in the glow of the fire, with the unillusioned eye of a brother, and even so he had to admit that Minnie was more than ordinarily attractive. She had thrust her slim ankles out toward the smouldering coals, and Cal would be more, or less, than human if he failed to take note of their neatness and their coquetry. Gander had many times suspected that Minnie was beautiful; now he knew it. The curve of her arm, the color of her cheek, the sparkle of firelight entrapped in her hair – in all these Gander saw Josephine Burge. When Gander really was stirred he thought of Josephine Burge. Or, more recently, of Jerry Chansley.

They were chatting happily, in the subtle thrust and parry of young people trying out each other's armor. Gander listened for some minutes; even caught his own name in the conversation; then, with a strange tingling in his cheeks, slipped away to his bedroom.

"I didn' mean to spy on 'em," he defended himself, "but I have to think o' Minn. He's got a halter-shank on her already." But a little later, "No, by gum! It's Minn that'll be leadin' him 'round on a rope, before he knows it."

Insofar as the duties of the farm would permit it Sunday was observed by the Stakes as a day of rest. It was not until eight o'clock next morning that Gander and Grit, hungry with their long fast, filed in to the table in the living room. The familiar whine of the cream separator filled the air, and when Gander glanced toward the corner in which the machine stood his eye was arrested by the unprecedented sight of Calvin Beach turning the handle, while Minnie, with an apron pinned about her, superintended the operation.

"She's got a snare hitch on him already," said Gander to himself. He grinned at Grit, who returned the grimace, the elliptic parenthesis about his mouth almost meeting in a genial circle of amusement.

After breakfast they discussed the incident together as they lounged at the sunny side of the horse-stable.

"I mind once a place where I worked where they useta run the churn with a mastiff," said Grit, "but this is the first time I ever seen a cream separator hitched to a D.D."

"He'll soon get fed up on that," Gander prophesied. "It's no job for a man." A touch of annoyance had crept into his voice with a realization of the possible effects of Cal's misdemeanor. The new man had, at least by inference, suggested that turning the cream separator was a masculine occupation. After many arguments Gander had thought that point definitely settled, but now his mother undoubtedly would seize this precedent to re-open the subject. He fancied he could hear her saying, "Well, when Cal's here, he turns it —"

"Not while that pretty sister o' yours is around, I guess not," Grit broke in on him. "Did you see their heads, almost touchin' each other, when she was emp'yin' the milk?"

"Shut up, Grit!" said Gander, sharply. He had little relish for Grit's unexpected perspicacity.

"You can't be too kerful with them mystery men," Grit continued, quite unabashed. "We've got two mysteries here now. Three times – and out!"

At that moment Cal, clean shaven and dressed in his Sunday clothes, came around the corner of the building. His presence gave a new twist to the conversation.

"We was jus' sayin'," said Grit, "that you ought to rig up the Ford to run that milk buzzer. That shouldn't be hard for a man with a eddication."

"A D.D.," Gander added, more specifically.

The new hired man insisted upon retaining his good humor, and after some conversation, in which he seemed to argue that the women on the farm had too much to do, or some such heresy, went off by himself for a ramble in the fields.

"Queer duck," Gander commented, when Cal was well out of hearing, and Grit tapped his head with his finger, significantly.

The whole household attended church at Willow Green in the afternoon. Gander drove the Dodge, with his father and mother, Hamilton, Grit, and Reed. It seemed that Cal and Minnie had elected to walk. They passed them on the way, swinging along on the grass by the side of the road, their hands not far apart. That much Gander had noticed, even while his chief attention was reserved for Fraser Fyfe's Ford. Yes, there she was, all right. Jerry. He saw her with Elsie at the door of the church, the centre of many eyes, for this was her first public appearance at Willow Green. The young farm lads would be having remarks to make. Well, let Gander hear them, that was all; just let him hear them. . . .

After the service Gander, on the pretence that one of Fraser Fyfe's tires was going slack, found occasion to approach the enchanted circle. Mrs. Fyfe, ample and warm, although it was only May, occupied the greater part of the front seat; her husband crowded himself into the remaining space by the simple process of closing the door. It was one of Mrs. Fyfe's whims always to ride in the front seat, so that she could be of immediate assistance to her husband in case of emergency. Elsie and Geraldine were seated behind, looking very cool and fresh in their spring hats and dresses.

"Think your off front tire is down a bit, don't you, Mr. Fyfe?" Gander ventured. "Looks a bit flat."

Double F studied the tire for a moment with much absorption.

"Does look a little flat at the bottom," he observed at length, "but the rest of it is all right. Guess it'll do till we get home. Want a lift, Gander? Jump in!"

Gander glanced at his own car, where he saw his father had taken the place of honor at the wheel.

"Well, might do that, too," he agreed, "if you ain't crowded."

"Crowded nothin'! Sit over, girls, an' make room for Gander. By the way, you know my niece, Miss —"

"Yes, thank you, Uncle; we've met." It was Jerry who spoke. And she smiled at Gander, and sat over, not too far, making room for him beside her.

Gander never knew just how that afternoon was passed, except that it was the most eventful day of his life. He stayed at Double F's for tea, and in the evening, when Elsie's attentions were monopolized by Hamilton, he went walking with Jerry. They took the road to the lake, and, when they reached it, stood for a long while skipping stones on the water, or watching the deepening hues of the mirrored sunset. Jerry had an eye for color. The prairie sunsets charmed her, she admitted. And Gander had an eye for Jerry. She charmed him, but his courage failed him short of confession. She seemed so far beyond him that he hardly dared let himself dream – It had been quite different with Jo. He never had thought of Jo as being beyond him. This girl, with her fine face, her small hands, her careful speech, was a new revelation. For all his self-esteem Gander could hardly think it possible that she might care for him. For the first time in his life he began to regret that he had not gone to school more regularly; that he had not read books; that he had nothing to talk about!

Darkness was deep about them as they walked homeward, and she took his arm, drawing him gently out of his shyness. Then, when she had loosened his tongue a little, she asked him if he never had thought of going to the city. "At least for a winter," she said. "It would do you good."

"But I thought you liked the country?" he answered.

"So I do; its beauty, its quiet, its peace. They make it very lovely. I wouldn't ask you to leave the country altogether. But for a few months – it would do you good."

"How?" Gander was interested. He wanted to know. But she had not the heart to tell him. She wanted him to know that he was clumsy and ill-kempt and uninformed, and she couldn't tell him those things. But he had intelligence, too; he had some sterling quality that appealed to her more than she cared to admit.

She could say only, "It would do you good. My brother has a garage business, and you are handy with machines. Some day if you decide to come, I will speak to him to give you a job. Then you can spend your nights at a technical school, and brush up – all those things you have neglected so much, Gander."

So that was it. He had known it in his heart all along. He wasn't good enough for her. He should go to school again, like a child. It was all right for him to dumbly realize this for himself; it was another thing to be told it by her pretty, tantalizing lips; to hear his defects suggested by that voice which seemed always on the verge of laughter. Only, to-night it had been serious enough. Gander was too inexperienced to appraise that seriousness at its real value. All he saw was her attitude of superiority. It was like the sergeant, drilling his raw recruits. "Form fours!"

They were at Fraser Fyfe's gate, and Gander was holding his indignation well in hand. He listened quietly in the darkness while she sketched to him the advantages of contact with many people. "That is what you lack here, Gander," she said. "You don't see enough people. New people give you new ideas, and make life more worth living. Don't you see? They draw you out. I know you have given me new ideas, and perhaps I —"

"Yes," he interrupted. "You've gave me new ideas, too. You make it quite clear I ain't good enough for you. Well, let me make one thing clear, too; I ain't asked you yet!"

"Gander!"

"Yes, Gander! You think because you're from the city, an' have been to school more'n I have, an' wear fine clo'es, an' have pretty little clean fingers, I ain't good enough for you. Perhaps I ain't. But I ain't asked you. An' when I want you I won't ask you – I'll take you, see?" Something of the mood in which he had terrified Jo Burge on the school section was upon him;

even the figure of Jo herself was floating before him, confusedly floating in and out between himself and Jerry. He had thrust his face close to hers. "When I want you I'll take you," he repeated. "Like this!"

He had thrown an arm about her; he drew her slim body to his. He crushed her weak efforts, holding her fast, until his lips found hers. For a long minute he held her. Life seemed to seep from her; her little frame went limp in his arms.

With a sudden fear he let her sink in the grass and, turning, almost ran through the poplar groves to his own home.

The next evening he learned from Hamilton that Elsie's cousin had gone back to the city.

NINETEEN

C al's arrival proved to be but the beginning of changes on the Stake farm. Cal had a perfect mania for changes. After his day's work was done in the fields, and he should have been content to rest and smoke, he was busy piling up the firewood that lay in a heap in front of the house, hauling gravel to fill mud holes in the yard, straightening into neat rows the farm implements and vehicles. He even dragged the pig pen from its convenient location near the well out on to a sod knoll behind the farm buildings. With the aid of a team and skids he lined up the two portable granaries and the blacksmith shop, making a sort of street, which Gander and Grit appropriately christened "Beach Boulevard."

In all these operations Cal had the active support of the little boy Reed, and sometimes of Hamilton, but Gander and Grit held aloof. They regarded these changes with suspicion. That an ignorant, college-bred man, who knew not so much as how to hitch a team when he came to the farm less than two weeks before, should take such liberties was nothing short of presumption. Gander would have told him so with engaging frankness, but it was evident that Cal had the advantage of the knowledge and consent of Jackson Stake, who never before had been known to care whether the buildings were in line or out of line, or whether the wood was piled or left where it fell from the saw, or whether the water trough slopped over and made little ponds in the yard for the convenience of the ducks and geese and the family sow.

"I tell you, it's a mystery," said Grit. "I said that all along. Wait till we see what we see next."

Gander tried to keep his annoyance within bounds, and the ache which he carried in his heart – the double ache, now; one for Jo Claus and one for Jerry Chansley – made it no easier. It was plain that he was being ousted out of the premier position on his own father's farm and supplanted by this mysterious man and boy who had come over-night from nowhere. He had heard his father boasting of Cal to Fraser Fyfe, and he had surprised his mother sitting in "the room" with Reed on her knee, singing to him one of the lullabies she had sung to Gander twenty years before. His Adam's apple had seemed to swell until it almost choked him at that sight. It tugged at something in his throat and whisked Joey Burge into his vision for a moment or two. Still, he didn't mind Reed; he liked Reed. But Cal! The man was always genial and good humored; he gave no occasion for a quarrel, but he was deep, deep. There was something behind all this.

On Sunday – the Sunday after his walk with Jerry Chansley – Gander had a hint of what that something might be. Minnie was home for the week-end, and in the sunny morning she spoke with Gander in the yard.

"Well, that's a change," she remarked, with undisguised approval. "Begins to look civilized."

"Oho!" said Gander to himself, recalling how often Minnie had protested against the haphazard methods of the farm. He had set it down to something in her which he called pride – a reprehensible kind of pride, which concerned itself with appearances, and with what people might think. This fellow Cal was like that, too; shaving in the middle of the week, and washing before every meal. And Cal had brought Minnie out from town the night before in his rickety Ford. The two were as thick as thieves already. . . .

But Gander's attention, for the time at any rate, was almost immediately demanded by another and more surprising development. His missing brother came home! As unheralded as he had gone, young Jackson Stake returned one Saturday morning in June. He had caught a ride from Plainville as far as the road which led into the Stake homestead; then he turned in along the trail through the poplar groves, following twists and turns unchanged through all the years of his absence. Only, the trees were taller, the dapple of leaf-shadows on the trail was darker, the ruts were a little deeper than when, as a youth of eighteen, he last had walked that road before. When he entered the farmyard he was struck with a sense of neatness and prosperity; the Dodge car, the portable granaries, the orderly arrangement of the machinery and vehicles arrested his attention.

"Looks as if they had struggled along without me, after a fashion," Jackie commented to himself as he took in the surroundings. "Wonder if the old man'll fall on my neck, and kick me."

Gander was tinkering with something about the pump under the windmill when he saw a stranger approaching; a tall, dark man of thirty or thereabouts, stouter than Gander and dressed in a suit that still gave signs of good material. He wore a celluloid collar and a tie pierced with a cheap but resplendent pin. Over his arm hung a raincoat, but he apparently was unburdened by any other baggage.

"Lookin' for a job, or a hand-out," Gander remarked to himself. Then, aloud, and politely enough —

"Well, how's she goin'?"

The stranger regarded him for a moment without reply. He had picked up some local information from his driver on the way from Plainville, and had no doubt that this tall young man was Gander, the direct descendant of his little brother Bill. He took a chance:

"Well, Gander, I see you don't know me. I'm the prodigal son."

Gander studied him with narrowing eyes.

"So you're Jackie," he said, at length. "I thought you had been killed in the war."

"That was a good idea," said Jackie. "A fine idea. But, you see, it didn't happen – to either of us."

The tone in which he said "To either of us" did not escape Gander's notice, but he had no immediate answer.

"Well, here I am," Jackie continued. "Your long-lost brother, and what are we going to do about it?"

"You can settle that with Dad," said Gander, curtly. "I didn't know he had sent for you."

"Oh, you didn't? Well, neither did he. But – we'll see," and he went off toward the house.

The return of Jackie was the last thing Gander had expected, and for a number of reasons it annoyed him. It demolished the subterfuge behind which his self-respect had taken some protection, that the first-born of the family had been a sacrifice to the war. He resented the ready sneer which Jackie had thrown at his own neglect to become a war-time casualty. Besides, he disliked Jackie. In childhood Gander had been the younger son, to be cuffed and ordered about by his big brother, and it was against his nature to take orders. And he was deeply attached to his father. Now Jackie would try to worm in between —

"He'll come back now an' sponge on Dad," said Gander, bitterly. "Try to get into his good graces, but it was me that stuck to him when he needed help. Dad'll not forget that."

He took some comfort from the confident hope that his father would be true to him against the devices of his elder brother. In that moment the possible rivalry of Calvin Beach became a very secondary matter. Jackie was his own flesh and blood, his father's natural heir.

The inheritance of the farm, until that moment, never had crossed Gander's mind. He looked upon the farm as the common possession of his father and himself, with Hamilton, Minnie, and his mother holding secondary interests. That his father would one day die was a contingency upon which he never had dwelt. Jackie's unexpected return put a new face on the whole situation. For the first time Gander began to realize that his father was growing old. It might not be so many years —

The bitterness of these reflections, and of the sinister motives which he attributed to Jackie, so enveloped Gander that he found it hard to treat his brother with any degree of civility, and there were times when he was near bringing disgrace upon the family by a physical outburst. He held his young blood in check on his father's account.

There was one ray of hope. Jackson, senior, had laid down the law that if Jackie remained he must do his share of work on the farm. During the summer season work was not pressing, and was left mainly to Grit and Cal, but harvest would be a time of hard labor and long hours, with Jackson, senior, playing no favorites. Gander looked forward with some confidence to his brother's disappearance about the time the stooking would commence.

He was puzzled, however, by a friendship which had sprung up between Cal and Jackie. They often were together, and once or twice he had surprised them in deep conversation. Jackie also seemed to have taken a fancy to Reed. As he thought these things over Gander came to the conclusion that these three had somewhere known each other before. There was something behind all this. Perhaps their meeting on the Stake farm was not such a chance affair as it seemed.

Although he suspected the two of being involved in something that was not apparent on the surface, Gander's attitude toward Cal was much more friendly than toward his brother. Cal had recently become self-absorbed and less genial than in the early days of his apprenticeship on the farm, but his goodwill toward Gander was too obvious to be doubted. Perhaps this was a reflection of his growing intimacy with Minnie, but in any case it made him easy of approach on the matter that was troubling Gander's mind.

He seized the opportunity one evening after supper as Cal hunted for a chain to attach to his plough, now that he was busy with the summer-fallow. Gander helped him explore among the weeds for some minutes, then suddenly shot a question at him.

"How're you hittin' it off with this big brother o' mine?" he asked. "I see you an' him together quite a bit."

It may have been his imagination, but Gander was quite sure that Cal was startled by that question. His answer did not come so readily as usual, and when he spoke he kept on hunting among the weeds, instead of looking Gander in the face.

"Oh, all right," he said. "I really haven't seen very much of him."

Gander put that down against him. If it wasn't quite a lie, it wasn't quite the truth. He had seen them together too much for that. It was plain that Cal was holding something back.

"Ever see him before?" Gander persisted.

"No – never." There was no hesitation about this answer, and it left Gander more mystified than before. He decided on a new tack.

"Jackie seems quite taken up with Reed, too," he remarked.

Cal's interest could not be feigned. He stopped his hunting and looked Gander sharply in the face. "Do you see any sign of that?" he demanded.

"Oh, see 'em around together now an' then."

Then Cal came partly out of his shell. "I wish, Gander, you'd try and keep Reed away from him, as much as you can, without saying anything about it. Will you do that for me, like a good fellow? And don't say anything about it, to anybody?"

More mystified than ever, Gander gave his promise.

"Sure, I'll do that, if I can. I like Reed. Fine kid. You know, Cal, you've never told us about Reed. Who he is, or anythin'?"

"Haven't I?" said Cal, and again Gander doubted his sincerity. "Oh, I guess it was Minnie I told. Well, there isn't much to say about it. He's my sister's son. She's dead, and I've raised him since he was a little baby."

"Father dead, too?" Gander persisted.

Cal's answer did not seem to come quite so readily. "Killed in the war," he said, shortly.

Gander turned these things over in his mind for a minute or two. Then —

"But Reed would be quite a chunk of a boy before the war, and you say you raised him since he was a little baby?"

Cal turned on him, almost angrily. "So I did. Gander, why are you grilling me like this? Do you think I'm lying to you?"

"Oh, no. Nothin'. Jus' was wonderin' about the boy," said Gander, but the incident left him more puzzled than ever.

So passed the days and weeks on the Stake farm; outwardly tranquil, while the warm earth suckled the young crops, and Cal's black parallelogram of summer-fallow widened with every day's labor. But underneath was a sense of unrest, like a storm brooding in the heat of a still afternoon. Suddenly the storm broke, lashing the fields, but without clearing the atmosphere.

It was a Saturday morning, again, when Gander, feeding his horses in the stable, noticed that Cal's team had been unattended. Big Jim was whinnying in disgust and surprise before his empty manger.

"Ho, Grit!" he called. "Seen anythin' o' Cal?"

"No, I ain't," said Grit, as he came up and helped Gander and Big Jim contemplate the absence of hay and oats.

"Never been late before," said Gander.

"Nope. He was out buzzin' somewhere las' night in that fly-trap o' his, him an' the boy. Maybe slep' in."

"Well, let him sleep," said Gander, generously. "Grit, you feed up his horses."

"Where's Cal an' Reed?" said Mrs. Stake, when their places were vacant at the breakfast table.

All present looked at each other. "Saturday mornin'," said Jackson Stake, with sudden inspiration. "No school, an' Reed's sleepin' in."

"That don't account for Cal," said Jackie.

"Sleepin' in, too, an' I don' blame him," the farmer retorted. "He does more work in a day than you've done since you 'returned to the parental roof,' as the Plainville *Progress* had it."

But Mrs. Stake was not so readily satisfied. "Maybe he's sick," she said. "He ain't been lookin' jus' the best lately, nor eatin' hearty at all. Gander, go out an' see."

Gander gulped the few remaining spoonfuls of his porridge and then did as he was directed. It was high morning, seven o'clock under a cloudless sky, and if Gander had known Browning's great apostrophe it would have stirred in his soul as he strode across the yard to Cal's granary. But Gander's feelings had no outlet in poetry, and his reflections were to the effect that there was but one cure for Cal's kind of sickness. "In Plainville last night, I guess," he commented. "Up till all hours with Minnie."

Finding the door of the granary closed, Gander confidently addressed the wooden panels.

"Cal! Oh, Cal!" he shouted. "Seven o'clock. Hooraw!"

No answer.

Gander raised his voice. "Cal, you've slep' in! Roll out! It's seven o'clock!" But there was neither voice nor sound from within.

With a sudden foreboding Gander opened the door. It revealed the room, stark empty. Everything was gone except a little table Cal had built, a lamp which he had borrowed from the house, and one or two trinkets not worth moving.

Gander beheld the scene as though it were a tomb. Then, suddenly recalling that he had not noticed the Ford in the yard, he rushed out into the open air. The old car was gone.

It took him a moment to realize the situation. Cal gone! Reed gone! The old Ford gone! Without a word! A sudden thought that perhaps the car had broken down, and they had not returned from Plainville, had to be as suddenly dismissed. The complete clearance of their effects from the granary showed premeditation. He started toward the house, then turned again to the granary. Perhaps he would find a clue.

He did. Secured under the lamp was an envelope addressed to Jackson Stake, Sr. Without compunction Gander tore it open. It contained a small sum of money, but not a word.

Gander replaced the money, folded the torn end of the envelope, and slowly retraced his way to the house.

"Well, I guess we got a real mystery on our hands now," he announced, as he stood silhouetted against the sunlight in the door. "They're gone. Both of 'em."

"Gone!" The voices around the table joined in chorus. But Mrs. Stake repeated, in a tone in which incredulity mingled with alarm, "Gone! Not gone? Reed's not gone?"

It was young Jackson Stake who suddenly broke out in laughter. "Gone? Of course they're gone. Birds of passage. What did you expect?"

His father silenced him with a bang of his great fist on the table.

"They're not gone!" he shouted. "Broke down, or somethin'. We'll be hearin' from Cal on the 'phone any minute. Gander, get the Dodge ready to go out for him."

"Well, my guess is as good as yours," said Jackie, "and I guess the next time you hear Cal there'll be wings on him."

The old farmer opened his mouth as though to answer violently, then suddenly dropped into a tone of wheedling curiosity.

"Say, you seem to know a lot about this," he addressed Jackie. "Let us all into the secret."

"No secret," Jackie replied. "Simple enough. Cal got out when the gettin' was good."

For a moment Gander attached no significance to Jackie's remark; then suddenly his backbone tingled and the blood went rushing to his head. His hand fell on Jackie's collar.

"Look here, you – you –" he hissed. "If you mean what I think you mean I'll knock you so far it'll cost you a dollar to send a post card home."

"Oh, I heard that speech years ago," said Jackie. "You'll have to brush up on your bright sayings, Gander."

"Here, cut it out!" said the farmer, who, for all his amiability, had the rigidity of Gibraltar in a pinch. "Cut it out. I tell you they've broke down somewhere an' 'll come buzzin' in here one o' these minutes draggin' that peradventure o' theirs behind 'em."

Gander had now cooled down enough for reason. "I'd like to believe it, Dad," he said, "but the facts is against you. Everythin's gone out o' the granary, clean as your plate. But he left this."

He handed his father the envelope, and the old man counted the money slowly, as though working his way out of a puzzle.

"Well, I guess he's gone," he said at length, in a sort of stunned voice. "I had paid him in advance a little on his wages, an' this looks like the difference. I guess he's gone. There ain't nothin' missin'?"

In the same breath he apologized for that reflection on Cal's honesty. "Of course not," he answered himself. "Nothin' crooked about Cal. If there was he wouldn't ha' left the change. . . . But why did he go, without a word?"

Mrs. Stake, grimly pacing between the table and the stove, was almost in tears. "My little boy, my poor little boy!" she kept repeating.

"I'll let you into a secret," said her husband. "Cal an' Minnie had come to an understandin'. He spoke to me about it, an' I wasn't makin' no kick —"

"Do you call that a secret?" Jackie interrupted. "Everybody knew that."

His father fixed him in a gaze of scorn. "Oh, did they? Say, you seem to know so much, why not tell us all about it?"

"Well, I suggested one answer. Perhaps —"

But Gander had had an idea, and was struggling with his Adam's apple.

"What you doin', Gander?" Jackson Stake asked him. "Swallowin' a tonsil?"

"I'm goin' to Plainville," said Gander, with decision. "Right off. But everybody leave the telephone alone. We don' want this peddled over the country until we know the facts."

"That's good sense," his father agreed. "No 'phonin'. An' you beat it into town an' see what Minnie knows about it."

"If he can find her," young Jackson added.

TWENTY

For all his confidence in Minnie, Gander had been seized with sudden misgivings. In spite of its repugnance – or, perhaps, because of it – Jackie's suggestion was infecting his thought. Suppose – He refused to suppose. With his mind in a turmoil he rushed the car into the yard, down the trail which wound through the poplar groves, and away dragging a cloud of dust along the highroad to Plainville. Into the sleepy prairie town he swept in disregard of the painted notice which threatened vengeance on all who exceeded fifteen miles per hour, and brought his car up in front of the office of Bradshaw & Tonnerfeldt. Without knocking he flung open the door and found Minnie taking dictation from Mr. Bradshaw.

"Why, Gander! What's wrong?" the girl cried, caught by her brother's excited appearance.

So she was here, anyway. She knew nothing about it. That might be good – or bad.

"Maybe nothin'," he answered her, trying to control his agitation. "Maybe a good deal. Can I talk to you a minute, Minn?"

Mr. Bradshaw sent them into his private office, and there Gander told her of Cal's disappearance.

Minnie went white with the impact of the news. "Oh, Gander, it can't be!" she cried. "Surely – he must have gone only on some little trip; he'll be back by night; perhaps he's back now. He wouldn't go – he couldn't go – altogether – without leaving a word!"

The girl's limbs were trembling under her as she slowly sank into a chair. Gander was not reassured by his sister's distress, but his loyalty to her revived in her presence. He essayed some clumsy words of comfort, while an unanswered question was battering at his heart.

Presently Mr. Bradshaw announced through the door that Miss Stake was wanted on the telephone. She pulled herself together and hurried to her desk. "This will be news," she had said to Gander.

It was. It was young Jackson on the line, with the information that Annie Frawdic, the school teacher at Willow Green, also had disappeared. It seemed Cal had been visiting at Ernton's, where Annie boarded, the previous evening. That much had been established. Annie had told Mrs. Ernton she expected friends to call for her in the night. In the morning she was gone. Straight case —

"I don't believe – I don't believe –" was all Minnie could fight back into the telephone. Then suddenly the room swam, something smashed, and the next she knew was the feel of water on her face.

"She's coming to; she'll be all right," she heard Mr. Bradshaw's reassuring voice. Then she began to know that she was lying across a desk, with her head downwards, resting on a chair. She struggled into a more dignified position.

"I'm all right," she protested. "I'm all right. Gander, what has happened? Oh!" With a stab consciousness came back upon her.

"I don't believe it," she murmured again. She walked over to a window, and for a moment her eyes fled across the undulating prairies, now rich in the midsummer green of their growing crops. She did not believe that Cal had deserted her. There would be an explanation; she would hear from him soon. And in any case she must play the game. Minnie had quality in her; she was a Stake. Her fair skin, her bronze hair, the curves of her lovely figure, were not all she had inherited from her father's side. She had his amiability, his cheerfulness of disposition, but also she had that rigidity of Gibraltar in the face of storm.

Without seeing the prairies, heaving green into their absorption with the infinite blue beyond, Minnie feasted upon them and restored her soul. Presently she walked with steady step back to her desk, and took up her note-book and pencil.

"I am ready, Mr. Bradshaw," she said. "Thank you, Gander, for coming in. You're a dear boy. And give them all my love at home."

Her composure, now that the shock was over, did much to set Gander at ease, and, as there was nothing else to do, he withdrew from the office of Bradshaw & Tonnerfeldt and drove, more soberly, home again.

But before leaving the town, from force of habit he called at the post office for the mail. There were one or two papers, a circular offering a bargain in farm paint, and a little envelope. He was in the act of stuffing all into his pocket when the address on the envelope caught his attention. "Mr. Gander Stake," it read, "Plainville, Manitoba."

Gander spelled it out, over and over again, driving slowly as he held the envelope between this thumb and the steering-wheel. A letter was an unheard-of incident in his life. His first impulse was to connect it with Cal, but his instinct gave him better guidance. This letter was not from Cal.

He drove until he was well out of town; then, in a spot where there was little traffic on the road, he stopped. He opened the envelope carefully with his knife, as though afraid he might hurt something inside, and drew forth a single folded sheet of note paper. The hand was fine and regular, and even Gander found it not very hard to read:

"Dear Gander – You were very rude, and I should not write you at all, but I just want you to know that my offer stands. When you begin to feel how much you need – all I told you about – come, and bring this letter. It will put you in line for a job. J. C."

J. C. Jo Claus! The name darted into Gander's consciousness. Strange he had not noticed the coincidence before!

"Well, I ain't out of a job," he said, tossing the letter from the car. But a hundred yards further on he stopped, went back, and picked it up again. A second time he read it, thinking how wonderful it must be to be able to write so much like a copybook. He noticed now a faint perfume from the sheet. After all, it was the first real letter ever he had had. Feeling foolish and guilty he tucked it away in the inside pocket of his coat.

When he was almost home Gander delivered himself of a reflection. "Old Bill was right," he said. "You have to treat 'em rough."

When Gander reached home it was to report that Minnie had known nothing at all of Cal's disappearance. It had been a blow to her, but she had pulled herself together and gone back to work. "Minnie's a brick," said Gander. "She's got as much sand in her as a stucco house."

The theory advanced by Jackie that Cal had gone away with Annie Frawdic, the school teacher, was not readily accepted, and as the day wore on evidence accumulated against it. True, there had been some indications of friendship between Annie and Cal, but Annie was known to be somewhat prodigal with her affections. It also was true that Cal had been at Ernton's the night before, and had sat late with Annie in the maple grove which protects the buildings from the west, while Reed and Jimmie Ernton played that they were Indians encamped about the smudge-fire in the yard. But Jimmie was quite positive in his testimony that Cal and Reed eventually went home.

That evening Gander determined to drive over to Ernton's and make some inquiries on his own account, but where the Ernton road turns in from the highway his intention weakened, and he continued on a purposeless course through the farming district to the southeast of Willow Green. The long twilight was full of the odor of growing wheat; the tinkle of a cow-bell, or the sound of voices, came up from amazing distances as though it were near at hand. Mother Wild Duck, piloting her fluffy brood, paused on the white surface of a prairie pond to watch the car speed by.

But Gander had no thought for any of these things. He was concerned about Cal, and about Minnie. He was concerned about that intangible sense of ill-omen which had brooded over the Stake homestead, and of which to-day's events had been the first fruition. How much did Jackie know? There was something between them. And Reed? He remembered his mother's pacing up and down, with a cry of bereavement on her lips, "My little boy – my little boy."

There was also the letter to think about. He had been telling himself that he had forgotten Jerry Chansley. He had lost his head over her for a little while, but he had "taken it out on her" – that was how he justified his outrageous behavior – and it was all over. And now came the letter, to stir within him again something he did not understand. At first he had been disposed to resent the idea of being offered a "job" by a girl. But as he wound over the still prairies in the light of the long summer evening he realized that it was more than that.

"She wants me near her," he said at last. "That's it."

And even as he reached this comfortable conclusion his thoughts would turn again to Josephine Burge. Since her marriage to Dick he really had been trying to dismiss her from his mind; Gander belonged to the old school to whom marriage still is marriage. Only – she wouldn't go! He told himself he was through with Jo; told himself so definitely that he avoided her apparent efforts of conversation when they met at Willow Green. No use keeping the old fire burning when its heat gave torture instead of warmth. And he had told himself that the flame was stamped out, only in a moment like this to find it burst up again within him. It is in the hour of crises that we return to our fundamentals.

The long twilight had settled into summer darkness when Gander turned his car toward home. He was humming along the country roads, solacing his soul with the pleasant purr of machinery, and as his engine hummed he thought of Jo – a little – as he had done in the days gone by. He wondered how she was getting along with Dick, and whether she was, really, as happy as she seemed. It was neighborhood news that Dick was in a bad way with his lungs. Gander had heard the opinion casually expressed that another winter would finish Dick, but never had stopped to think just what significance that fact might have for him. He sometimes wondered how, in his precarious health, Dick kept the farm going at all.

"I might run over an' give him a few days' work, now that we ain't so busy," said Gander to himself, and the thought came out of a heart clean of any ulterior motive. "Ought to give him a hand, I guess. He's like he is – on my account."

It was the first time Gander had admitted so much. Never until to-night had he held himself to answer for doing less than his share in the great struggle that had made of Dick a piece of wreckage and had sent Tommy Burge and Walter Peters and a million others headlong into the unknown. If it were true that they had

"Bade the world 'Good Morning'
When the world had said 'Good Night'"

Gander knew nothing of it; all he knew was they were dead. But that seemed not so very dreadful now; not so very, very dreadful. It was, at least, a way of escape. What was the use of living without – without —

"Yes, I'll have to go over an' give him a lift," said Gander. "Should ha' done it long ago."

He felt better for this resolution and was almost happy again. Suddenly his headlights cut across the figure of a woman on the road. She stepped aside to let him pass, but not quite out of the circle of light. It limned her face against the darkness, and he saw – Jo Claus!

Gander brought his car to a stop a few feet beyond her. "Come on, Jo; have a lift?" he called back.

"Oh, it's you, Gander?" he heard her say. He had backed up; he had opened the door; she was stepping in beside him.

"Thanks, Gander; that's good of you," she said. "But what's the matter? You're out of your beat a little, are you not, to-night?"

He could not see her so well now that she was seated beside him, but her voice was the same, only there was a sadness in it, a sort of resignation, which he had not known before. It touched his pity. Things were not so good with Jo. Her appearance of happiness at Willow Green was a mask, a camouflage —

"Oh, jus' rovin' around," he tried to explain. "No-where in partic'lar. In fact – where am I?"

"About half way between Martin Burge's and the place that I call home," she told him.

Yes, Gander had his bearings, now. He had not been lost. He knew the country so well that he travelled it sub-consciously. Now why had she said "The place that I call home?"

"I was just walking across," she continued, "when you happened along." He knew that she had turned to look at him in the darkness.

They could not be more than a few hundred yards from her door. They would be there in a minute. Gander reached a quick resolution.

"Jo," he said, "will you go for a ride with me? I want to talk to you."

She hesitated. "Not far, Gander," she conceded. "Dick will be expecting me."

"I'll come back whenever you say," he promised, and took a cross-road running south.

For some distance they spun along without speech. Gander was conscious of a thrill of adventure; a sense of impropriety that was very enticing, especially as he knew, and Jo knew, that it was quite all right. Jo trusted him; after all, Jo trusted him. That was what made him so very happy. But what would she think if she knew – about that other J. C.?

"Haven' seen much of you, lately, Jo," he ventured, when it became apparent that she would wait for him to speak.

"No. Often wished you would come over, Gander. Dick would be glad to see you."

"Strange thing, Jo," – he was laughing now, with happiness – "strange thing, but I was jus' thinkin' o' that, when I caught up on you, there. Had jus' said to myself, 'Must go over an' give Dick a few days' help with a team.'"

Her hand found his arm, and although the pressure was but a featherweight it went tingling to his fingertips.

"That would be very kind of you," she said. "Only, I don't know – Dick might not like it. No" – she seemed at once to have sensed his recoil – "not that. But Dick is proud. He won't admit defeat. Oh, Gander, you have no idea of the bravery of that boy!"

This was not exactly what he had expected. "He has a good booster in his little wife," he remarked.

"He should have. He's a good boy. Fighting away on the farm, when he should be in bed, or away somewhere on a holiday, camping out, perhaps, under the green boughs – Oh, I know what he needs, Gander. And I can't give it to him."

Gander's inherent generosity surged within him. "Jo, can I help? I'm not much of a cashier, but Dad's got some kale, an' he'd come through if I asked him."

The pressure of her hand tightened a little. "That's kind of you again. Very kind, indeed, Gander – after – after all –" She hesitated, and he knew what was in her mind. "But, you see, that would be like helping with the team. He wouldn't have it. He would call that defeat, and he won't admit defeat."

They ran on in silence, each busy with thoughts which

remained unexpressed. Presently she motioned that they turn toward home. "Dick will be waiting for me," she said.

It was not until he had turned his car that the day's events in the Stake household crushed back into Gander's mind. For half an hour the stimulating presence of Jo Burge had swept him clear of that perplexing problem. Should he tell Jo? Yes! She must learn of it, anyway; why not from his own lips? So he told her briefly of Cal's disappearance.

"I don' know what to make of it, Jo," he concluded. "We always used Cal well, and there ain't any reason – there shouldn' be any reason – for this."

"I wouldn't worry," said Jo, and he was struck by the maturity with which she spoke. This was no longer the child of his school days, the girl of his adolescence; this, beside him, was a woman, schooled in the responsibilities of the world; accustomed to facing difficulties without panic. She seemed to mother him now. "I wouldn't worry," she said. "He's likely one of these rovers; he roved in, and he roved out again. After all, don't you think, Gander, they are the wise people? Here we are, you and I, tied down to our farms; it doesn't matter how sick we get of it, there's the unending routine. But Cal! He kisses his fingers to it, and flits away in the night!"

She sighed, and Gander took an unpremeditated plunge. "Would you – flit away like that, too – Jo, if you could?"

"If I could, perhaps. But I can't. I've got Dick. He needs me. Oh, Gander, you've no idea how much he needs me! So, you see, I can't."

She answered as though Gander had been urging such a course upon her. And he hadn't. He had merely asked a question. Was it her own heart she was answering? Gander wondered, but had not the courage to inquire.

He reverted to the other matter in his mind.

"I'd like to believe what you say, about Cal, but I'm not so sure. The fact is, Jo, he an' Minnie have been pretty good friends. I guess they were plannin' to make a match of it. He told Dad as much. An' now he lights out without a word to Minn; she didn' know a thing about it."

"Oh, I'm so sorry!" said Jo. "Minnie's a fine girl, and this will hit her hard. But she'll get over it. We all do. Over everything."

"Do we?"

"Yes." She said the word with finality, as though all things were settled.

They were nearing Jo's home, and Gander felt that he had not managed to make clear his real misgivings. But how to make them clearer he did not know.

"So you think there's nothin' strange about Cal lightin' out?" he blundered. "Jus' get engaged to a girl an' then beat it? You think there's nothin' – nothin' – suspicious – about that?"

"Suspicious? It's not things that are suspicious, Gander, nor actions; it's people. And that depends on the kind of person you are. Now, I'm not suspicious. If I were perhaps I wouldn't have gone with you for a drive, Gander. A suspicious person might —"

"I know what you're thinkin'. You're thinkin' about what a – what a fool I made o' myself, that day. Jo, I'm awful sorry. I've been sorry ever since."

"I know." Her words were tender and quiet, as though nothing now could make any difference between them. "And for a while I was frightened of you, but I'm not – any more. And I wouldn't worry over Cal and Minnie. Perhaps he got engaged without intending to; just sort o' stumbled into it, and took the first chance to stumble out again. It's not very heroic, but it's quite natural. And maybe, after he's thought it over for a few days, he'll change his mind again. We do that kind of thing, Gander. Look out you don't find Cal back, Ford and boy and all, in your farmyard one of these mornings!"

They were now stopped at Jo's gate, and there seemed nothing more to be said.

"Won't you come in?" she asked him, when they had sat a minute or two without speaking. "Dick will be glad to see you."

"No, not to-night, I guess. Maybe some other time."

"All right, Gander. Any time. And thanks so much for the ride – and the conversation."

She gave him her hand, and he held it a moment, as an old friend. Then she disappeared up the path that led to her house.

Gander drove slowly home, a mixture of emotions. Jo had changed so much, and yet, in some ways, not at all. She had taken on responsibilities, with her invalid husband and all the work of the farm. He had noticed that her hand was as hard as his; not like Minnie's, or Jerry's. But how wise she was! She had set his mind at rest, and filled his heart with a peace it had not known for years.

"And she's so good to Dick," Gander commented, as he rehearsed their conversation while he guided his car along the prairie trails back to the Stake homestead. "She's a reg'lar mother to him."

A mother! Yes, that was what she was. Caring for her sick boy. But a wife? Gander wondered.

TWENTY-ONE

The days went by without any word of Cal or Reed. The summer-fallowing on the Stake farm was finished, and Gander and Grit, Hamilton, and Jackson Stake were now busy in the fragrant hay. Young Jackson still stayed about the farm but took little part in its labor; in spite of the conditions laid down by his father he spent most of his time fishing in the lake, shooting gophers, or roaming over the prairie. Once or twice he drove the Dodge into Plainville and brought Minnie home for her week-end visits on the farm. The girl seemed in need of these holidays; she was paler than Gander could remember having seen her, and her brave pretence of light-heartedness was more pathetic than frank dejection.

Then suddenly one day in mid-week she came tearing home in a hired automobile. Gander knew nothing about it until he returned to the house at noon, when he found his father and mother in a state of unusual excitement. Mrs. Stake's black eyes had a flash of moisture in them, and there was a nervous spring in her step as she walked the endless treadmill between the table and the stove.

"Well, there's word o' Cal," said the old farmer, who never for a moment had lost faith in his runaway hired man. "Minnie's had a telegram."

"An' Reed's sick – that's why," his wife added. She was caught between concern over the boy's illness and relief that at last something definite had been learned.

"Yes, an' Minnie's gone to look after him; Jackie's took her in the car."

By degrees it came out that Minnie had had a telegram from Cal, dated from somewhere in Saskatchewan, saying that Reed was dangerously ill and appealing to her for help. The train connections were bad, and Jackie had volunteered to drive her out.

"That ain't like our son an' heir," said Gander. "There's more in this than'll come off with shavin'."

"Well, it's one good turn he done, so let him have the credit," his father retorted.

"Maybe when Reed's well enough to move they'll all be back," ventured Mrs. Stake. "We'll give him a room upstairs —"

"But why did they light out?" Gander wanted to know. "An' so far? Couldn' they get sick nearer home?"

"Minnie'll find all that out, don' you fear," Jackson Stake assured him. "The mystery is about to be eloocidated, as the Plainville *Progress* would say."

In a few days came a brief note from Minnie with the news that they had found Cal and Reed, and the boy was down with typhoid fever. "It's a case of nursing," she said, "and I am doing the best I can." Other notes followed from time to time, reporting Reed's progress toward recovery, but without a word of explanation of Cal's strange behavior.

"For a girl that's got an eddication Minnie can take longer to say less than anybody I know," Gander grumbled. "This mystery is clearin' up like the beginnin' of a steady rain."

But at length came a letter from Minnie; a real letter, with news. Mrs. Stake read it to her assembled family, between the fried pork and the raisin pie one day at noon, while the harvest stood waiting in the fields.

"My dear Mother," she began, then paused to wipe her glasses with her apron, in a fruitless effort to remove a mist that had gathered somewhere else. "My dear Mother – At last I have a breathing spell and, fortunately, note paper, which Cal has just brought from town. Now if I had my typewriter you might expect a real epistle. It is a hardship to have to write with two fingers after you have learned to pound it out with ten.

"Picture me, if you can, in the country home of a certain Mr. Mason, who is enjoying a holiday somewhere in the East, and who is expected back shortly. Mr. Mason's residence is about the size of Cal's old granary, with a low roof that lets in the heat in daytime, when you don't want it, and lets it out at night, when it wouldn't go amiss. Alongside of me is Reed, bundled up in an easy chair which Cal made out of the staves of an old barrel. He's thin and white – Reed, I mean – but out of danger, thanks to a competent nurse, so Dr. Thompson says. He has had a racket, poor little chap, but he's worth all the fight we've made for him. All the time now he is wondering when we are going back to see Grandma. When he was delirious he would talk about no one but Grandma, and one night he tried to sing that verse of yours about 'Borne on the night winds, voices of yore come from that far-off shore.'"

Mrs. Stake coughed and wiped her glasses again. "I'll have to be gettin' these glasses changed, Jackson," she said. "They don' seem to fit me like they did." Then, resuming —

"When Cal came out here he fell in with this Mr. Mason, who wanted some one to take charge of his farm for a few weeks, so Cal took the job. I guess the water wasn't very good, and the first thing he knew Reed was down with typhoid. So then he sent that telegram. This is a sparsely settled district, and there was no chance of getting help nearer at hand. When Jackie and I drove up we found Cal on the shady side of the shanty – it's just a shanty – doing the family washing. He was a picture! But the house was spotless – you remember how Cal used to keep his granary —"

"Too much Cal in this," Gander interrupted. "Cal! Cal! —"

"California," Grit added, brilliantly.

"Well, what of it?" Jackson Stake demanded, impatiently. "Go on, Mother."

"— used to keep his granary? – it was just like that. *Perhaps* he was glad to see us. But the first thing was to look after Reed, and that is what I have been busy with, right until now.

"I suppose you are wondering when we will be back. Well, it all depends on Mr. Mason. Cal cannot leave the stock, and besides, the crop is coming in, and he'll have to start the binder in a day or two. It will be some time, at any rate, before Reed is able to travel. And Jackie has left us. He's a bird of passage, as you know, and one night, when Cal was in town, Jackie said to me, 'I'm going to hit the trail again,' and away he went. Cal followed him with the car, but Jackie beat him to The Siding, where he boarded a freight train, and —"

"Then Minn an' Cal's up there alone," said Gander. "That ain't quite the thing —"

"Shut up, Gander!" The interruption was from an un-expected quarter; the silent Hamilton had spoken. "Minn's a nurse now, and a nurse can do – most anything, and it's all right. I mean —"

"Wisdom from our young son," Gander retorted. "Who told you that? Elsie Fyfe?"

"Well, what else is she goin' to do?" Jackson Stake wanted to know. "Get up an' leave the little sick boy? If you got a nickel, Gander, for every fool remark you could pay the national debt. Go on, Mother."

"— he boarded a freight train, and we haven't seen him since. But we're hoping that by the time Mr. Mason is back Reed will be well enough to move, and then, home we come! I guess I'll have to drive the Dodge alone, or else we'll hitch the Ford behind."

"I bet they'll hitch the Ford behind," said Grit Wilson, with subtle humor.

"Of course," Mrs. Stake continued reading, "we haven't all the accommodation here that we could use, but we get along. Cal sleeps in the old Ford, drawn up within calling distance in case he should be needed. The other night it rained a downpour, and I know he was soaked, although I offered him the hospitality of one end of the shack. In the morning I told him he was very chivalrous —"

"Shiverous? What's that?" Grit inquired.

"From gettin' wet. Cold rain," Gander explained. "Go on, Mother."

"— and he said – well, I may as well tell you, Mother, that Cal and I have come to a complete understanding. I hope you and Dad will be pleased; it cannot be altogether a surprise to you."

Mrs. Stake laid down the letter and took off her glasses.

"Minnie – it seems like yesterday she was just a baby in my arms." The thin old face began to twist, and Jackson Stake got up, blustering, from the table.

"Get off to the fields, you fellows!" he commanded. "Hangin' around like the washin' on the line! 'S all right, Mother. They'll make as fine a pair as ever – Get off, I tell you!"

"We haven't had our pie yet," Hamilton protested.

"For the soul or sake o' me, so you haven't!" Mrs. Stake exclaimed, as she found safety from her emotions in serving fat wedges of raisin pie. "I clean forgot."

There was a moment's pause from conversation as the pie disappeared amazingly. Then Gander, gulping his last crumb, returned to the matter on his mind.

"But she don' say why he went away," he reminded them. "The mystery's as deep as ever." . . .

Bill Powers' threshing outfit was humming in the wheat-fields when Cal and Minnie came back to Jackson Stake's. Reed was almost himself again; a little wobbly, like a calf, as Gander said, but rapidly getting back on his feet. Cal dropped into the work of the farm as though he never had left, and Minnie returned to her typewriter in Plainville. But in the late autumn Cal made negotiations for a strip of land down by the lake, considered of little value because it would not grow wheat, and commanded only a burst of scenery and a few acres of standing trees. During the winter months he cut down and hauled logs to a spot which he had cleared close to the beach, and there, in the early spring, he built his bungalow, Jackson Stake and Gander lending a neighborly hand.

In May Cal and Minnie were married. Mrs. Stake's table groaned under the wedding dinner, and the guests groaned around it before the feast was finished. Then Cal and Minnie, with Reed in the back seat, took their honeymoon trip in the old Ford along the rough timber trail which leads from the Stake farm down to the lake. Hamilton had slipped out of the company and gone down ahead, and when the bridal party arrived there was a blazing fire in the boulder fireplace which almost filled one end of the bungalow. But the boy had slipped away again, as quietly as before. Slowly he tramped the trail back to the farm, thinking of Elsie Fyfe.

Gander was surprised to find how much he missed Cal, and Minnie, and Reed. He doubted the possibility of anyone making a living by writing for magazines, as Cal proposed to do, and had every expectation that before long he would be back working on the farm for Jackson Stake. In the meantime he found excuse as often as seemed reasonable to spend an hour or two down at the bungalow.

In those days Cal and Minnie puzzled him a good deal. They were admittedly fond of each other. To be admittedly fond of a member of one's family had always been regarded by Gander Stake as a mark of weakness. True, there had been moments, back in those war-ridden days, when he had put his hand on his father's shoulder, but never for more than a moment, and always shame-facedly. And Cal and Minnie were brazen about it! Also, although the whole country was a-rush with seeding operations, they lived in a disgracefully leisurely fashion, remaining in bed until seven in the morning, and spending hours sitting by the lake or rambling through the trees on the little estate. There were times, it is true, when he found them at work – or at what they called work – Cal dictating and Minnie pounding her typewriter, but these were rare occasions; mostly they seemed to have nothing to do. They would sit and look at the sunset on the lake with something in their eyes that puzzled Gander beyond words.

Perhaps it was some of these things, or all of them, that

turned Gander's thoughts, in spite of himself, more and more toward Josephine Claus. Jerry Chansley had become only a memory. He had not answered her letter, partly through shyness, and partly because he was ashamed of his bad writing, and she had not written to him again. But he knew now that what he had seen in her for the moment had really been Josephine Claus; always it was Jo – the same Jo. Jerry had been merely a brief deflection in his constancy to Jo.

He had kept track of Dick during the winter; learned that he had had rather a bad time of it. Much of the work of the farm was falling to Jo, and it was known in the Willow Green district that Dick's father was having to help out financially. Others in the community began to feel that the responsibility lay partly on them as well. Among them Jackson Stake.

"I hear that Dick Claus is behind a bit in his seedin'," he said one day to Gander. "In fact, ain't gettin much done but what others do for him. We're pretty well through an' I was thinkin' you might give him a day or two with a team an' drill."

Gander's heart thumped. It was what he had been thinking of all spring and had not had the courage to mention. Gander tried to show no enthusiasm.

"Do you suppose he would like that?" he asked, remembering what Jo had told him. "Perhaps he'd think we were meddlin' —"

"Well, what if we are? He meddled for us – that's how he got his lungs as full o' holes as last year's underwear. Now you hitch up to-morrow mornin' an' go over an' meddle a little for him. An' take along a few bushels o' seed, jus' in case he don' happen to have any ready."

Early next day Gander's four-horse team, hitched to a seed-drill, with a wagon dragging behind, pulled into the yard on Dick Claus' farm. The morning was warm and sunny, as is the habit toward the end of May, and Gander was warm and sunny inside, too, albeit his Adam's apple was performing gymnastics within the narrow limits of his thin neck, and he had some misgivings as to how his visit would be received. Dick was proud. Well, the Stakes were proud, too, after a fashion, and this was their way of paying a debt.

As Gander was waiting in the yard, wondering how he should announce his errand, Jo herself came up from the stables. She was carrying two pails of milk; her head drooped forward, and her eyes were on the ground. She was almost beside him before she was aware of his presence.

"Oh, Gander!" she exclaimed, when she saw him. "Where did you come from? You gave me quite a start."

"Oh, jus' blew in with the weather," said Gander, nonchalantly. "Cows seem to be doin' pretty well, Jo?"

"Not so bad, Gander. Well, they should, in May, if they're ever going to. The cows and the hens – they're our mainstay, Gander."

"How about the crop? Fact is, Jo, I came over to give a little lift with the seedin', if I can."

She had set down her pails and raised her head. The lines were beginning to deepen about her mouth and eyes, and Jo was only twenty-three – not more than twenty-four! It was yesterday that, in her little calico dress, he had rescued her from prisoner's base! Something tugged chokingly at Gander's throat. He had liked Jo, always, but this was more than liking; this was – sympathy, he told himself. Her dress was rough and drab, with a button missing at the neck; her hair was none too tidy; her whole attire suggested haste and over-work. This was not the Jo of the days he had known; not even the Jo of the afternoon church services at Willow Green; this was the real Jo – Jo Claus, at home, at work, with the responsibilities of her sick man and her profitless farm dragging down upon her. Yet, under that white, fair skin were the same little freckle spots shining through; the hair had its same old lustre; her brave little smile was more bewitching than any coquetry.

"Jo!" Gander exclaimed, and there were worlds in his one word.

"I must see Dick," she answered him, hastily. "He has not been so well – he is not able to do much about the farm. Father has put in most of the crop, but, what with not having Tommy any more –" She left the sentence unfinished and hurried to the house.

In a few minutes she came out again, and it was apparent that she had herself in hand. "Dick isn't up yet," she said, casually, "and I haven't got the house in shape for visitors. It'll be better at noon. But I told him what you had come for, and he asked me to say it was a real neighborly thing. There's no ploughing ready, but he thought you might stubble-in some oats or barley at the low end of the farm. You'll find seed in the granary —"

"I brought some oats with me, jus' in case you might be short."

"You shouldn't have done that, Gander. But you can keep track of the bushels, and we'll pay you – when we can."

"I don' want no pay, Jo; I don' want no pay from you – or Dick." Gander noticed that the horizon had suddenly gone blurry. How wonderful she was!

"You'll be in for dinner at twelve?" she said, as he started his team. "Dick will be able to see you then."

Gander had not thought of that. "Well, yes, I guess," he agreed.

All morning he worked in a strange intoxication. He told himself he was glad to be able to do this for one who had suffered in the war. In his heart he knew he was delighted to be serving Jo. And there was so much that might be done! A glance about the farm yard had shown many spots where a man's muscle and management were needed. It was a shame he had not come sooner. He must make up for it. There would be summer-fallowing, and haying —

The forenoon was gone before he knew it. Gander brought his horses into the yard, watered, and stabled them. Then he went up to the house.

The ground floor of Dick's house consisted of a single room, which was used for kitchen, dining, and general living purposes. At one end a stairway led to the upper story. Jo was busy preparing dinner as Gander's shadow fell across the door, but Dick rose from his chair and welcomed him with his hand.

"This is good of you, Gander, old man; just like a Stake," he said. Gander took his hand. It was slender and soft; not like Jo's. Dick was even more frail than he had expected. Gander shook hands gently, as though afraid of breaking something. Then Dick asked him if he wanted to wash, and Jo hurried with a basin of hot water to a bench in a corner of the room. With a deftness that was almost sleight-of-hand she whipped a soiled towel from its nail and hung a clean one in its place.

The meal was rather difficult. It was so hard to find anything to talk about. Dick was interested in the progress of seeding in the neighborhood, but Gander's mind was whirling around two different centres – Dick and Jo. He noted how she waited on him, and how he accepted her services. There was tenderness between them, somewhat as between Cal and Minnie; yet not quite the same. Gander's intuition sensed the difference, but his mind was unable to analyze it.

After dinner Dick invited Gander to smoke and began talking about the old school days at Willow Green. He recalled many a prank of those happy times; he seemed bent on making Gander feel again that they were just schoolmates together. Meanwhile Jo worked with her dishes at the end of the room; her body bent over a table, her back toward them. As Gander glanced toward her he saw a hole in her stocking; it may have been the shape of a silver dollar, and the white skin shining through. . . .

"Remember the day I blew up the ink bottle?" Dick was saying. "I see the marks on the ceiling yet, once in a while, when I get over to church. Say – I've heard a few explosions since, but never anything that made such consternation."

He laughed with the memory, then quickly drew a handkerchief and pressed it to his lips. Jo, warned by instinct, was at his side in a moment. One hand slipped around his head; the other drew the white cloth from his fingers. As she folded it over Gander noticed a slight stain of red.

"Mustn't over-do yourself, Dick," she was saying. She was like a mother brooding over him. "Perhaps you had better lie down again. Gander will be back in the evening. Then you can talk."

"I'm all right now," he insisted, but weakly enough. "Gets me once in a while, Gander. Some day – Oh, I'd be all right if I could get about a little. I'm very useless, Gander. Just a load on – everybody."

"Hush, Dick," she murmured. "You mustn't say that."

And Gander, awkwardly remarking that by this time his horses must have finished feeding, got up and resumed his work at the lower end of the farm.

TWENTY-TWO

For three days Gander worked on the Claus farm, until he had finished "stubbling-in" all the land that was suitable to that treatment. These days gave him time to observe Dick and Jo, and to evolve in his slow mind a conclusion that seemed inescapable. Jo was mothering Dick; she was giving her life to Dick; but she liked to have Gander about the farm!

If he had doubt in the matter it was Jo herself who set it at rest. On the third afternoon, as he was nearing the end of his job, he saw her coming across the fields. She was waiting for him at the end of his row when his horses came swinging up, their great heads nodding, their harness straining with the drag of the heavy drill.

He went over to where she stood in the shade of a clump of willows. She seemed flushed a little, perhaps with her walk across the fields, and with the weight of a basket which she had set down at her feet. But her hair was drawn neatly beneath her hat; her dress, although cheap, was fresh from the ironing-board, and there was something like a smile on her wistful, troubled lips.

"It's pretty warm for May," she said, "and I thought you might like a cool drink, and a sandwich or two."

"You shouldn' have bothered, Jo," he protested. "I was all right."

Her eyes looked full in his. "You're not bothering at all, are you?" she demanded. She motioned to the grass and they sat down together. She poured him cold water from a bottle and fed him thick sandwiches of bread and ham. Gander remembered a time she had brought him water, years ago, and his face still stung with that recollection.

Gander did not dally over his food. With him even such a lunch as this was to be taken seriously and with despatch. When he had finished he stretched himself approvingly.

"That's good, Jo," he commended. "Puts a little pep in a fellow in the middle of the afternoon. Now I'll get along."

"You'll finish easily to-night, won't you?"

Gander measured the unseeded distance with his eye, "Yep. Ought to make it in a couple o' hours."

"Then what's the hurry? I mean," she added, confusedly, "you can stay and chat a minute?"

He settled back on the grass. "Yes, if you like."

Her hand fell on his arm. "I just want to tell you, Gander, how much we – how much I – appreciate what you are doing for us. You've been a real friend."

"Oh, that's nothin'. Anyway, it was Dad that sent me."

"But you weren't hard to send, were you, Gander?"

She was looking into his face, and there was no mis-understanding. Her hand had slipped down to his and he clasped it in his palm.

"No, Jo," he said. "I'm not hard to send – where you are."

They sat for a minute in silence, gazing across the green prairies into an infinite sky where puffs of white cloud floated like swans on a transparent sea.

Then said Gander, swallowing hard: "I thought, Jo, you wouldn' ever want me to come near you again, after what – after I'd been – such a fool."

Her fingers tightened a little on his. "We're all fools, sometimes," she answered.

Then he took a great plunge. "Do you mean, Jo, that if you had everythin' to do over again, you'd do it diff'rent?"

She waited a minute, and when she spoke she seemed to choose her words slowly and carefully. "I'm not saying that, Gander. I don't suppose we ever know what we really would have done if we hadn't done what we did, if you understand. But Dick is a good boy, and I – I —"

"Do you love him, Jo?"

"He's my husband, and I love him, and will serve him – to the end."

There was a sadness in those last words which stirred all of Gander's latent sympathy. She would serve him – to the end. Jo would do that, because she was faithful and true. But love? Gander was not so sure.

"Can't anythin' be done for him?" he asked. "Couldn' we – is there nothin' more that we can do?"

She shook her head. "He could go to one of those Government hospitals," she said, "but he won't. Says it wouldn't really make any difference, and he wants to stay at home and help with the farm, although this spring – well, you can see for yourself. He worries, too, on my account."

She turned her head from Gander now, and he, with a lump in his throat, waited for her to speak again.

"I don't want you to misunderstand me, Gander," she

went on. "I said we're all sometimes fools, but what I've done I've done. And I won't go back on him, Gander, ever."

She turned toward him again, and Gander saw how bravely she was fighting the tremble in her lip. "I won't go back on him," she repeated, as though in self-defence. Then for one moment her fortitude gave way. "But oh, Gander," she cried, "I made a mistake!"

Tears were welling in her eyes, and Gander felt his own head swimming. He would have comforted her in his arms, but she drew gently away. "No, no. Gander, I have said too much. I didn't mean —"

"You see," she went on again, "he has done so much. He has made such a sacrifice. For you, for me, for all of us, Gander. For you, Gander – have you thought of that?"

"Yes, Jo; yes, I have."

"Of course," she continued, more cheerfully, "he has a pension for partial disability. Might have had more, if he had pressed for it, but Dick has always made light of his trouble. With his allowance, and what we are able to do on the farm, and what some of our friends" – here she glanced into Gander's face a moment – "do for us, we get along."

They sat together in silence for some minutes, each with many thoughts but without words. Then she brushed a few crumbs from her dress, took the basket in her hand, and arose to her feet.

"Must be getting back, Gander," she explained. "Good-bye."

"Good-bye, Jo." He said it solemnly, as though they were parting for the last time, and turned to his seeder.

When he had finished the field Gander drove straight home, without stopping at the house. He did not want to be embarrassed by Dick's thanks. Besides, he was wrestling with an idea in his mind.

He took the first opportunity to consult Cal about it. He found him down by the lake, thumping on Minnie's typewriter, which he had set up in the shade of a cottonwood tree.

"Hello, Gander!" Cal called cheerily. "I'm learning to ride this velocipede myself. Can you read that?" He drew a sheet from the machine, and Gander puzzled over it for a moment.

"Looks a good bit like a code, I admit," said Cal, "But Minnie is getting able to follow it in places. As a matter of fact, you may not know it, but that is a very learned article which I am writing for a magazine on The Industrial Assimilation of the Ex-Soldier. That's a good title, Gander, and I expect to get the price of an acre of wheat out of it."

"Never could understand how you manage to get paid for – words," Gander confessed, frankly. "But I've jus' come to swap a few with you myself. Somethin' along the line of that – whatever it was you said."

"Yes?" said Cal, curiously. It was not often that Gander came to consult him.

"You know Dick Claus?" Gander began. "Him that got his lungs all busted up in the war?"

"I've heard of him," said Cal. "Trying to work a farm, under difficulties, isn't he?"

"Yep. Fact is, I've been helpin' him out with a little late seedin' for the last day or two. He's pretty well up against it, Cal. Not able to carry on. I was – that is – I was wonderin' if we couldn' do somethin' about it."

Blushing for his generous thought, Gander seated himself on a stump beside Cal's tree and got out his pocket knife to whittle. The shavings curling from a dry branch restored his confidence, and he went on:

"I've been helpin' him out for a day or two, an' kind o' gettin' the lie o' the land. Went to school with Dick, an' with his wife. Jo Burge she use' to be." He paused. Even the mention of her name was delicious on his tongue. "Well, he's goin' to snuff out one o' these times, an' I thought maybe we could make it as easy for him as possible."

"You think he can't pull through? Why doesn't he go to a sanitorium? There are places where he could have special attention for his trouble. I don't know how much they could do for him, but it would be worth trying."

"He won't go. Thinks it's no use, an' besides, he won't leave Jo."

Cal puckered his brow. "What do you suggest?"

"I'm not much of a suggester, Cal, but I got the idea that maybe if he was down here by the lake, where things are pleasant an' quiet, an' away from the worry of the farm, it might go easier with him. I was wonderin' if we couldn' arrange that, Cal?"

Cal turned the idea over in his mind for a minute. "Maybe," he said. "What about his wife? Would she come, too?"

"No, I suppose she'd want to stay on the farm. Pretty near have to, to keep things goin'. But she could run down here every little while —"

Cal looked at Gander quizzically, and Gander wondered how much he knew, or suspected. His answer gave no light on that question.

"It's up to us to do what we can," Cal continued, "and I suppose it could be managed. Minnie's a real little nurse, let me tell you, and if we could get Dick away from his worries it might do him more good than you imagine – more good than you imagine." Gander did not like that repetition, but Cal went on briskly, "I'll talk it over with Minnie and see what can be done about it."

The outcome was that Cal and Gander built a little shelter, just large enough for a bed and table and, as Cal said, "room to drop his boots," in a grove of leafy trees close to the bungalow. They made the roof water-tight and screened the walls against mosquitoes, and Cal, out of the depths of his inventiveness, arranged a bell that would ring in the house when pulled from Dick's bedside.

Persuading Dick to make the change was no easier than they had expected, but finally, with Jo's urgings added to their own, and Gander's promise to bring Jo down to see him at least three times a week, he consented. He looked a fine patient when, after bumping down the hill in Gander's car, he settled to rest in the clean white sheets which Minnie had provided.

"This is wonderful of you boys," he said. "I do believe I'll feel better here."

"You'll be as right as rain," Cal assured him. "In a month or two you won't know yourself."

The month or two wore away. Gander, faithful to his promise, drove over to Jo's house three or four times a week and took her down to visit the patient at the lake. Once in a while she stayed all night, sitting by Dick's bedside and encouraging him with reports of the progress of the farm until he fell asleep, and then keeping her vigil until the light of dawn began to filter through the haze hanging across the lake. In the morning Cal would drive her home in his old Ford. But generally she went back with Gander the same evening, after darkness had settled down, and they wound their way across the fragrant prairies in the still warmth of the summer night.

On these drives Gander found himself peculiarly hampered for speech. There was a joy in Jo's presence which he dared not try to explain, even to himself, and which kept his lips sealed. When she praised him, as she did on every occasion, for his generosity and his kindness, he turned it off with a nervous laugh and a declaration that it was nothing. And when, at the door of her house, she would give him her hand and say good night, Gander again had no words that could sound above the thumping of his heart.

It was an evening in July, with blue thunder-clouds gathering in the west, and the air heavy with the smell of heading wheat. They had gone to the lake early, for Gander had wanted a swim, and had found Dick out of his arbor and resting in the sand down by the water. He was brighter than usual; the lake breezes or the setting sun had whipped a dash of color into his cheeks; his long, thin legs straightened under him, and, with the help of his stick, held him steady and erect when they came up beside him.

"You see, Jo, I'm on my feet; I'm on my feet again!" he cried. "I'm going to make it, Jo; I'm going to make it!"

He held out his arm, and drew his wife's face to his. "I believe I'm going to make it after all," he whispered. "I'm getting stronger, and I seem to be able to fill my lungs again."

Gander would have drawn away, but Dick caught him with his eye. "Don't go, old man," he said. "It is you I have to thank for this; you, and Cal, and Minnie – yes, and Reed; his little, wise, boyish talk has made me young again."

But Gander slipped away to have his swim, and to think.

Later in the evening he sat beside Dick's bed, his hand in Dick's, while the little wrist watch on the table ticked the minutes busily away.

"It's a wonderful thing to have been boys together," Dick was saying. "To go to school, to grow up, to go through – all these things – and still to be – together."

"Yes," said Gander.

"I have often thought, as I lay here in this quiet place, of all these things," he went on. "Gander, when I came down here I didn't expect to go back. Now I do. Gander, don't imagine I don't understand. I do. I've seen some brave things – some brave men – but nothing braver than this."

His eyes closed, and the slightest film of moisture glistened on his lashes. Then he sank quietly into his pillow and lay so still and white that Gander found himself in the grip of a fear which suddenly deepened into panic.

"Jo! Minn!" he cried, leaping to his feet.

"What is the matter, Gander?" said Dick, opening his eyes.

"No – nothin'. You're all right, are you, Dick?"

"All right, but tired. Now I'm going to have a sleep. Good night, Gander."

Gander stretched his legs along the sand beach that skirts the lake. Around a little jutting point of land he came upon Cal, trolling in a bay.

"Our patient seems to be picking up, Gander, don't you think?" said Cal, as he drew in his line. "Better spirits to-day than he has shown for a long while. Seems really to have made up his mind that he may get better."

"Yes, I was talkin' to him," Gander answered, briefly, wondering why he could not bring more enthusiasm into his voice.

"Trouble about it," Cal went on, "is that that may be a good sign, and it may be a bad one. It all depends."

"How do you mean, 'It all depends'?"

"You know how a lamp flickers up before it goes out? It may be that. Or it may be really settling down to a steady flame. We should know in a few days."

The drive home that night with Jo was even more silent than usual. She sat very quiet, as though lost in thought, until they reached her door. The night was dark, and Gander could sense, rather than see, her presence at his side.

When he had stopped the car she remained in her seat, and he waited for her to speak.

"Gander," she said at length, "I believe – I hope – he's going to get better, after all."

"Yes, I think so. I hope he is," said Gander.

She arose slowly, and slowly stepped down from the car.

"Good night, Gander."

"Good night, Jo."

During the days that followed Gander watched that flame of which Cal had spoken with fascinated interest. Would it flicker out, or would it settle down to a steady glow? Every evening found him at the lake, and every evening seemed to see Dick a little stronger than before. Hope, most wonderful of all medicines, had returned, and was surging in his veins. Hope and gratitude. His gratitude he lavished on Gander, overwhelming him with appreciation. He talked continually of their boyhood days, and of his rich good fortune in having such a friend. Afterwards Gander would slip away in silence, lonely and ashamed.

One evening when Gander had brought Jo down to see him Dick was particularly vivacious. He was planning that he would be able to help a little in the harvest; by winter he would be as good as ever.

"That sister of yours, Gander – she's wonderful. You're all wonderful. You pulled me out of No Man's Land as sure as did ever any soldier in the trenches. Only you won't get any V. C. for it."

Gander's thought flew back to the day of the accident at Bill Powers' threshing mill, when the men had jestingly suggested a V. C. for him, and Jo had come to his defence. Jo had been true to him always. Always.

TWENTY-THREE

Gander turned from Dick's company, and from Jo's, to stroll alone by the side of the lake. Life was pressing in upon him. Never even to himself had he admitted what he feared – or hoped? – might be the outcome of Dick's illness. He acknowledged only one wish in that connection. And yet – something was filling his throat; his stomach was gone; there was a vast desolation within him.

Presently he found a flat stone, and sat down. He was unaccountably tired. The desire to smoke was upon him, and he drew his pipe from his pocket, filled it with tobacco, and felt for matches. But without success. He usually could count on his right vest pocket, but not to-night. Through pocket after pocket he went in that sudden mild panic which assails every smoker under the threat of no matches. Finally his search produced, not matches, but a crumpled and badly soiled envelope. He studied it for a moment, curiously, wondering from where it had come. Then, all at once, he knew!

With something akin to a great tenderness he drew the note from its battered covering, and spelled it out again in the mauve light which flowed up from the lake in reflection to the sky overhead. Yes, Jerry had been a strange but tender incident in his life. She must have cared for him, a little, at least, or she would not have written that note. Perhaps, even yet —

Light footsteps sounded on the gravel, and in confusion he stuffed the letter back into his pocket. A pair of soft hands folded quickly over his eyes and held him in a friendly vice.

"You're moody, Gander," said Minnie's voice. "You're worrying."

There was a tenderness in her tone which told Gander his sister had sought out this hour to talk with him.

"Oh, I'm all right," he answered. "Kind o' tired, to-night."

She sat down beside him, her hand on his.

"You're making long days of it, with your work on the farm, and looking after Dick – and Jo."

"Oh, it's not that. I'm all right."

"Gander, are you sure? I've wanted for weeks to talk to you, and to-night, when I saw you go away by yourself – I followed. You don't mind, do you? I only want to help."

"Help what?" he said, his eyes on the ground. "I'm all right."

"I haven't been spying, Gander," she went on, disregarding his manner, which invited no confidence, "but I couldn't help seeing things. They've been so evident. And I'm sorry for you, Gander."

"Sorry for me? Why?"

She slipped her arm about his neck and turned his face to hers, and as he looked into her deep brown eyes Gander knew what she was about to say.

"Because you are in love with Jo Claus!"

"I'm not – I tell you I'm not!" He sprang to his feet. "Minn, I tell you that is not true! I never –" Then, as though his strength had suddenly seeped from him he sank beside her again. His head rested between his hands; his body shook with the paroxysm of a stifled sob.

"Gander!"

Her arms were both about him now, steadying her brother.

"Yes, Minnie, it's true," he confessed, almost inaudibly. "I can't help it. It's been that way – always – ever since we were little children. I've not done anythin' wrong, Minnie, but I can't help what I feel – in here!" He struck his breast with his hand. "I've tried to play fair. I've done the best I could – for Dick."

"Yes, you have. Every one must say you have been very noble. *Dick knows.* Don't imagine he doesn't know. But it's turning out differently from what all of us – including Dick – expected. And now what are you going to do about it?"

"Do about it? Nothin'. What can I do about it?"

She held him close to her for a minute, weighing Gander's disposition, his reserve, his independence, his rejection of all discipline, wondering how far she could go. Then —

"If I were you, I would get out, Gander. The world is big. If you get out you may forget – at least, you will get away from the edge of the precipice. If you stay here you will always be in danger of slipping over."

She was not prepared for his retort. "Is that why Cal got out?" he demanded.

He felt her body stiffen, and knew he had struck a vulnerable point. Well, this was a good time to strike. *She* was not sparing him.

"Is that why Cal got out?" he repeated. "Nobody has ever told us yet why he beat it, like he did. Nor who that boy is. You know, Minn, and you – you don' dare tell!"

"Don't ask me that, Gander," she breathed. She was on the defensive now. "It is better not. Believe me, I could explain, but it is better not."

"Well, you don't hesitate to dig into *my* affairs," he answered. "Suppose I dig a little into yours? Who is Reed, and why did Cal sneak out at night like a coward?"

"Cal is no coward!" There was fire in Minnie's voice. "You wouldn't call him that!"

"I didn't say he was a coward; I just said he acted like one. Now if you can put it in a different light, go ahead. I'm listenin'."

The girl was silent, and both of them, for long minutes, gazed with unseeing eyes over the rose-colored waters of the lake. At length she spoke:

"Gander, I had decided I never would tell, but if it will help you, in your fight, to know what another man did in his, then I will bring you that help. But it must be a secret of honor between us. Is it?"

"All right; shoot!"

Minnie settled herself to a more comfortable position. "Reed is the son of Cal's sister, Celesta," she began. "Celesta died when Reed was born. She never had been married."

Gander stirred, but did not interrupt.

"Cal promised he would bring the boy up as his own, with no knowledge of the shame that surrounded his birth. That is why he let Reed call him Daddy X; x, the unknown quantity, you know – or perhaps you don't. And all went well until they came here, and until Jackie came."

"What had Jackie to do with it?"

She paused for a moment, as though she could not trust herself with the next revelation. Then, almost inaudibly, "Gander, Jackie is Reed's father!"

"What!"

"It's true! I didn't know until I went West, to nurse him up in that little homestead shanty in Saskatchewan. Then —"

"Then Cal told you?"

"He did not. Jackie told me. You see, he had been plotting against Cal – plotting ever since he knew. But when Reed was sick, and Jackie was there, all of a sudden he grew very fond of the boy. And one day, when Cal was away, he told me the whole story – the whole sordid story. That night he disappeared. I think he had seen things in their true light, and for Reed's sake he disappeared. Just as, for Reed's sake, Cal left here, that the secret might be safe."

She stopped, and it was a long while before Gander spoke. "Then Mother is Reed's grandmother?" he said at length. Even in such a moment it seemed to her strange that that should be Gander's first reaction.

"Yes."

"Does she know?"

"No one has told her. But something – deeper than words – must have carried it to her heart. Do you remember how she took to him from the first? How she used to hold him on her knee, and sing that little hymn about 'Voices of yore, Come from that far-off shore.'"

"Yes – yes. And it was for him that Cal ran away?"

"For him – yes. To save Reed, and to keep his promise to his dead sister."

Gander had risen to his feet. "I'm sorry for what I said, Minnie. Sometimes it is the brave man that runs away, isn't it?"

Minnie's eyes were wet, but her voice was filled with a great happiness. She had reached her brother's heart – that strange, loyal, proud, distant heart which so few could reach.

"Yes," she repeated, holding him again in her arms, "sometimes it is the brave man who runs away. There are *some* good men, Gander. . . . I have often thought life is like a thresher, pouring out its cloud of straw and chaff and dust, and a little grain. A little hard, yellow, golden grain, that has in it the essence of life, Gander!"

A bank of cloud was gathering in the west, threatening rain, and presently Gander and Jo took their way homeward. Once or twice their road was lit up with a blaze of lightning, and when they reached the house a few big drops were splashing in the dust.

"Won't you come in?" she asked him. "Until it blows over?"

"Oh, I guess I better keep on a-goin'," he told her. But he went in.

She lighted a lamp and drew the blinds to shut out the storm. Then she motioned him to a chair.

"Make yourself at home. You have something to smoke?"

He felt mechanically in his pocket and found pipe and tobacco. His heart was pounding above the lash of the rain on the windows.

"Dick is getting along," she said, when his pipe was going.

"Yes."

They sat for a long while in silence, wondering how far they might interpret each other's thought. At length Jo got up and started a fire in the stove. She set a little supper before Gander and herself. Gander ate as one who chokes on morsels. His throat was full.

"You don't say much," she chided him.

"No. Too busy thinkin'," he answered.

The storm, instead of blowing over, increased in intensity. The rain lashed on the windows and against the thin board walls of the house. And the little clock up on the wall ticked on, its chatter drowned in the roar of the elements.

At midnight Gander sprang to his feet.

"I must be goin', Jo," he said, hurriedly. "No idea it was so late."

"You can't drive over those roads now," she protested. "They're running in water. It isn't safe."

"Oh, I'll make it."

"It isn't safe, Gander. You can stay for the night as well as not. I'll fix Dick's couch up for you and you'll be comfortable enough. You can't go in that."

As though to prove her words she opened the door. The wedge of light from the lamp penetrated a few feet into a slanting storm of rain. A flash of lightning disclosed two rivulets of water flowing down the road which led through the yard. For a moment they watched it together; then she closed the door.

"You see, you can't," she said.

"Jo, I must. What will people say?"

"If they haven't said already they needn't start now. I'll be up early and make your breakfast, and you can get away at the peep of dawn. Then you will have daylight, anyway."

She arranged sheets and blankets on Dick's couch in a corner of the living-room. Gander could see her tucking them deftly into place; patting them tenderly, he may have thought. But he smoked on in silence.

It took Jo a long time to arrange everything, but at last it was finished. Then she lighted another lamp, and paused for a moment beside Gander's chair.

"Good night, Gander," she said.

"Good night, Jo."

Then she went up the stairs at the end of the room.

Gander waited until he could no longer hear her moving about on the thin boards which creaked with every pressure of her foot. And even after he went to bed he lay awake for a long while, thinking, listening to the splash of the rain, to its drip and gurgle from the eaves, to its drumming on the windows, its patter on the board walls. It brought back in memory that night in the old house on the farm; that night when Fraser Fyfe came plodding across the flooded fields to see how he and Minnie were faring through the storm. With a start it came to Gander that then, too, Jo had been the centre of his imaginings. Years ago – and she was still the same Jo. But now she was Dick Claus' wife.

Slowly and in order he recalled the incidents of that night. How he had counted himself a coward, until Minnie had praised him for his bravery. How she had crawled into his arms for comfort and protection. . . .

He lay for a long while, thinking. . . .

And, while his thought circled many fields, always it came back to one centre. . . . As he lay there, fighting through a mist that was not of the rain, for the first time in his life he looked Gander Stake in the face.

"You haven' made much of it, Gander, have you?" he demanded, bitterly. "Not very much of it. You wouldn' take discipline – I think that's what they call it, that 'Form fours' stuff – and here you are. . . . Here you are." Then, with a bitter jest at himself, "And where are you?"

Minnie's revelation about Cal and Reed came back to him. How little he had guessed! And the honor of the Stake family —

That was a point that hurt. The honor of the Stake family!

And here it was involved again, in him.

Slowly he began to see that there was only one way. Minnie was right.

Upstairs Jo Claus was sleeping. Or was she? He remembered that day on the school section, and wondered if she had been sleeping then. . . .

There was only one way. It came to him slowly, but when he saw, he saw.

"Gander," he said at length, "now you will take your medicine, and you will take it from yourself. Form fours!"

He got up and drew on his clothes. It was still raining, although not so violently. There would be light as soon as the clouds lifted.

He touched a match to the lamp; found an old envelope and a pencil. Then, in his wobbly hand, he scrawled a little message.

"Dear Jo," it read, "I forgot to tell you that I have to leave on the mornin' train for the city. I've got a good job in a garrage. I like workin' about machines. Hope the oats will come all right, and Dick, too."

He was about to sign it "Gander," but a sudden dignity was upon him. He inscribed his initials, "W. H. S."

Then he stole silently through the door and started his car.

Jo, awake in her room upstairs, fancied she heard the sound of the motor. She ran to her window just as a flash of lightning revealed Gander's car lurching down the muddy road.

W ithin this novel about the education of a character who has little "need for words" and finds
books "bothersome," Robert Stead, the consum-
mate local journalist, continually honours the artistry of the
unbookish. As he was writing *Grain*, he revised many passages,
such as this one describing Tommy Burge, to emphasize the
vitality of the vernacular:

> [*Typescript*:] he was as slim as Gander, with long legs and
> a fair face peppered with large freckles.

> [*Manuscript revision as published*:] . . . a fair face
> peppered with freckles, in large flakes like oatmeal, a
> circumstance which had gained for him the cognomen
> of Porridge.

The metaphor of the oatmeal (more exactly a simile, a more
commonplace literary figure appropriate to the voice of
Plainville) adds to the description a hint of the community
itself speaking. By creating a delightfully indigestible

metaphorical meal of porridge and pepper, Stead turns his own prose in the direction of his subjects.

The Robert Stead Collection in the National Archives of Canada contains no manuscript of *Grain*, only a typescript entitled "Gander" (dated 29 September 1924). This lightly edited typescript indicates that Stead did not rewrite obsessively: key passages, such as his ecstatic prose poem on the song of the binder and the architecture of stooking, apparently reach print more or less as first drafted. Many of the revisions he did make taste of the porridge and pepper of unpremeditated vernacular metaphor. But in the same breath he may mix in the "book-learning" of a remote Latinism, such as "cognomen." Implausibly, on another occasion, Gander's simple "need of a hair cut" (in the typescript) becomes "need of tonsorial attention" (in the published version).

In rewriting "Gander," Stead often writes himself into such uneasy contradictions. Generally, he revises to temper the rhetoric of sentimental romance on which he relied heavily in six earlier novels, from *The Bail Jumper* (1914) to a companion piece to *Grain*, *The Smoking Flax* (1924). But when he turns a "haircut" into "tonsorial attention," he falls into the very pseudo-literary pomposity that his novel generally tries to avoid. Frequently he revises to exploit the sounds and smells of untutored metaphor, but elsewhere he seems to replace plain(ville) talking with pretentious circumlocutions, which might originate in his post-journalism career in public relations (first for the Canadian Pacific Railway, and, after 1919, for the Department of Immigration and Colonization). Yet overwriting, where Stead inclines to an extravagant Dickensian metaphor admirable for its verbal imagination, if not for its subtlety, provides some of the best moments in *Grain*. And contradictions, of course, are not necessarily flaws – the very explicitness of the paradoxes in *Grain* make it the most worthwhile of Stead's novels to read.

Many novelists begin their careers writing more-or-less autobiographical novels about growing up. Stead turned to this more usually apprentice genre near what was to be the end of his career as a publishing novelist. (*Grain* sold considerably fewer copies than his earlier formula romances.) The title "Gander," under which Stead submitted the novel to his publisher, implied a *bildungsroman*. He had tried several other titles: "A Son of the Soil," "A Soldier of the Soil," "Aftermath," "No Man's Orders," "Half a Hero." Eventually, his publisher proposed the title "Grain," highlighting, perhaps, the element of economic history (and, of course, the metaphorical potential) in the work. The shifting possible titles imply that *Grain* is several different novels: by the mid-1920s Stead was moving away from muscular Methodist romance (Ralph Connor was a family friend), such as his own *Dennison Grant* (1920), and reaching for, if not quite finding, something different. Again, the appeal of reading the novel is mulling the resulting contradictions. Although he was writing about a boy's education, Stead kept halting the narrative to indulge in documentary detail about pioneer farming. But as much as he aspired to authenticity, his doctrine of realism insisted that grand romance was true to life. And although Stead believed passionately in the romance of empire, as several earlier books of his patriotic verse revealed, his war novel keeps slipping sceptically towards pacifism.

When *Maclean's* magazine serialized *Grain*, the editor, H. Napier Moore, wrote to Stead that more favourable letters had been received about it than about any previous serialization in the magazine: "These letters are not only from farmers, who highly praise the accuracy and detail of the pictures you have drawn, but from city dwellers as well." To many of his immediate readers the documentary element was obviously welcome. For readers more remote from early twentieth-century prairie culture, localizing detail is still central to the book's appeal. Stead reports affectionately that the poplar shingles on the Stake house curl until the knots pop out and provide a window to the night sky; he records the rules for the schoolyard game of "Pom, Pom, Pull-away"; he notices a mother prairie hen and her chicks taking shelter in a clump of willows (in Gander's mind's eye such details of animal life are more likely to evoke his prairie than pictures of landscape). But the rhetoric of "high enterprise," as it shapes material success or human love, is always close at hand.

Stead *argues* these ambiguities of romance and documentary in his conception of character: Gander, reading the romance of the machine, is not "closely observant," but the author/narrator and *alter ego* is. However productive this tension, the marketplace, despite the success in *Maclean's*, did not respond. After *Grain*, Stead's writing career turned toward more public addresses (on the machine age, Canadian-American comparisons, imperialism), articles on home-steading history, and autobiography; in the face of declining sales figures, further fiction in the style of *Grain* had little lure for him.

In *Grain* Stead moved as far away from the popular romance as he was able; he seemed suspended between a career as sentimental novelist and journalist. Something of his dilemma echoes in a letter to John McClelland (22 July 1935) bemoaning the rejection of his subsequent manuscript "Dry Water" by New York publishers:

It may be granted at once that *Dry Water* is not an
"action" story. It was not designed to be. . . . It is a
character story in which the effect of prairie farm
environment on a number of persons . . . is, I think,
faithfully portrayed against an authentic background.
To introduce action which is not native to that background would I think do violence to the whole book.

The tone of this lament may suggest that the paradox I
have been describing as key to the appeal of *Grain*, and to the
characterization of Gander, was enacted in Stead's own life.
Certainly the persona conveyed by the material preserved in
the National Archives is of the solid public servant. Stead's
letters are businesslike: they rarely comment on aesthetics or
politics, and are almost never jocular. Seldom does he refer to
wife, family, or even the weather. Presumably more personal
letters were destroyed; his diaries were meticulously digested,
leaving only chronologies of external events for the public
record. Even the diaries he kept of vacation trips consist
mainly of painstaking accounts: each mile driven is recorded,
as is each five-dollar bill he doles out to his wife.

Any colourful personality resides in the novels – and in
one archival glimpse of eccentricity. I find it hard to imagine
this dedicated civil servant (Stead once described the profession as "brain-fagged") venturing near anything impractical.
But a report from a handwriting analyst, dated 20 September
1923, was obviously important enough for Stead to preserve.
Perhaps, given the date, the analyst's comments stimulated the
novelist just as he was contemplating writing *Grain*: "The cool
calculating, analytic thinking," Mr. F. Jacob advised under
"Vocational Suggestions," "plus the sense of rhythm and

responsiveness to all beauty, should make for a musical style of writing and the happy selection of words and phrases." Twenty years later, Stead addressed the Ottawa Rotary Club: his topic, deemed important enough that the Club published the address as a small monograph, was simply "Words." Although he advises his audience to be restrained – "always prefer the short and common word if it will express what you mean" – his speculations are most stimulating when he argues with himself about the relation between language and thinking. An Alberta rancher's "vocabulary was limited," he notes, but "when he employed profanity . . . he could be amazingly descriptive and explicit."

Although Canadian readers of 1926 were not ready for much profanity, no matter how descriptive, in their fiction, Stead's commitment to the resonance of the working farmer's language implies some reconciliation of the contradictions which the novel and archival papers pose. The monograph on "Words" is a hesitant manifesto for the unruly plunging and bucking of what academics call the restricted code, speech patterns for everyday living. "Culture had not yet demanded in these rural districts," Stead reminds us in Chapter 7 of *Grain*, "its severe price of contempt for the untrained."

When Jackson Stake first contemplates the effect of the war on grain prices, Stead has him exclaiming "By God, yes." In revision, this phrase becomes less blasphemous, and more local: "Jumpin' jack rabbits! Yes!" Switching to a natural speech metaphor provides both an image of the prairie (recognized, again, through the fauna rather than through topographical features) and a sense of the Stakes' relationship to the natural world, since metaphors of animal life jump most readily into their speech. By such writing, Stead counters in *Grain* a contempt for the untrained, and thus anticipates the verbal ingenuity of Margaret Laurence's Christie Logan.

Another revision toward Plainville's commonplace yet exuberant metaphor shapes this passage on William Stake's nickname:

> [*Typescript*:] "Hello, Gander!" they greeted him as he joined their group, and the name stuck. By the time he was eighteen . . .

> [*Manuscript revision as published*:] . . . joined their group. William's Adam's apple fled for cover, and his long neck twisted in boyish confusion. The name stuck. By the time he was eighteen . . .

In this revision, not only does Stead elaborate the Dickensian grotesqueness of his character, he also reinforces the imagery of battle and war which permeates the novel. (The typescript's original "Gander threw himself into the task" becomes "Gander attacked the ripened fields.") As he rewrites in such passages for a more visual and tactile sense of character, he works to reinforce, subliminally, his pacifist theme: the battle for grain, for food, is as crucial to a nation's self-ideal as is a battle in the mud of France. Perhaps Stead, even in 1926, was rewriting the received story of Canada's own growing up – the national *bildungsroman* – where the battles of World War One are often the turning point of the narrative.

Stead's ambivalence between romance and realism, between pacifism and militarism, is also apparently grounded in issues of gender. Certainly his editors saw his fiction in such terms. Warning him that his "American audience is largely women," Z.C. Brandt, the New York literary agent, wrote to him concerning *Grain*: "An audience of women, like myself, would fall into two classes – either 'lowbrow', who want the story value, or 'highbrow', who want the delineation of types, and the creation of real personages. . . . You must carry your book either on a love story or on the lovableness or pathos of some character" (5 March 1926). In response to such criticism, presumably, Stead added to the novel an extended account of Gander's encounter with Geraldine Chansley, and the opening of chapter 23 in which Stead tries to justify the much maligned – but satisfyingly mysterious – ending of the novel. Several aspects of the novel suggest that Stead was interested in engaging more significant issues of gender than those required to pander to some editor's presumptuous bifurcation of the female audience. He had come to distrust the lovable characters of the lowbrow love story, but was not quite able to escape the clichés and create a strong female character. Like Gander, Stead almost recognizes "that in some way she [here I think of Geraldine, to whom the passage refers, but also of Jo, and of his mother] was stronger than he." Had he continued in this vein Stead might some day have written a feminist novel: he deleted from the beginning of the typescript a three-page section which elaborates at length on Susie Stake's psychological stress, caused by a physician too drunk to attend at the birth of her first child. It is a moving passage that again suggests how *Grain* is a novel on the way to being something else – an *As For Me and My House*, perhaps.

But neither the dust nor uninterrupted skylines of Sinclair Ross's quintessential prairie novel have much prominence in *Grain*. A more immediate connection can be found in a letter from Stead to John McClelland (14 January 1926). Stead mentions a "wag friend's" suggestion that "it is quite appropriate that 'Gander' should come after 'Wild Geese'!" I detect just enough evidence in *Grain* and Stead's own papers to be convinced that the influence of the high romance and female politics of Martha Ostenso's *Wild Geese* (1925) goes beyond a passing joke.

But like *Wild Geese* before it, and *As For Me and My House* after, Stead's novel complicates its own complications often enough that we *want* to keep looking at it and reading it in new contexts. *Grain* is neither the definitive prairie novel nor a novel of consistent verbal mastery. It is a novel between worlds, a patchwork genre, whose greatest attraction is Stead's ear for the taciturn yet surprisingly verbally inventive people who are his subjects. The prairie vernacular in written form appears here more than in Frederick Philip Grove, or Frederick John Niven, or Laura Goodman Salverson, or Martha Ostenso. And the novel adeptly catches a peculiarly matter-of-fact prairie humour, that self-deprecating jocularity that Stead sometimes shares with his characters. When asked to write about his favourite Canadian books, he found four, all works of *fiction* and "imaginative genius of a high order": the *Canadian Newspaper Directory*, *Hansard*, *Who's Who in Canada*, and the *Telephone Directory*. In many passages from *Grain* we recognize the slightly quirky sensibility that can discover high art in such unbookish books. As Stead's notes for a 1942 public lecture confirm, he looks for the potential artist in every farmer:

It was possible for every farmer to be an artist.

My father's first furrow in the prairie.

The perfect stack.

> *The well-kept farm yard.*
> *I can look at any farmer's woodpile and tell whether*
> *   he is an artist.*
> *Farmers still have these opportunities to express*
> *   themselves – art is fundamentally the business of*
> *   creating something which gives expression to*
> *   personality.*

The novel Stead wanted to write may have been beyond his reach, but in *Grain*, within his grasp, is the portrait of the venerably eccentric character, the colour of dialect, the expressiveness of local metaphor, and the fine art of the first furrow – at its best, a novel where the textures of language are a continuing presence in the reader's mind.

BY ROBERT STEAD

FICTION

The Bail Jumper (1914)

The Homesteaders: A Novel of the Canadian West (1916)

The Cow Puncher (1918)

Dennison Grant: A Novel of Today (1920)

Neighbours (1922)

The Smoking Flax (1924)

Grain (1926)

The Copper Disc (1931)

Dry Water: A Novel of Western Canada (1983)

POETRY

The Empire Builders and Other Poems (1908)

Prairie Born, and Other Poems (1911)

Songs of the Prairie (1911)

Kitchener, and Other Poems (1917)

Why Don't They Cheer? (1918)